UNDERTOW

Arlene Hunt is originally from Wicklow and now lives in Dublin with her husband, daughter and mêlée of useless, overweight animals. *Undertow* is her fifth novel.

Also by Arlene Hunt
Vicious Circle
False Intentions
Black Sheep
Missing Presumed Dead

ARLENE HUNT

UNDERTOW

HACHETTE
BOOKS
IRELAND

First published in Ireland in 2008 by Hachette Books Ireland

1

Copyright © 2008 Arlene Hunt

ABERDEENSHIRE LIBRARY AND INFORMATION SERVICES	
2631783	
HJ	704251
MYS PBK	£11.99
AD	AF

ISBN 9 780 340 97728 6

All characters in this publication are fictitious and any resemblance to real
persons, living or dead, is purely coincidental.

Typeset in Sabon MT by Hachette Books Ireland
Printed and bound by Mackays of Chatham Ltd, Chatham, Kent

Hachette Books Ireland policy is to use papers that are natural, renewable
and recyclable products and made from wood grown in sustainable forests.
The logging and manufacturing processes are expected to conform to the
environmental regulations of the country of origin.

Hachette Books Ireland
8 Castlecourt Centre, Castleknock, Dublin 15, Ireland.
A division of Hachette Livre UK Ltd, 338 Euston Road,
London NW1 3BH, England

www.hbgi.ie

For Anna, the Lady of the Manor

1

For as long as Lorcan Wallace could remember, he had been angry. He had been angry as a boy, angry as teenager and now, at the ripe old age of twenty, he was an angry young man. He woke up angry and went to sleep angry. It didn't seem to matter the circumstances, his temper was always there, bubbling and churning below the surface.

When his mother had been alive, Lorcan had managed to keep a tighter rein on his volatile emotions. He knew his temper upset her terribly.

'Why, Lorcan, why did you do this? Why can't you behave yourself?' she had asked him one afternoon, having been called to the school to remove him from the premises.

Lorcan had explained as best he could. He had been minding his own business in class, carefully crafting a sheep from plasticine, when he had overheard Brian Flynn laughing at him. Brian, a big-mouthed doctor's son, was a bullying thug, who dished out Chinese burns on unsuspecting girls and stole pencil sharpeners. He and Lorcan had never liked each other, so when Lorcan had heard him mock his work it was inevitable that the red mist would come down.

And come down it had. One minute the class was busy creating creatures from Noah's Ark, the next Múinteoir Fellim was trying to prevent Brian swallowing his tongue. Lorcan had explained all this, but his mother had only sighed and put another cigarette to her lips. In the hullabaloo that followed, the school management concluded two things. The first was that Lorcan could do with some therapy, and the second, that he might be better off in a different school.

In an effort to comply with at least one of those conclusions and stave off the other, Lorcan's mother had insisted he see a child psychiatrist – almost unheard of back in those days. Certainly Lorcan's father Darren was against it, describing it as 'the biggest bloody waste of everyone's time and his money I've ever heard of', but his mother had persisted. That was why Lorcan, aged six and a half, had found himself sitting at a tiny table in a cheery yellow and green office, drawing pictures and describing how he had felt when he had done what he had to Brian.

After three sessions of picture-drawing and role play, the quack in question reported that Lorcan suffered from 'paranoid fantasies and delusions of persecution'.

On hearing this assessment of his only son, his old man had said, 'So what? Everyone suffers from that.' And that was the last time they had attended the quack's cheery yellow and green office.

Lorcan had carried on being angry, but for the most part managed to keep himself in check, and when he couldn't, his father beat a little less rage into him. The status quo held for a few years and might have continued to do so had not his mother died.

So he was angry. He was used to it.

But it amazed him, utterly amazed him, that whenever he and Orie Kavlar were together he didn't feel angry. He wasn't even close to it. He was, he noted, feeling pretty damn good about himself.

That was the effect Orie had on him. Hell, that was the effect Orie had on everybody. He was a twenty-two-year-old Polish lover boy, darkly handsome, with an easy smile and permanent calm manner that worked like a soothing balm on Lorcan's troubled mind. Orie made Lorcan laugh. He made Lorcan feel clever. He made Lorcan think his shit didn't stink. He made Lorcan think nothing mattered except whatever moment they existed in.

Though he would never have admitted it, Lorcan thought Orie was the coolest person he'd ever met. They'd been friends for around eight months and, as far as Lorcan was concerned, they were soulmates.

'Always she want to know what I am doing. Where I am going, who I am talk to. It is not good. You know?'

Lorcan nodded. Orie was talking about his girlfriend again – the skank, as Lorcan thought of her. Orie and the skank fought a lot, and from what Lorcan could make out they'd had a real humdinger of a row before the trip. Orie had been upset about it. Lorcan had met the skank once and couldn't understand what a man like Orie, so handsome and funny, saw in a spotty teenager who chewed gum with her mouth open.

'So I take phone and I throw it, but stupid! It breaks against wall.' Orie shook his head. 'Stupid, uh? Now I have no phone.'

'What did she say?'

'Ah!' Orie threw up his hands. 'Nothing, but I am fool. Now I must buy new phone.'

'Women.'

'Women,' Orie agreed, 'always the same. They take you to the drink.'

'They sure do,' Lorcan said. He didn't know the first thing about women other than that they existed. He'd met plenty of them in the casinos over the past few months, heavily made-up tarts in barely-there dresses. Ever since he and Orie had gone to work for Mink, the women had paid them special attention. Orie lapped it up, but Lorcan barely gave them the time of day. It wasn't that he disliked women, just that he didn't think of them much at all. He had a sister, but sisters didn't count.

'Yo, Lorc, there is garage. Pull in.'

Lorcan did as he was asked unhesitatingly.

'You want I get something for you?'

'Nah, I'm good.'

'You are baby!' Orie shot him with imaginary pistols and jumped out.

Lorcan watched him cross the forecourt and pull open the door into the shop, walking with that cocksure swagger. Orie, his black hair glistening under the lights, chatting up the cashier, a bored tubby girl with a nose piercing – Lorcan wouldn't have looked at her twice. Orie was beaming at her, as if she was a beauty queen, acting like he hadn't a care in the world, as though they didn't have a delivery to make.

To say Orie Kavlar was a bad man would be something of a lie. He wasn't bad so much as operating in a morals-free zone. Whatever inbuilt system the average Joe on the street had to keep them on the straight and narrow, Orie seemed to lack. Lorcan understood that. He liked to listen to Orie as his friend explained human nature. Orie always said that there were two types of people in the world, the sheep and the wolves; he himself was a wolf. He said Lorcan was a wolf too.

Lorcan loved that image, of him and Orie, two lone wolves. His father had been a wolf once – everybody said so – but age and so-called respectability had turned that once great man into a lamb. Now Darren Wallace was nothing but another slave to the clock.

Lorcan frowned. He didn't want to think of his father. They'd exchanged furious words the day before, and even now Lorcan felt the heat flare in his cheeks. What had the old man called him?

A waste of space.

Lorcan popped another cigarette into his mouth and lit it, clicking shut his Zippo by snapping it against his thigh. He'd show him.

In the shop, Orie was paying for his things, shooting the breeze. The chubby girl smiled at something he said. She smiled the way women always smiled at Orie, whether they wanted to or not. Whatever Orie had ought to be bottled – they'd make a bloody fortune selling it, better than Viagra.

Lorcan's upper lip curled gently.

Dumb bitch. As if.

Orie came out and climbed into the truck's cab. 'Here, comrade, I bring you gift.'

'What?'

Orie grinned, tossed him a packet of Maltesers and opened a bar of Cadbury's Dairy Milk. 'Good, yes?'

'You made us stop for chocolate? I thought you needed fags or something.'

'You don't want?'

'Yeah, I'll have them.'

'What we talking about?'

Your skank, Lorcan thought. 'The club we're gonna open once we have the bucks.'

'Oh, baby!' Orie said. It was their favourite topic of conversation.

They drove on through the night, heading south, making

11

good time along the almost-deserted M50. They were on their way to meet Jimmy McKellen, a sharp-eyed Northerner and Mink's right-hand man. Jimmy made Lorcan anxious. He couldn't shake the feeling that Jimmy was always laughing at him behind his back, not that he'd ever seen him crack a smile, let alone laugh. As far as Lorcan was concerned, the less time he spent around Jimmy McKellen the better.

The vehicle Lorcan was driving was a 1998 Mitsubishi Camper, a squat boxy little number that belonged to Jimmy's doddery boss, Ian Maguire. Jimmy's own van, the one they normally used for this trip, was in the shop getting new shocks put in. It was a risk using the Camper, but riskier still to take a van that might break down, and riskiest of all not to go.

'When I am rich man,' Orie jerked his thumb at a Mercedes passing them on the right, 'I am going to drive one of these.'

'A Merc? Nah, my old lad drives one. They're all right, but if I was rich I'd get a Lamborghini.'

Orie laughed. 'Too . . . in the face. Too many people see you.'

'I wouldn't give a shit. I'd want people to see me. I'd get it in red too. What's the point in having all that dough if you don't show it off?'

'To have is enough.'

'No way, Orie. I'm gonna be living it up, flash car, flash pad, flash everything.'

'Flash Lorcan!'

'You know it.'

'Are you going to game next week?'

'The Chinks set up? Dunno – it's a grand a hand, minimum.'

'You must spend money to make money.'

'Shit, I know that, but I'm pretty tapped out. I'm still paying off Slim, remember.'

Orie nodded. 'You win big, you free from him. Open club. Buy Lamborghini.'

'Yeah.' Lorcan took another drag of his cigarette. 'I suppose there is that.'

Lorcan didn't want to think about Slim. Lately the loan shark had had a nasty habit of invading his thoughts on a regular basis.

Orie sighed deeply.

'What?'

'Without money, I am thinking we are bits players.'

'Bit players.'

'Yes. We do this, we pay, we take risk, we pay, we do work, we pay.'

'I know.' Lorcan cleared his throat. 'Not for long, though, yeah? You're known now. You speak the lingo. We can start making our own forays.'

'Forez?'

'Trips. Soon as I sell the car we can get a van. Or a truck.'

'And Mink?'

'Fuck Mink. We won't need him.'

'Then,' Orie slapped his hands together, 'we will make the big money.'

'Yeah, we will. Then we can open our club. You think any more about a name? Got to be something classy, like . . . like . . . Pizzazz!'

Orie snorted a laugh but Lorcan didn't care: he knew Orie wasn't laughing at him. Orie never laughed at him.

Jimmy McKellen stood in the dark just inside the warehouse doors and smoked. The boys – as Mink called them – were late. Boys. Jimmy didn't consider them boys, he considered them idiots. At least Lorcan was, dumb as a box of hair, and that was being generous. How in hell Darren Wallace had produced such a son was a mystery to him. He knew Darren from back in the day, and the last thing he could be called was stupid. That was the only reason Mink had taken Lorcan on. But, as Jimmy never tired of pointing out, the kid was a Wallace in name only.

Jimmy glared at the car parked in front of a warehouse, Lorcan's black and silver Honda Civic, complete with spoiler, alloy wheels and body kit. Dumb.

At twenty past ten the Camper pulled into the yard. Jimmy immediately rolled back the warehouse door. Lorcan drove straight inside and Jimmy closed it behind him.

Lorcan switched off the lights and engine and jumped down from the cab. 'Hey, Jimmy.'

'You're late,' Jimmy said. 'What did I tell you about that car? Why didn't you park it round the back?'

'Give it a rest, Jimmy.'

'Jimmy.' Orie jerked his head in greeting and continued on to the back of the van.

'Stow that car round back and let's get a move on.'

'What difference does it make?'

Jimmy was smaller than Lorcan, but he was a tough and wiry man who didn't like his authority challenged. 'It matters, you fucking eejit, because people remember cars. They especially remember fancy-arsed cars. I've told you about it before, but for some reason you don't seem to understand what I'm tellin' you. So maybe you'll understand this. If you can't work within the rules then you don't work this gig. I'm not doing a spell inside because you can't follow simple fucking instructions. We do not attract attention. You got that, kid?'

'Hey, Jimmy, you don't need to talk to me like that. I'm not fucking stupid, you know?'

'What's that got to do with anything?'

Muscles bunched in Lorcan's jaw. 'You don't need to speak to me like that. I'm not stupid.'

'Yeah, OK, keep your shit together. I'm just asking you to move the car.'

Lorcan stalked off.

A minute later, Jimmy heard the Honda rev and tear round the back of the warehouse. Stupid little shit. He couldn't even do that quietly.

Jimmy jammed an unlit cigarette into his mouth and walked to the back of the van where Orie was waiting. He climbed up, unsnapped the locks and threw the bolt. The double doors opened, revealing a selection of wardrobes and assorted piles of junk. 'Let's go.'

Orie climbed up, and together they unloaded the second-hand furniture in silence, removing two massive mattresses last.

'All right, ladies.' Jimmy clapped his hands. 'Look lively.'

A group of women were huddled to the rear of the cab. They blinked and got to their feet. They were dazed and exhausted after their journey.

Jimmy waved at them impatiently. 'Come on, ladies, we haven't got all night.'

They began to emerge, but two hung back. One was stretched out full-length on the floor, the other girl kneeling by her head, patting her face.

'Hey, move it there.'

The kneeling girl looked up. She was pretty, with long dark hair and huge luminous eyes. She said something to Jimmy in a language he couldn't understand. 'What's she saying, Orie?'

Orie spoke to her.

The girl looked at him and began to babble, her words tumbling over each other as she clung to the prone girl.

'What the fuck's she saying?'

'She say girl is sick.' Orie glanced at Jimmy and shrugged. 'She say there was no air. She say she have epilepsy. The man, the first man, he take bags, she has medicine there, she—'

'Tell her to calm down. She's freaking the others out.'

'She says she fell down. With fit.'

Jimmy walked towards them and squatted down. He patted the supine girl on the face. 'Hey, sweetie, rise and shine there.'

There was no response. She looked pretty out of it.

Lorcan jumped up onto the trailer. 'What's wrong?'

'Fucked if I know. This one's out cold.'

'Did she take something?'

'Don't think so.' Jimmy grabbed the collapsed girl by the arm. He began to drag her towards the doors to take a better look, but as he did so the other girl screamed and beat at him.

Jimmy raised his arm to ward off the blows. 'What the fuck—'

'Is her sister,' Orie said.

'Tell her to fucking relax, tell her—'

Lorcan stepped forward and backhanded the girl across the face. She fell heavily enough to make Jimmy wince. Some of the girls who had climbed down from the truck were crying now.

'What the fuck did you do that for?'

'She was screaming.'

'You bloody gobshite. You don't hit them in the face,' Jimmy said. 'There'd better not be a mark on her.'

'She's fine.'

'Go and keep an eye on the rest of them,' Jimmy said. 'Orie, get her up. Tell her it'll be all right. Tell her we'll look after her sister. What's her name?'

Orie helped the dazed girl to her feet. He wiped the blood from her split lip with his thumb and spoke softly to her. 'She say her name is Nadia.'

'Right. Well, you tell Nadia not to worry, we'll get her sister some help, and she'll be on her feet in no time, and then she can join the others.'

Orie repeated this. Nadia shook her head and muttered to him. 'She want to stay with her sister.'

16

'Well, she fucking can't. Tell her to go on ahead,' Jimmy said. 'Once this one gets better she can catch up.'

Orie again repeated everything. Nadia tried to pull away but Orie held her hand. Her huge eyes searched Jimmy's face, seeking any sign of humanity, anything to prove he was telling the truth.

'Lorcan, take her and the others to the storage room at the back. The camera's set up.'

Lorcan grasped the girl by her arm. 'Come on.'

She started to keen, dropped to her knees and grabbed her sister's hands. Lorcan dragged her along the floor of the van. Before he managed to get her down, she cast one long, anguished look at the unconscious girl and began to weep. Jimmy knew she had already worked out there would be no Hallmark reunion.

Lorcan herded the women out of view, half-carrying the crying woman under his arm, as if she was a handbag. Eventually her cries died away.

'Is bad?' Orie said.

Jimmy lifted the girl and carried her outside. He gestured to Orie to close the doors as he lowered her to the floor. He tilted her head back. There was dried foam and blood around her mouth. When he lifted the lids, only the whites of her eyes were in evidence. She couldn't have been much more than fourteen or fifteen, with long glossy hair and the kind of pale, clear complexion he knew would have fetched plenty of offers. 'Where did this one come from?'

'Balkans.'

'She's fucked, too far gone.' Jimmy glared at the unconscious girl as though she had personally offended him by slipping into a coma. 'This is fucked up, Orie.'

'We can bring to hospital.'

'We can't bring her to a bloody hospital.'

Orie stared at him. 'She will die without doctor.'

Jimmy felt the girl's pulse. It was weak and unsteady. 'It can't be helped. We weren't to know she was sick. Listen to me. We've got to get rid of her.'

Orie blessed himself.

Jimmy stared at him, incredulous. 'You're fucking with me, right, Orie?'

'Jimmy—'

'Jesus fucking Christ. Look, I'll take care of her, but you get rid of her.'

'What?' Orie looked sick.

'Look, you stupid Polack, we can't have her here. I need to get these girls ready. Poppy's going to be here any second. Now, snap out of it. Shit happens. I'm not asking you to do anything except take her out of here.'

Orie put his hands into his pockets. 'OK, I take.'

Jimmy checked the girl's pockets for anything that might identify her, but there was nothing. He put his hand over her mouth and pinched her nostrils closed.

She never stirred. She died on the dirty floor of a warehouse in Ballyfermot, far away from home.

Jimmy checked her for a pulse. 'Right, she's done. Let's stick her in the back of the van. Now, listen to me, Orie. Drive under the speed limit, right? Don't go no faster than that and don't break no red lights. You get stopped, you stole this truck.'

'Shit.' Orie stuck a cigarette into his mouth. His hands were trembling.

'Yeah, shit – we're in it. Now, grab her legs and let's get her the fuck out of here.'

2

Sarah Kenny lay with one arm folded behind her head. Though the night was cold, she had kicked the covers to the bottom of the bed and now she felt chilled.

She made no move to cover herself as she watched the light from the cars on the streets below track across the ceiling of her bedroom. She didn't mind the cold. She hadn't slept properly in days, but although she was tired and midnight was approaching, she knew she wouldn't fall asleep any time soon.

Another car went past. Who were all these night travellers? Where were they going?

How often, she wondered, had she lain here as a child, watching the same shadows, listening to the same sounds? It had been countless times and yet, somehow, oddly, it all felt so alien to her. She felt unanchored, free-falling, as though she and the room had sprung out of another dimension.

She needed to go to the bathroom, but she ignored it. As long as she lay there she could almost avoid the dread that seemed to accompany her through every step of the day. She didn't want to get up. She didn't want to pull on her dressing gown. She didn't want to see her face in the mirror, to have to endure another day of pretending everything was normal.

She wanted to be still, to lie in the dark and watch the light play on the ceiling. She wanted to be in the same bed she had slept in as a child, when life was simple, when she was safe.

It had been three weeks since her deranged ex-boyfriend Victor had attacked her, three weeks since she had fought the omnipresent threat of his dark menace. Three weeks since her past had caught up with her and her future had been vaporised in a single deadly blow. She had plunged a kitchen knife deep into Victor's chest and sent his body out to sea. She had sat and watched as he bobbed in the inky blackness before the undertow caught him and spirited him away. It had been three weeks of guilt and fear, of sleeplessness and nightmares.

Three weeks.

It felt like a lifetime.

Why did he have to come back into her life? Everything she had worked so hard to rebuild was ruined – her private detective agency, her home, her family – he had infected it all. A solitary tear rolled down her cheek onto her pillow. Disgusted, she swung her legs over the side of the bed and stood up.

She crossed the landing to the old-fashioned bathroom, pausing at her mother's bedroom door. She did not need to switch on any lights: she knew the house like the back of her hand, every creak and draught, every shadow, every scent. She opened the door and stepped into her mother's room.

Deirdre Kenny was not there. She was staying with Helen, Sarah's older sister. Helen had offered to look after her for a few weeks until Sarah had recovered from her 'mugging'. Hah. It had been the only excuse she could come up with to explain the injuries Vic had inflicted on her.

The bed was neatly made up and her mother's dressing table bare. The air still reeked of Clinique Happy. Sarah remembered how her mother had flung the bottle at her all those weeks before, lashing out in frustration and confusion. Alzheimer's was a cruel disease, and it pained Sarah that her mother was slipping further and further into its foggy grasp every day.

She would have to come home soon, Sarah supposed. Helen had said she was fine at the house, that everything was going well. Belinda, their mother's nurse, had no problem going the extra distance to Helen's home. Helen had even claimed that the latest round of tablets their mother was on seemed to be having the desired effect. Certainly they seemed to keep Deirdre calmer. Some days, Helen said, it was almost possible to think of her and not the disease that was ravaging her brain.

Sarah knew Helen was lying.

She closed her mother's door and stepped into the bathroom. She used the toilet and then washed her hands in the old ceramic sink. She pulled the cord and waited for the fluorescent bar over the mirror to hum into life.

It never failed to startle her how awful she looked, these days. The bruises were fading, and her eyes were no longer swollen, but she was gaunt, yellowed, frail somehow.

Victor had really done a number on her, no doubt about that. She closed her eyes and leaned her forehead against the cabinet.

And she had really done a number on him.

It didn't matter how many times she played the scenario in her head. It didn't matter how many times she washed her hands. It didn't matter that she had burned her clothes. It didn't matter that he was gone. It didn't matter. None of it mattered.

He was dead, yet he was haunting her.

When she closed her eyes, she saw him outlined against the light from the distant shore, felt the splash of his hot blood on her hand, heard the sound he'd made as he fell to his knees, saw his fingers as he reached for her. In moments of stillness she imagined the sound as he fought to breathe while his lungs filled with blood.

Victor.

She washed her hands again.

She thought she saw him sometimes. She knew it was impossible, but in those moments she was convinced that maybe somehow he'd survived. Well, was that so crazy? He had stalked and haunted her in life, why not in death? She owed him, didn't she? She had taken his life. She had plunged a knife into his body and pushed it into the sea.

She opened her eyes and stared at her reflection.

She wouldn't think of it from his perspective. Vic had been a monster. Killing him had been an act of self-defence, pure and simple. Victor had run her sister Jackie off the road, destroyed her office, attacked Rodney Mitchell – the solicitor who worked on the floor below her – and threatened her family. He had beaten her and mocked her as he had done it. Why did he deserve anything other than death? He had been a dangerous animal and she had put him down. Why was she questioning herself now?

Her hands shook. She tried to steady them. She opened the cabinet and took out a packet of painkillers. She swallowed two tablets with some water and ran her wrists under the cold tap until her heart slowed and her breathing calmed. She took a last look at herself in the mirror. She would wait in the shadows and think about Victor until it was time to face another grey, sleepless dawn.

3

Lorcan and Jimmy drove into town in silence. They were on their way to meet Orie on Ormond Quay. It was twenty past one and the streets were filling with late-night revellers. As they pulled in, a gang of girls stumbled off the Ha'penny Bridge, screeching and catcalling, tumbling out of their heels and boob tubes.

Orie climbed into the back seat. He handed Jimmy the keys to the Camper. He was pale and dishevelled. 'The van is there.' He pointed across the road.

'Where did you put her?'

'Up in mountains.'

'Is she well hidden?'

'I think so.'

'You think? You think?'

'I put in woods.'

Lorcan scowled as one of the girls collided with his car.

'Off the road at least?' Jimmy said.

Orie nodded.

Jimmy passed him a brown envelope. Orie took it and flicked through the banknotes it contained.

'Don't do that here.'

'Fuck it,' Lorcan said. 'Let him count his money if he wants.'

Jimmy glanced at him, about to say something, but Lorcan's face was tight and furious. He turned back to Orie. 'I've spoken to Mink. You guys are off this gig for a few weeks.'

'What?'

'No more trips.'

Orie's eyes met Lorcan's.

'Don't look at him, look at me,' Jimmy said. 'You're going to hang low, at least until we're sure this shit has blown over.'

'I already told you' – Lorcan glowered at Jimmy – 'that we can't afford not to work.'

'Too bad. It's not your decision.'

'Yeah, but I need the money, Jimmy. I owe Slim. How am I supposed to pay him if you're cutting us out?'

'Not my problem.'

'It wasn't our fault.'

'Are you deaf? It's Mink's contact, and he says you're out for a few weeks. Get it into your thick skulls.'

'I want to talk to Mink.'

Jimmy moved fast. He grabbed Lorcan by the front of his shirt and dragged him across the handbrake. 'Listen, dipshit, I speak for Mink. And trust me, boyo, you don't want to be talking to Mink right now.'

'All right, all right. I'm just saying this is shit, man, what you're doing to us.'

'To us?' Jimmy shoved Lorcan away. 'What are you on about? This isn't about you! That girl's dead, you fucked up.'

'But what about our money?'

'What about it?' Jimmy snapped. 'If you're that stuck why

don't you ask your old man for a hand-out? It's not like he's short of a few bob.'

Lorcan's upper lip curled. 'I'm not asking him for anything.'

'Well, that's your business. I'll be in touch when we need you again.' Jimmy got out of the car and hurried across the road to where Orie had parked the van.

He climbed in and sat there for a moment. He knew the two younger men were hurting, that they'd be scheming and plotting. They were degenerate gamblers, the pair of them.

Never work with morons. He ought to have that tattooed on his body somewhere.

He took out his mobile and called Mink.

'They ain't happy.' Jimmy watched Lorcan drive away. 'Let me get rid of this truck first.'

Lorcan drove down the Quays, smarting about Jimmy handling him like that in front of Orie.

'You are OK?' Orie was riding shotgun again.

'He's a bastard, that McKellen.'

'He is,' Orie agreed glumly. 'Mink too.'

'I don't give a shit what he says. He can't tell us what to do. I need that money. I owe Slim and he won't wait. I've got to have money for him next week.'

'You will ask your father?'

'Nah, Orie, you know he won't help. He'd lose his rag if he knew I owed someone like Slim that much.' Lorcan drummed his fingers on the steering wheel, trying to think. He could probably steal another cheque out of the old man's book. He'd done that a few times, never for more than two grand a pop. The old man didn't use his personal account and, as far as Lorcan knew, he hadn't noticed the extra stubs.

Maybe he could hit up his sister Caoimhe for some funds. She'd help him out, he was sure.

But that would still only buy him time. Maybe it was time to branch out. That way they wouldn't be at the mercy of freaks like Mink and Jimmy McKellen. They'd been talking about it for long enough. Why not now? This could be a golden opportunity to step up.

'Orie, listen.' He glanced at his friend. 'Them guys we get the girls from. They don't give a shit who picks them up, right?'

Orie shrugged his shoulders. 'They are Russian. You pay, they are happy.'

'Right, that's what I'm saying, and it would be easy to arrange a buyer for them over here, or even just get them into a few places ourselves. Look, it's like what we were talking about. We do the work and we get the shit end of the money. You know, my old lad's always saying, "In business when one door closes another opens."'

'He says this?'

'All the bloody time. McKellen and Mink just shut our door tonight. I think it's time we opened another.'

'Mink will be—'

'Fuck him. He was happy enough to take our money in the casino, wasn't he? We need to be our own bosses, Orie. That way no one talks to us the way McKellen did tonight. We get to decide what we do and when we do it.'

Orie stuck a cigarette into his mouth. 'Is a risk.'

'So? We're taking risks as it is, aren't we? Least this way we're taking the risk for ourselves.'

'We can make good money,' Orie conceded.

'Yeah, exactly! Imagine what you and me could do together! We'd be rolling in it. We could open the club sooner, make serious money. Shit, we could be high rollers, you know what I mean?'

Orie's eyes were gleaming. 'We could have women, all women.'

'Yeah, well, whatever, we could have serious action. Orie, come on, we've been talking about it for months, right? Well, now's our chance. You in?'

Orie was grinning now. 'I'm in.'

'Say it with me, bro! I'm in!'

'I'm in!'

They knocked knuckles.

'All right,' Lorcan said. 'Now we just need to raise the initial outlay and we're in business.'

'Ah,' Orie said.

'Don't worry, we'll think of something,' Lorcan said.

4

For as long as he could remember, Anthony Dunlop had been called Mink. Never Tony or Anto or any other abbreviation of his Christian name, just Mink. By the time he was old enough to question this peculiarity, the name had stuck, and its origins were lost in the mists of time (although his older sister had once informed him it was because he was a rat bastard, only sneakier).

And, like dogs that came to resemble their owners, eventually Mink grew to fit his moniker. At barely five foot four, he was hardly a remarkable specimen of raw masculinity. He was slight and dainty, prone to giggling, which did nothing to defuse the rumours that he was as bent as a six-pound note. Mink, of course, knew about the rumours but cared little for what other people thought. Gay, straight, into barnyard animals, it was all the same to Mink. The truth was he was straight by design but asexual by choice. Frankly, he found the whole idea of sex messy and slightly distasteful.

Everything about Mink was sleek. He had a delicate face with sharply pointed features. He had a thin pencil moustache, and his hair, which he wore greased back, was jet black (Noir Nights) and shone like polished ebony. His skin, unblemished by the sun – he claimed he was allergic to it – was alabaster white.

His floor manager and assistant, Poppy, sometimes referred to him as Gomez, but only when she was absolutely positive he was nowhere within earshot. He would not have found it amusing. And he was not a man to irk.

Mink was the youngest of a big working-class family from the East Wall. His father, Charlie, had worked in a factory out at Bray and only returned to the family home at weekends, when he would spend his time coughing, drinking and generally whiling away the hours until he could escape his family again. Bray was not far away, but it was obvious to everyone that Charlie liked this arrangement, living in relative peace, away from his sprawling brood and domineering wife.

Mink's abiding memory of his father was of a slight, ineffectual man, who liked to pretend he was asleep when approached by members of his immediate family. He had died from lung cancer when Mink was fifteen. After his funeral, he was quickly and quietly forgotten about, almost as though he had never existed.

Celia Dunlop, Mink's mother, was something else entirely. Big and loud, with arms like a sailor and a shock of wiry black hair, she ruled her roost with an iron fist and a tongue that could scrape the skin off a child at twenty paces. She had borne Charlie ten children – which had amazed Mink when it dawned on him the effort Charlie must have had to make in impregnating his mother – of whom seven had survived, Mink being the youngest.

Celia or Cece as her few friends called her, was a flighty woman who had been backed into life's yoke and fought against it with every fibre of her being. Poor, yet well read and prone to fits of unbelievable temper, she could be sweet as treacle one minute and cold as ice the next. She kept the home together through sheer force of will and insisted that all of her children remained at school and got an education so that they might live better lives than the one she had been forced to endure. And they had followed her wishes to a T.

According to anyone who knew her, Cece was a holy terror. But, like Mink, she cared little for what others thought. She was ambitious, pushy and cavalier in attitude, though not ignorant of the hurt she caused in others. On the contrary, she was a master manipulator of emotion. She didn't need to threaten her children physically: her words were enough to inflict the deepest pain. Her tongue was as vicious as a bull-whip. She ridiculed her brood regularly, finding soft spots and, like a blowfly to a corpse, zoning in with uncanny accuracy. If they got poor marks, she belittled them; she played off one against another, praising one to the heavens while sneering at the rest. It had made the Dunlop children ultra-competitive and disdainful of weakness.

By the time he was seventeen, Mink hated her more than anyone in the world. And when his older brother Charles had killed himself rather than come home and tell his mother he had been let go from his job with the Bank of Ireland – the first white-collar Dunlop, as Cece had called him – Mink had decided there and then to have nothing more to do with her. He also decided that 'white-collar' was a load of his ever-loving hoop and only a mug would aspire to it.

He had left home the day after Charles's funeral, and never returned.

At first, life had not been easy for Mink, but at eighteen he travelled to London where a whole new world had opened up to him. It was the early eighties and, compared to recession-squeezed Ireland, England's capital was awash with money and young people eager to spend it. Mink, ever the pragmatist, followed the money trail, which led him unsurprisingly to the East End, where working-class men like himself toiled hard and played harder still. He landed his first casino gig aged nineteen, and by twenty-two had become one of the best-known faces in the business.

In the casinos, Mink had learned some valuable life lessons. Regardless of outside forces, the economic or personal situation, men and women liked to gamble, and a potent mix of alcohol, sex and food encouraged them to part with their money. The surroundings were important: plush was good, over-the-top was better, and no-expense-spared was best. He found that the personal touch was everything: knowing a client by name, offering a complimentary drink here, a meal there, an introduction to a glamorous woman, it all helped.

But money was everything, the bottom line. And you could make it through girls, food, everything and anything. He had seen several fortunes won and lost – mostly lost – over the years and understood that wealth could be fleeting. When you were down, you stayed down: friends drifted away from losers for fear of contamination. He was determined never to find himself in that position.

Mink missed no opportunity to learn, and by the time he returned to Ireland in 1992, just as the Celtic Tiger was sharpening its claws, he was a formidable businessman, but an even more formidable crook. He had little compunction and few weaknesses. He concerned himself with only one thing: money – how to get it, how to keep it, how to make more of it.

He now had two casinos, in Galway and in Dublin. The Dublin one was called the Mariposa, Spanish for 'butterfly', housed in a white Edwardian building just off Ely Place. When asked about the name, Mink liked to say that anyone could come in as a caterpillar with a few quid in their pocket, but if Lady Luck smiled on them they could leave as a butterfly. He also owned Cherries, a 'high-end' lap-dancing club on Fitzwilliam Street, and it was from the floor above it that he managed his empire.

Behind the glamorous façade of the casinos he also ran a string of high-class escort agencies dotted across the country. They were a useful and highly lucrative tie-in with his legitimate interests. Men liked a beautiful hostess. They gambled more money with greater abandon when they had a lady on their arm. If they lost, the lady smiled and told them whatever they needed to hear to make them feel like winners again. The men felt like kings and the ladies didn't do shabbily either. To Mink it seemed an ideal arrangement.

Of course he didn't want to be associated with the escort side. Even the manager of the main agency in Dublin didn't know that Mink's money had founded the penthouse. Mink's assistant, Poppy, had convinced her it was an associate's. And that was the way Mink wanted it kept. He felt no need to advertise his acumen. He did not like publicity, never felt the need to be photographed or appear in the society pages of a newspaper. No, Mink liked the life, the trappings and the money. Publicity left him cold.

And he disliked problems as much as he disliked publicity.

It seemed to him, as he listened to Jimmy McKellen recount the evening's tale of woe, that Lorcan Wallace and his pal Orie had become a major problem.

'I told you Lorcan was a loose cannon. I warned you about him from the start,' Jimmy ranted.

'He can be unreasonable, but he spends a lot of money. I like people who spend a lot of money at my tables.'

Jimmy grunted. 'Unreasonable? He's as thick as bottled shite. You can't talk to him, Mink – he flies off the handle if you so much as look crooked at him. I'm telling you, he's not right in the head.'

'His old man used to be one of the best safe men in the business, did you know that?'

'Brains must skip a generation.'

'And the Polack?'

'I don't trust him at all. He's smarter for one thing.' Jimmy shifted in his seat. 'Look, Mink, you're asking me and I'm telling you, we can't trust them. If that girl surfaces, we need a fall guy.'

'We can't touch Lorcan,' Mink said, his eyes drifting to the monitor on his desk. The cameras were fixed over the private booths in the club downstairs, and Sofia, one of his girls, was gyrating slowly before a man who was pink-faced with hooch and lust.

'I'd rather be rid of him than the Polack. At least the Polack's useful on the other side.'

'I know, but Lorcan's connected. Darren might be retired, but you can be sure he still knows people. We don't need that kind of trouble, Jimmy.'

'So, because his old man's an ex-con we're stuck with him.'

'Thems the breaks.'

'Yeah, I know, but I'm telling you, I don't like him.'

Mink got up and strode to the window. He lifted the shade and gazed down on the late-night traffic as it moved along Fitzwilliam Street. 'Without the Polack Lorcan will soon fall into line.'

'I wouldn't be so sure,' Jimmy said. 'You didn't see the little fuck tonight. He's frothing because he owes money to Slim.'

'Ah.'

Somebody knocked at Mink's office door.

'Come in.'

'I got confirmation on all the tables for big games. The charity poker night's gonna be knockout and I mean knock-bloomin'-out.' Poppy strode in as she spoke, a file open in her hands. She nodded briefly to Jimmy. Mink turned and watched her as she crossed the floor.

Poppy was a London girl, born and raised. She spoke like an *EastEnders* reject. She was a small, busty, platinum blonde with a pixie cut, who owned a king's ransom in high heels. People underestimated her because of her size and her accent, which he knew she hammed up. Beneath the dolly-bird front she was as sharp as a tack. Mink had head hunted her from another casino after watching her work the room three nights in a row. She was his right-hand woman, and sometimes he thought she knew him better than he knew himself.

'What we need is a few names to liven it up. I'm talking about models, rugby players, anyone media-related. There's a PR firm we can hire and we need . . .' She stopped and glanced from Jimmy to Mink. 'Everything all right, boss? You look like you just found a toe in your yoghurt.'

'No digits in my dairy.'

'I've got the preliminary guest list here if you want to look over it.'

'Leave it there. I'll take a look at it in a while. And tell Magda the photos for last night's new IDs are slightly blurred. What's the point in having photo ID if you can't tell who a person is from their card? They can be cleaned up, but it's not to happen again.'

'Right.'

'I'm not happy about last night's girls, Poppy. That tall redhead was wearing flats in the Mariposa. I won't have that. It looks ugly.'

'Right.'

'I mean, whatever next? They'll be coming in wearing tracksuits and those camel-coloured sheepskin boots.'

'Uggs.'

Mink pulled a face. 'If I see anyone wearing flats that girl is out on her ear.'

'I'll take care of it.'

'Standards, Poppy, we have to keep them up.'

'Right.'

'That's all.' Mink clasped his hands behind his back.

Jimmy watched Poppy go. 'So what do you want to do?'

'Get rid of the Polack. That'll soften Lorcan's cough.'

'When?'

'No time like the present.'

5

Lorcan dropped Orie off on O'Connell Bridge and headed back across Westmoreland Street. He parked in an empty loading bay on Drury Street and crossed the road. He turned left onto Fade Street and walked briskly along until he had passed the entrance to the Market Bar. Two doors down he paused and glanced around. Satisfied that no one was watching, he rang a discreet bell.

Seconds later, the door was opened by a behemoth known only to him as Ga-Ga.

'Hey, Ga-Ga. He here?'

The behemoth jerked his head towards a narrow set of stairs. 'Go on up.'

Lorcan slipped past the big man and took the stairs three at a time. He stopped outside a reinforced metal door and knocked. He had made the mistake of barging in without knocking only once: the blow he had received to the back of the head had almost put out his lights permanently.

The door opened and a second man, who made Ga-Ga look like an elf, peered out.

'Hey, Dolan, it's me.'

Dolan closed the door in his face without uttering a word. Lorcan waited, drying his damp palms on the legs of his jeans.

After what seemed an age, the door opened again, and Lorcan stepped into the one-bedroomed apartment from which Teddy 'Slim' Keane ran his one-stop loan shop.

'Hey, Slim.'

Slim was in his usual position, his near three-hundred-pound frame wedged into a reclining chair, PlayStation console gripped in his fat fingers. He was playing the latest Grand Theft Auto game. The space around his seat was littered with takeaway boxes and empty Coke cans. He didn't so much as look up at Lorcan.

'You got the money?' His voice was barely above a wheeze, but it made the hairs on the back of Lorcan's neck stiffen.

'Yes.'

'Give it to Dolan.'

Dolan held out his hand. Lorcan removed three grand of the five he had made that evening from his pocket and passed it over.

Dolan took it to a table where he counted it quickly and methodically. Once he was certain it was exactly right, he carried it into another room.

'Business must be picking up,' Slim said.

'It's OK.'

'You still following the gee-gees?'

'Now and then.'

Slim produced some sound that Lorcan guessed was a laugh. It was either that or the man was losing a lung.

'How's your father?'

'Yeah, he's good. Look, Slim, that interest is killing me.'

'Yeah?'

'Can't you just drop it a bit? Even half a per cent? Just until I get my feet under me a bit. You know I'm good for it. Me and Orie, we're going into business and—'

'Dolan will show you out,' the fat man said, using his screen car to plough through a group of screaming pedestrians. 'See you next week.'

'Slim—'

'Let's go.' Dolan reappeared and waved his hand towards the outer door. Lorcan bit his lip and turned to leave.

'Kid.'

He turned back. Slim still had not taken his eye from the screen, but somehow Lorcan knew he could see him.

'Don't fuck with me on this issue. You asked for my help, I gave it. You knew the terms, no one held a gun to your head. But, trust me, that will be the case if you try to fuck with me. Have yourself a pleasant evening.'

Dolan moved between them and guided Lorcan to the door. In less than a minute he was out on the street. He checked his wallet. He was down to two grand, just like that.

He walked back towards his car. How the hell had it come to this? He was in a hole to the tune of almost eighty grand to Slim, and with the twenty per cent interest rate he'd never be free of it. He was shelling out serious money and barely making a dent.

He reached his car and stopped. A bright yellow clamp was attached to the rear wheel and a sticker plastered across the driver's window. Lorcan took out his mobile phone and called the number printed on it.

Half an hour later, a white clamper van pulled up, and a tall, Nordic-looking man alighted.

'Good evening.'

Lorcan nodded to him.

'You want to pay cash or credit card?'

Without a word, Lorcan paid him the eighty euro required to

free his car. The man pocketed the money and wrote him a receipt, which Lorcan also accepted silently.

The man set to work. He squatted and unlocked the clamp, took it off and stowed it in the back of the van.

While he did this, Lorcan took a tyre iron from the boot of the Honda, carried it to the front of the clamper van and smashed in the windscreen and passenger windows. He threatened to do the same to the man when it looked as if he was about to intervene.

After he'd put out the headlight, he replaced the tyre iron in the boot and stared at the shaken clamper, who had retreated to the footpath where a crowd of late-night revellers had gathered to cheer and clap.

'You're fucking crazy,' the clamper said. 'I have your number, I'm calling the guards.'

'Have yourself a pleasant evening,' Lorcan told him, then climbed into his car and roared off down the street.

6

Orie Kavlar flung his cards down in disgust. 'Fold.'

'I don't think the cards favour you tonight, my friend.'

Orie tried not to rise to the bait, even though Chippy, the dealer, an odious slanty-eyed toad from God knew where, had spoken in that smug way he hated. He checked his watch. It didn't look as though Lorcan was coming to the game after all.

'Maybe it's time to call it quits.'

'What are you – my wife?' Orie could barely bring himself to watch Chippy drag the money from the centre of the table towards himself. The dealer's undisguised glee was just too hard to take. 'Deal and mind your own fucking business.'

Chippy collected the cards and shuffled, his expert fingers moving and cutting in a continuous blur. 'Are you sure you want—'

'Too much talk. Deal cards.'

Chippy dealt hard and fast. There were six of them seated around the table. Orie, Chippy and four other Chinese, three men and a woman. The Chinese smoked incessantly and never seemed to sweat.

Orie peered at his cards and contained a groan. Another shit hand. He flung them into the centre of the table. 'Fold. I go for a piss.'

Chippy beamed at him. The Chinese exchanged glances. Were they smirking? How the hell could anyone tell?

Orie grabbed his jacket and left the basement. He heard the Chinese jibber-jabbering among themselves and cursed. He hated playing with them. He hated playing in this dump, but what choice did he have? He was barred from most of the casinos, and he owed money all round town.

He slumped against the wall of the underground passage and dug out a cigarette. That manky Chippy with his grins and his sly digs. It was always bad doing business with the Chinese. They were hard to read, their fades and tells not as easy to spot. Plus they'd sit there all night. Degenerate gamblers, the lot of them.

Orie pulled the smoke down deep into his lungs and held it there, savouring it, thinking.

The dead girl troubled him. Jimmy McKellen had been as freaked out as Orie had ever seen him. It made him feel twitchy. He didn't like working with the man at the best of times.

The alternative wasn't so hot either.

Orie took another drag. Lorcan's plan was simple, but dangerous. First, the Russians were an unpredictable lot, and even guaranteeing they could do business with them was no easy task. On top of that, they were Mink's contacts. Now, Orie wasn't stupid. The main guy – the guy who spoke Polish and English and probably half a dozen other languages – didn't give a shit who he dealt with as long as he got paid. His only caveat was that he wouldn't work with fools.

First problem: Orie liked Lorcan well enough in short bursts, but Lorcan was far from smart – he was flash, a mouthpiece who attracted attention. The second problem was that Lorcan suffered from weird mood swings. He went from green to red in a heartbeat. He was impetuous and flighty, quick to anger and slow to cool. And he held a grudge like no other. He was worse when he drank. He couldn't hold his drink or his bloody tongue. And Lorcan drank a lot.

And then there was the money. Money seemed to pass through Lorcan's hands like water. Orie had never seen anything like it. He knew Lorcan had a gambling problem. Shit, Orie liked to gamble too, but Lorcan bet on whether or not the sun would rise. He patted his breast pocket, alarmed at how flat it felt compared to earlier. He had hoped to double or even triple the cash he had earned from the girls, but somehow it just hadn't happened.

The early clouds had cleared, and he could make out a star here and there in the night sky.

He'd had a bad run of luck, that was all. Maybe he ought to call it a night, head home and catch some shut-eye. Tomorrow was another day.

A bottle clinked in the alley to his left.

Orie peered into the shadows and felt a prickle of unease. He sensed rather than saw movement. He squinted, but the shadows remained impenetrable. He reached behind him to feel for the knife he always carried in his belt. 'Who's there?'

Nothing.

'Who's there?'

'Hey, Orie, it's only me.'

Orie was surprised to see Jimmy McKellen appear out of the gloom. Surprised and alarmed. 'Jimmy. What you doing here?'

'Nice night.'

Orie didn't reply.

'Mink wants a chat.'

'I am busy now.'

'I know how it is.' Jimmy twisted out a smile. 'Are you having a good night?'

'No.'

'Me neither.'

Orie waved a hand dismissively as he straightened up, but he kept his right hand concealed. He knew the man was as dangerous as a cornered rattlesnake. He tried to think. If he went back inside, the Chinese would be of no use to him so he should aim for the street.

'Why don't you come on over to the club? I had a hell of a job tracking you down. Is your phone not working?'

'Is broke. Why does Mink want to talk tonight?'

'Search me. He just asked me to come and pick you up. I think he might have another job or two for you. So, you coming or what?'

'Sure.' Orie raised one shoulder. 'I will go to club after game.'

'I think you should probably come with me now.'

It wasn't a suggestion, and the over-friendly semi-cajoling tone was gone. Orie knew his card had been marked. Mink must have been more than unhappy about the girl. 'Sure.' He pitched away his cigarette and turned to the door.

'Don't do that, Orie,' Jimmy McKellen said, and something in his voice made Orie pause and look around.

'I get coat.'

Jimmy did not respond, but when he met Orie's gaze, Orie could see his eyes were as flat as bottomless pools. Whatever Jimmy McKellen had planned, whatever duty Mink had ordered him to perform, it was clear he had not a single qualm about doing it.

'You have your coat.'

Orie casually loosened the clip of the knife scabbard and transferred his weight to his heels. If Jimmy McKellen thought he'd go easy he was making a mistake. He wouldn't give up without a fight.

Before either man moved, the metal door opened and a patch of yellow light flooded the alley. 'Orie? You out here?'

'Lorcan!'

'Hey, Chippy said you'd better hurry up if you want in on the next hand.'

Lorcan's eyes drifted to where Jimmy McKellen had taken a step backwards towards the concrete steps.

'What are you doing here?'

'Hey, Lorcan.'

'What are you doing here?' Lorcan repeated and glanced at Orie. 'Everything all right?'

'Jimmy was telling me that Mink wanted to see me.'

'Oh, yeah?' Lorcan stepped into the alley but kept the door ajar with his foot. 'Why's that? He offering us our work back?'

'No, look, it was nothing major, just a chat,' Jimmy said, smiling. Everyone knew that Lorcan was a martial-arts fanatic, but that didn't mean jack shit in most street fights. 'Sure it can wait if you've a game on.'

Lorcan's eyes narrowed. 'Was it just Orie he wanted to see? He didn't want to talk to me about anything? Like maybe how sorry he is for fucking us over some dead girl?'

Jimmy shrugged. 'I told you, you'll have to take that up with him.'

'Nah, forget it, I'm not taking anything up with anyone. You can tell him that. Me an Orie here, we've decided—'

Orie put up his hand. 'Lorcan, wait—'

'We've decided to branch out on our own. So you can find two other fools to do your runs for you. I won't be putting no more money into his club neither. We're done.'

Jimmy McKellen laughed. 'You're branching out? What the fuck do you think this is? Some kind of co-op?'

'Maybe you ought to head on back to your side of tracks, Jimmy,' Lorcan said, in a low voice.

'You threatening me, kid?' Jimmy said, and now there wasn't a hint of laughter in his voice. 'You think that because some of your old man's juice didn't dribble down yer mam's leg you can threaten me?'

'You want to start something with me, Jimmy, you'd better be prepared to finish it.'

Jimmy's hands bunched, but after a moment they relaxed. 'You're not fucking worth the time or the trouble.'

Lorcan's lip curled. 'Come on, Orie, let's get a hand in before Chippy calls it a night.'

Orie moved off the wall and slipped behind his friend.

'Orie.' Jimmy raised his voice a touch. 'Mink will still want to talk to you.'

'You can tell Mink anything he has to say to Orie he can say to me,' Lorcan said.

'You don't want to play it like this, Lorcan,' Jimmy said. 'You aren't *that* stupid.'

Lorcan backed into the doorway. 'Fuck you, Jimmy, fuck you and fuck Mink. You can pass that message on tonight.'

He let the metal door close, casting Jimmy McKellen back into the shadows where he belonged.

7

Detective Sergeant Ray Devlin clamped a cigarette between his lips and rubbed his hands, hoping to get the circulation going. His feet were sinking in the freezing mud and a sharp wind ripped through the trees, lifting the flap of his overcoat and chilling him to the bone. It was well after midnight, but bad luck and a mean duty sergeant had him covering for another officer who was sick. He leaned over the crime-scene tape. 'Well?'

Assistant State Pathologist Colm Furlong put down his camera. 'Don't light that here.'

'I won't. What have we got? You reckon she was dumped, right?'

'Of course she was. Lividity suggests she didn't die here.'

'So what happened to her? Can you see anything out of the ordinary?'

'I would hope none of this is ordinary to you, Sergeant.'

'Come on, man, you know what I mean.'

'Sergeant, there are five manners of death. Did you know that?'

'You don't say.'

'Natural, accidental, suicidal, homicidal and undetermined.'

'So what are we looking at here?'

'Well, we have a young girl in full rigor. I'd put her age to be fifteen, sixteen or thereabouts.'

'Junkie?'

'I don't know.'

'Any sign of injury?'

'No blunt trauma that I can see.'

'Right, so we've a young girl, dead, no sign of attack.'

'I didn't say she wasn't attacked; I said there's no visible sign of any blunt trauma.'

'Right. So it could have been a natural death.'

Furlong snorted softly.

Devlin waited. Sometimes, working with Furlong was like pulling teeth.

The pathologist picked up his torch. He checked the girl's arm again and shone the light on her hands. 'Hmm.'

'What?' Devlin inched slightly closer. Truth was, even after ten years on the force he still wasn't a big fan of bodies. He'd had the misfortune to attend a bloater during his third week in the job and had never really recovered from it. 'What am I supposed to be looking at?'

'Are you blind? Look, man.'

Devlin peered. 'Jesus—'

'Rats, they've had a good go at the fingers. Some of her nails are broken too.'

'—Christ.'

The pathologist laid her hand down and moved to her head. He shone the torch all around her face and into her mouth. 'Hmm,' he said again.

'I don't know yet.'

Devlin hopped from one foot to the other in consternation. He fancied he could see tiny eyes in the shadows, hairless tails twitching with anticipation. It was probably his imagination, but that didn't stop his stomach churning. He wished he had left for home before the call to cover had come in. He wished his boss Stafford didn't seem to have it in for him. He really didn't like bodies. 'Well, I'm sure you'll know more when you get her back to the lab.'

'Naturally.'

'Right. I'd better get on and see if I can get statements from the witnesses. I'll talk to you later.'

'Don't you want an answer?'

'An answer?'

'To your question.'

Devlin squinted at Furlong, but the tall man's morose face betrayed nothing. Still, he had long suspected Furlong of being a smart arse, and tonight's encounter had done nothing to disabuse him of that view. 'Go on,' he said cautiously.

Furlong straightened and jerked his gloved thumb towards the girl. 'I'm going to go with homicidal. I doubt she decided to smother herself.'

'She was smothered?'

'My guess would be yes.'

'Your guess?'

'My guess, until I examine her properly. And people don't generally smother themselves.'

'Clever,' Devlin said. 'Obvious you're not used to a live audience.'

'The dead try to tell us many things, Sergeant, but we don't always hear them.'

'Weirdo,' Devlin muttered, through a cigarette, as he stalked away. He lit it as he climbed the dog-shit-and-rubbish-strewn bank and jumped down onto the wooded path, hoping to take a quick statement and get the hell back to the station, then home to bed.

He should have known it wouldn't be that simple.

'G'wan to fuck. I'm not giving me name,' the male witness said, glancing around furtively, as though the trees might overhear. 'I told you we were just out for a walk.'

'You were out walking in the dark at this hour on a Sunday night?'

'That's right,' his female companion said. 'We were walking.'

Devlin looked her over. She wasn't dressed for walking. She was having a hard job keeping her high heels from sinking into the mud. 'A walk? From where? To where? There's nothing around here for miles.'

'Well, the car's in the car park.'

'So you parked it and walked down to a rubbish tip?' Devlin rubbed his nose with his thumb. 'Tell me from the top what happened.'

'I already did. We were just out walking and we found her there. Nearly set the heart crossways in me so it did.'

'Was she already dead when you found her?'

'She looked dead to me.'

'You didn't check to see if she had a pulse or if she was still breathing?'

'I didn't touch her. I'm telling you she was dead. Her eyes were open.'

'And what time was this?'

''Bout half eleven.'

'You didn't see anyone else around?'

'No. Sure it was almost pitch black.'

'You didn't notice anyone leave the area? A car or maybe a van?'

'There was no sign of anyone.'

'There wasn't,' the woman confirmed, pulling her coat closer around her. 'Look, I've gotta get home. I can't be out all night.'

'I still need your names.'

'You won't be getting them.' The man drew himself up to his full height, which stopped somewhere south of Devlin's chin.

'If you don't give them to me, I'm going to have to ask you to come in and sign a full statement.'

'Ask me hole,' the man said. 'We didn't do anything wrong.'

'We've got rights,' the woman added.

Devlin sighed again. It was going to be a long night.

8

'Ow – son of a bitch!' said John Quigley, private detective, devoted smoker and not very good carpenter. He shook his hand then held it up to the light for inspection. 'Jesus, will you look at that!'

'What is it?' DJ Clique, young, currently emo and probably a higher earner than John, looked up from his seat on the floor.

'Splinter.' John pulled it out with his teeth. 'I thought you said this thing'd be a doddle. I'm telling you, Click, half the screw holes don't match up.'

'Clique,' the young DJ corrected automatically. 'Not Click. Why do you always get it wrong?'

'Why does anyone do anything?'

'Oh, man, how has Sarah not killed you over the years?'

'Don't think the idea hasn't crossed her mind.'

The two men were in Rodney Mitchell's office, the solicitor from one floor below QuicK Investigation and one floor up from Freak FM, the pirate radio station where DJ Clique worked, which just so happened to be owned by John's slightly crooked pal Mike Brannigan. There was a clapped-out grocery on the ground floor of the dilapidated Georgian building, run by a crazy woman who insisted on leaving her empty cardboard boxes strewn about the communal hall, regardless of the local fire inspector's admonishments. This was the community.

Rodney was lying in the Mater Hospital, with his leg in traction. He had been working late on the evening an intruder had broken into John and Sarah's office. On hearing the disturbance upstairs, he had tried to stop whoever it was destroying the place. For his efforts he had received a severe beating, leaving him with a broken leg and concussion.

John had been in to see him regularly. He had refused to sneak him in any bottles of hooch, reasoning correctly that alcohol was the last thing Rodney – a borderline alcoholic – needed to mix with his medication. Instead, he had somehow wound up agreeing to put together some flat-pack furniture for him. The previous day he had found Clique gazing mournfully at a flat tyre on his moped and had offered to drive him home in exchange for his help. So here they were, the blind leading the blind.

Clique slicked his purple fringe out of his eyes and peered at the wood scattered about the office floor. 'Which piece do you have?'

'Eight.'

'I have eight.'

John tapped a nondescript section by his foot. 'Then what do I have?'

'Pass me the instructions.'

'Oh, right, 'cause you're so good with them.'

'I can't be any worse than you, man.'

John lit a cigarette. Kids these days, so forceful.

'Hmm.' Clique squinted at the paper, tilting it towards the light.

'Anything making sense?'

'It's says here we need to put the dowel into the third holes in pieces seven and eight.'

'And then what?'

'And then put the sixteen-millimetre screws into the backboard.'

'Which one is the backboard?'

'It must be the long bit.'

'I thought you said that was the door.'

Clique glanced at him, exasperated. 'You said it was the door.'

'It's the backboard,' another voice said.

Both men looked round.

Sarah Kenny leaned against the open doorway, a paper bag tucked under her arm and an amused smile on her lips. She wore dark trousers and a snow-white T-shirt under a black wool coat. Her straight dark hair hung loose over her shoulders. John was surprised to see her.

'DIY, John, you? Now I've seen it all. Hello, Clique.'

'Sarah, hey. Good to see you. How've you been?'

'Fine, thanks.'

John gave her the once-over. She was too thin, too pale, and the dark rings under her brown eyes had not lessened, but at least the bruises on her face were fading and her nose, though still scabbed, was returning to its normal shape and size. 'What are you doing here? I thought you were going to take today off.'

'I've had enough time off. It's boring, and there's only so much daytime television I can cope with. You wouldn't believe the rubbish they put on. Have you ever watched Jeremy Kyle?'

'Never heard of him.'

'Trust me, that's a good thing.' She nodded, a little curtly. 'How are you, Clique? How did he manage to drag you into this?'

'He played on my good nature.'

'Pfft! I played on your laziness, you mean. You could have said no to the lift.'

'And miss an opportunity to spend time in your thrilling company?'

'How's Rodney?' Sarah had changed the subject.

'Doing OK – I was in with him yesterday for a while,' John told her. 'They've lowered his pain medication, so he was bitching about that.'

'Are you going in today?'

'Maybe tomorrow.'

'Will you tell him I was asking for him?'

'Why don't you come with me? I know he'd love to see you.'

'Maybe later in the week.'

Clique glanced at his oversized watch. 'Dude, I've got a show in half an hour.'

Sarah straightened. 'I'm going to head upstairs, John. I've some paperwork that needs doing. Here, I brought you a roll.' She reached into the bag and handed him a small parcel wrapped in tinfoil.

'Cheers.'

'I'm sorry, Clique,' she went on, 'I didn't know you'd be here or I'd have brought you something too.'

Clique waved a hand. 'Don't worry, I wouldn't touch one of those if my life depended on it. All that grease and those trans-fats, man, yuck. That shit'll mess you up.'

'Yeah, right,' John snorted, 'but you'll smoke grass until you turn green at the gills.'

'All natural, man, totally different, not like that chemical stick you smoke. You should switch. There's been surveys done, and they prove grass can be beneficial to a man's well-being. You can't say that about cigarettes.'

'Where?'

'Where what?'

'Where were these surveys done?'

'I don't know – universities and places like that.'

'So, good unbiased sources, then.'

'Well,' Sarah said, 'I'll leave you to it.'

'I'll be up shortly.' John raised his roll. 'Thanks for the grub.'

As soon as she had left, John sat on the radiator to eat.

'She's so sad, isn't she?' Clique said, picking up the instructions again.

'Huh?'

'She seems so down. She got really banged up in that attack – and for what? A few quid, a phone?'

'I don't think he got anything. As far as I know, it was because he didn't take kindly to her resisting that she got so badly hurt.'

'Not worth it.'

'No, definitely not. I hope you'll remember that too.'

'This city, man,' Clique shook his head, 'it's getting more and more out there, you know? No one just argues any more – it's get a knife, kick someone's head in, stab them with a screwdriver. Society, you know? It's fucked up.'

'It sure is.'

John chewed and watched Clique hammer and glue in the dowels. He had plenty of his own questions about what had happened to Sarah. Not that he was getting any answers. That didn't stop him wondering why Sarah had been down by the shore that night. A lot of what she'd said simply didn't add up. Why had she brought her mother to her sister's house? That was so unlike her. Then there were her injuries: she'd taken an unusually vicious hiding over a mugging. Not that it wasn't possible, but something niggled at him about it.

Rodney and Sarah. The pair of them knew something about that night. But until either felt like sharing, John would have no clue as to what it might be. At one point he had even speculated that Sarah and Rodney had fought, but he dismissed that. The damage done to Rodney was not something Sarah could have inflicted, and Rodney would never have lifted his hand to a woman, no matter how blotto he'd gotten. No, it wasn't a fight between them, but there was something. What could they possibly be hiding? And, perhaps more importantly, why hide anything from him of all people?

Whatever had gone on, it had totally changed Sarah. Before John had left for England on their last case, he and Sarah had been on the cusp of something. They'd even shared a kiss in the office. OK, he had sprung it on her, but she had kissed him back, and there had been no mistaking the flirtation until then. But, since he'd returned, Sarah had been acting like a cat on a hot tin roof. At first she had been tearful and anxious; now she was aloof and withdrawn. She wouldn't discuss anything with him other than work, and even then she was stilted.

So what had happened? What had he done wrong? What had changed between them while he had been out of the country for three days?

John popped the last of the roll into his mouth, balled the tinfoil and tossed it into the bin. 'Right then, back to it.'

Clique climbed to his feet, pulling up the skinny jeans he wore halfway down his hips in a gravity-defying display. 'OK, let's see if that's the backboard or not.'

'Clique, if you want to go downstairs and set up, go ahead.'

'Why?'

John took the instructions out of his hands and studied them afresh. 'Mostly because you're about as much use as tits on a bull.'

DJ Clique squared his narrow shoulders and flicked his purple fringe out of his eyes.

'That hurts me right here, man.' He pointed to his heart.

'Really?'

The young man snorted. 'Yeah, can't you see my tears?'

'You can't cry,' John said. 'You'd mess up your eye make-up.'

'Not a chance.' Clique gathered up his things, a blazer two sizes too small for him and his leather laptop bag. 'Maybelline.'

'Huh?'

'Maybelline mascara and liner. Waterproof and smudgeproof.'

'Sweet Jesus.' John sighed. The youth of today. How did they manage to make him feel so bloody old?

9

Sarah let herself into the office and hung her coat on the stand behind the door.

This was her office, her place, not Vic's. He couldn't have it. He couldn't take it away from her. It wasn't much, but it was hers – well, hers and John's. It was a relief, she told herself, to be at work, a relief to be able to do something.

She just needed to keep busy. Do a day's work, behave completely normally.

She made a mug of instant coffee and took a seat behind her desk. She began to sift through her mail. She tried not to think about how vulnerable she felt, how the panic deep within her was ready to spring like a geyser if she let it.

Poor Rodney – he had looked so awful the day she had gone to visit him in hospital. Not that she had looked so hot herself. He had gazed into her eyes and had known immediately.

'What did you do?'

'He can't hurt either of us again, Rodney. I took care of it.'

'Oh, Sarah.'

He had turned away from her, ashen. But she had kept talking, forcing him to listen, forcing him to hear what she had done, filling his head with information he neither wanted to know nor deserved to have inflicted on him.

His face when she had finished. How could she have asked him to keep her secrets? How could she have used his affection for her like that? She could scarcely bring herself to think about the pain he had suffered because of her lies and deceit. The hurt in his eyes had been more than enough to send her spinning in a swirl of guilt and recrimination.

And then there was John. She had been avoiding him for the past week, happy to stay off his radar. John wasn't stupid. He knew something was wrong. He was concerned. She knew that, she knew he cared, she knew he had feelings for her. But she couldn't let him close to her, couldn't risk exposing herself to him. Not now. He'd never understand.

She had killed a man two years before – Patrick York, a drug-running psychopath – but that had been to save John. This was different. She had killed a man in cold blood. It had been premeditated. She had known she would do it before she'd left her home that night. There was no point in pretending otherwise. She had gone there with a knife, and she had killed Victor.

She put her cup down and rested her forehead on her fingertips. There. That was the truth. Didn't psychiatrists say you should face the truth to be set free? Maybe that was the key.

She had killed a man she had once loved. She had killed him and sent his body out to sea.

She needed to think about something else.

Impossible. She knew it was only a matter of time.

She had read the paper that morning, and now her whole world was hanging by a thread. Finally it was here, everything she had feared, everything she had known would happen.

A man's body had been found washed ashore in Wales, a nothing piece in the newspaper, barely five lines long. But reading it had sent her into a tailspin. The description had been vague, but she had known. It was Victor. And if she knew, it was possible that others soon would and then his body would be connected to her. It was only a matter of time before she would be made pay for her actions. Why try to pretend otherwise?

Why bother doing anything?

Stop it.

She glanced at the phone. Why didn't it ring? She'd even welcome a complaint or telesales – anyone. Maybe it was out of order. She lifted the receiver and listened to the dialling tone. It was working fine. She rang the estate agent who was handling the sale of her apartment in Patrick Street. Had they heard anything new? Had there been any more interested parties? No? Just one couple? Would she consider reducing the price a bit more? The market was competitive at the moment. Sure, why not? What did it matter now anyway?

She hung up and twiddled her fingers some more. Maybe some work.

She finished her mail, flicked through John's copy of the *Star*, drained her coffee, straightened her desk and checked the phone again. She was considering whether or not to clean the windows when the buzzer sounded.

She jumped, smashing her knee against the underside of her desk. Cursing, she hobbled to the intercom by the door. 'Hello?'

'I need to speak with the detectives, please.' The voice was young, female, a working-class Dublin accent.

'Come on up. We're on the top floor.'

Sarah buzzed her in and glanced round the room. Strangely, John's desk didn't look like a biohazard. He was making a big effort. He'd even stopped smoking in the office. He was doing it for her.

They had kissed here. A scattering of goose-bumps rose on her arm.

She checked her image in the mirror while she waited for the girl. She smoothed her hair and tugged down the hem of her shirt. *I'm a mess.*

She smiled, checking her teeth for lipstick. On the surface, she appeared a calm, professional woman, thirty-four, slim, tall, serious. Normal. On the surface she could have been anything. The surface would have to do. At that moment it was all she had.

She sat down and, seconds later, heard a soft tap on the door. 'Come in.'

The door opened and a heavily pregnant girl entered. She was short and fine-boned, with mid-brown shoulder-length hair and pale translucent skin. She wore a furry singlet over a gaudy pink tracksuit. The bottoms were stuffed into a pair of the filthy sheepskin Ugg-style boots that all the young seemed to live in. Sarah guessed her to be about eighteen. She looked uncomfortable, flurried, exhausted and more than a little breathless. Sarah guessed the three flights of stairs had been a struggle. 'Please, take a seat.'

The girl eased herself into the chair in front of Sarah's desk with a grateful sigh. She plopped a frayed canvas bag onto her lap and clutched it so hard her knuckles went white. 'Are you the detective?'

'I'm one of them. My name's Sarah Kenny. My partner, John Quigley, is out of the office at the moment.'

'I've read about you lot in the paper.'

The girl glanced around her, clearly not over-impressed by their office. Nobody ever was. Sarah often wondered what people expected to find in a building such as theirs. 'What can I do for you?'

'Stacy. Stacy Power. It's about my fella. He's gone missing. I want . . . I need you to look for him.'

'Your boyfriend?'

'Yeah. I can pay you up front.'

'We can talk about that later,' said Sarah. She pulled a pen from the jar on her desk and opened a notebook on a fresh page. She wrote Stacy's name at the top and 'Missing Person' beneath it. 'How long has your boyfriend been missing?'

'Since Saturday.'

Sarah glanced up. 'It's only Monday – are you sure he's actually missing? Maybe he spent the—'

'I know what missing means. And he's missing.'

'OK. Well, why don't you give me the details? Let's start with his name.'

'Orie Kavlar.'

'Kavlar? Unusual name. Is he Irish?'

'No.' Stacy's face remained impassive but her tone was confrontational. 'He's from Slovakia.'

'Right.' Sarah wrote this down too. 'And what is it that makes you think he's missing?'

'I told you, I haven't seen him since Saturday.'

'Is that unusual?'

'Well, yeah.'

'Has there been any contact at all?'

'He left a message on my phone in the early hours of Sunday morning. A weird one.'

'In what way?'

'He didn't sound like himself.'

'What did he say that was out of the ordinary?'

'He said he'd be gone for a few days but he'd be in touch.'

'I see. So he told you he'd be missing.'

'Look, he sounded weirded out, and then he said I wasn't to go anywhere near the flat.'

'Which flat? Yours?'

'His. We don't live together.'

'Why would he say that?'

'How should I know?'

'Where does Orie live?' Sarah raised an eyebrow.

'Up on Dorset Street. He's got a bedsit there. It's Flat 2, Number 90. It's in the basement. Sometimes I stay over and all but, like, mostly I live with my ma and da. We're getting a place, though, after the baby's born.'

'Can I have your address?'

'160 Cork Street.'

'Oh, we're practically neighbours.'

This didn't seem to impress Stacy any more than the office had done.

'Did he say anything else?'

'Just that he loved me. But something's going on and I'm worried about him.'

'What do you think's happened?'

'I don't know, do I?'

Sarah sighed.

'What?'

'Why do you think he's in trouble? Did he mention to you that he was?'

'No.'

'And he told you he'd be gone for a few days?'

'Yeah, but you didn't hear the way he said it. He was freaked out.'

'OK, then, and where does Orie work?'

'He doesn't have an exact thing. You know what I mean?'

'No, I'm afraid I don't.'

Stacy shifted uneasily on her chair. 'Like nothing regular, nothing nine to five.'

'Is he on the dole?'

'No, he can't get dole, can he? I told you, he's from Slovakia.'

'Sorry,' Sarah said, marvelling at how stupid the girl managed to make her feel. 'So what does he do?'

'He drives a cab part-time.'

'He can't get dole but he can drive a cab?'

'Look, you asked me what he does and I'm telling you, right? I don't need the third degree.'

'OK, OK.' Sarah wrote down 'taxi driver'. 'Can you give me the name of the company he's with?'

'No.'

'Excuse me?'

'Like, the thing is he's not at work. I checked with them. I did that before I came here.'

Sarah put down her pen and regarded the girl. 'Stacy, if you want me to find your boyfriend, you're going to have to trust me, and you're going to have to give me as much information to go on as you can. Otherwise I can't help you.'

'I don't want to get him into any trouble.'

'Why would you be getting him into trouble by telling me where he works?' Sarah asked.

'I dunno – I'm not even saying that, you know? Just . . . Orie's really private, that's all. Look, I don't know if this is such a good idea. I didn't think there'd be so many questions.' Stacy dug a packet of cigarettes out of her bag and opened them with her teeth.

'There's no smoking in here,' Sarah said.

Stacy pulled a face and put them back into her bag. She tugged a pale-blue pendant from under her top and fiddled with that instead. She was close to tears, Sarah could see.

'What about a description, then? Can you give me that? Do you have a recent photo?'

She opened the bag again and handed Sarah a snapshot, carefully pressed between clear plastic. 'He's about five foot eight. As you can see, he's got really dark hair, kind of long at the back. It's curly and shiny.'

Sarah took the photo and put it on her desk. 'How long have you and Orie being going out?'

'Almost a year now and . . . why are you looking at me like that? I know what you're thinking. Same as me folks, but I don't care nothing about it, and Orie doesn't either. He's me fella and so what how long we're going out?'

'What age are you?'

'I'll be eighteen in December.'

She said it so defiantly that Sarah couldn't help but smile. Oh, to be young and in love, brave and so foolhardy. 'When are you due?'

'In a fortnight.'

'Girl or boy?'

'I don't know.'

'Which would you like?'

'I don't mind either way.' Stacy had relaxed her guard a little: she no longer seemed angry and resentful, just scared and vulnerable. Sarah thought she preferred the former. 'Orie says he thinks it's a boy from the way I'm carrying. But we didn't want to know. And, anyway, we don't care long as it's healthy. That's what matters. Right?'

'Sure.' Sarah wanted to tell her she ought not to smoke if the baby's health was a priority, but she didn't. It was none of her business. And she didn't think Stacy would take kindly to her observation. 'So tell me what happened on Saturday? Did you have a row? Maybe he's cooling his heels for a few days.'

'No, there was no row. We hardly ever row about anything.'

Sarah said nothing to that, but she could tell from the way Stacy's expression froze that she had lied.

'I called over Saturday morning and we talked about stuff. Then Orie had to go because he had to work early. He's been covering extra shifts on account of the baby coming. He was doing the double shift on Saturday. He's, like, a really hard worker.'

'OK, that's good.'

'So, I said goodbye to him around eleven and that was the last I saw of him.'

'He didn't call or mention anything to you about needing to go anywhere this weekend?'

'No. And he would have done.'

'And you said you contacted the taxi company?'

'Yeah, and they keep telling me they don't know nothing either. Wouldn't even tell me if he was working his normal shifts. But that might be because of the work permit or something.'

'Have you gone to the guards?'

'No, and I won't. Orie would freak out.'

'Does he have a mobile?'

'It's broke.' She bit her lower lip, unsure again. 'I've left loads of messages in case he was checking voicemail.'

'What about friends? Would he maybe have gone to stay with one?'

'I don't really know any of them to talk to.'

'You don't know any of his friends?'

'That's what I said, isn't it?' Stacy pressed her hand to her stomach as though she was in pain.

'Are you OK?'

'I'm fine.'

'Do you want a glass of water?'

'No – I just want you to find Orie, OK? I don't care about anything else. I think something's happened to him. He wouldn't do this – he wouldn't just go off.'

'Has he ever gone off before?'

Stacy turned her head to the window. 'No, not really . . . not like this.'

'Like what, then?'

'Orie's not like everyone else, OK? I mean, he works a lot. He likes his down time, that's the way he is, but nothing like this, and the one time he did have to lie low for a few days it was mostly my old lad's fault.'

'Your father?'

She shrugged.

'I take it he was unhappy about the baby.'

Stacy shrugged again, but there was a shine in her eyes that no amount of bravado could cover.

'Is your father still angry with him?'

'He's not exactly over the moon, but what can he do? What's done is done. It's none of his business anyway. But I didn't come here to talk about me old lad. I just want you to find Orie.'

There was a faint sheen of perspiration on Stacy's upper lip, and the colour had drained from her face. Sarah watched her wince again and felt a flicker of alarm. 'Are you sure you're OK?'

'Yeah, can you pass me one of those tissues?'

Sarah handed her the box from her desk. Stacy took one and blew her nose furiously. She took a deep breath and composed herself as best she could. 'I know what the look was for, earlier. Everyone thinks he's done a runner 'cause of the baby, but it's not like that. Orie loves me, and he's happy about the baby. Jesus, he's nearly more excited about it than I am.'

'That's good.'

She blew her nose again, long and hard. 'It's a girl.'

'I thought you didn't know.'

'Orie thinks it's bad luck to find out beforehand, but I couldn't help it. I asked the nurse on my last scan. I didn't tell him.'

'I'm sure he doesn't need to know,' Sarah said kindly, wondering why Orie hadn't been with Stacy to her last scan if he was such a prince. 'But, Stacy, I meant what I said earlier. If you want me to find him you've got to give me more information than you have so far. I need to know at least where he works.'

'I don't want to get him in trouble.' She blinked and looked forlornly at Sarah.

Sarah waited. If the girl was serious about finding the missing boyfriend she had to play ball. If not, she could leave, and Sarah could go back to staring into space and worrying about her own mental health.

'All right,' Stacy said after a moment. 'He works for Ace Cabs. They're over on the North Circular Road.'

Sarah copied this information down. 'And Orie's from Slovakia?'

'Yeah.'

'How long has he been in Ireland?'

'Three years now.'

'Has he always lived at the place in Dorset Street?'

'I think so.'

'What kind of cab does he drive?'

'A Toyota Corolla, beige.'

'Do you have the registration number?'

With another scowl Stacy gave it to her.

'And is it his own car or the cab company's?'

'The cab company's. He shares it with another guy.'

'Can you give me his partner's name?'

'Gappy.'

'Gappy?'

Stacy nodded.

'Does this Gappy have a second name?'

'I don't know.'

Sarah put down her pen down. 'You don't know a whole lot about Orie, do you?'

'I know I love him and he loves me,' Stacy said.

Suddenly Sarah felt very sad – sad and old. 'OK, Stacy, give me everything you've got.'

Stacy did just that and, as Sarah had suspected, it didn't take long.

10

When she heard the front door close, Caoimhe Wallace glanced at the kitchen clock. It was ten past ten on a bright, cold Monday morning and she was alone in the Castleknock house she shared with her father. She put down her teacup and hurried into the hall, just in time to catch her younger brother shrug off his jacket and head for the stairs. 'Lorcan? What are you doing here?'

'I have to get something from the attic.' He stopped and scowled. 'What are you doing here?'

'I live here.'

'I thought you'd be in work.'

'Where the hell have you been? The Gardaí called here yesterday looking for you. Why didn't you answer your phone? I've been calling and calling.'

'I was asleep.'

'Asleep? All day yesterday?'

Lorcan didn't answer.

'Dad's going absolutely spare. What happened on Saturday night?'

Lorcan rolled his head. He was wrecked and the last thing he needed was to stand here and explain himself to his sister. He and Orie had played poker with the Chinese until the early hours of Sunday morning, and then they had headed back to his place to crash, thinking it safer for Orie than going back to his. By the time he had woken up late on Sunday evening Orie had vanished but he'd left a note telling him he'd call.

Lorcan had read the note, feeling hungry and hung-over. He had managed to fix one of those problems but not the other. To make things worse, he'd lost eight hundred to the Chinese and another five hundred on a supposed sure thing as Man United had lost to fucking Bolton.

What the hell was Caoimhe doing here anyway? He had planned to nip in, find his old lad's chequebook, write himself a cheque, take anything he was sure his old man wouldn't miss and sell it. Simple as that.

'Lorcan, answer me. What the hell's going on?'

He crossed the marble floor and went into the barely used drawing room. He poured himself a large whiskey from a selection on the hostess trolley and gulped it down.

'Lorcan.' Caoimhe stood by the door, her tawny eyes wide with concern.

She reminded him of his mother. He looked away. 'What?'

'What's happened to you? You look awful.'

'I had a late night.'

'Did you really smash up a clamping van?'

Lorcan poured himself another drink.

'Why did you do that?'

'He clamped me.'

'For God's sake, Lorcan, why the hell do you do such stupid things? Dad's talking about letting them take you in.'

'Figures.'

'He told them you'd present yourself within forty-eight hours to a local station. They left a card. Dad said you're to say nothing, but to ring Shankley before you go anywhere. I think he told Shankley he's to go with you if you want him. It might not be a bad idea.'

Lorcan snorted. Shankley was his father's solicitor, a miserable old fella who reeked of mothballs and Brylcreem. 'Big of him to have organised a buffer.'

'What would you have him do?'

'Me? Nothing. I don't need him to do anything for me.'

'Are you still taking your medication?'

'My anxiety medication?' Lorcan looked at her over the top of his glass. 'Of course.'

'Liar.'

'Why did you ask, then?'

'Why are you acting like this? It's that guy you're always hanging around with, isn't it? Orie. He's bad news, Lorcan.'

'Shut up about Orie. You don't know anything about him.'

'You know he's mixed up with bad people, Lorcan. You need to stay away from him, get your life back on track.'

'He's my friend.' Lorcan swirled the remains of his drink in the glass and tossed it back. He felt the fiery liquid burn the back of his throat. He was so tired, and his jaw ached from the lines of coke he'd done with Orie in the apartment. He wished Caoimhe hadn't seen him like this. He didn't give a shit what anyone else thought, but she had a way of getting under his skin. 'Were you worried about me, sis?'

Caoimhe walked across the room and rested her hand on his shoulder. 'Of course I was. I was going to call into your apartment this morning. I was worried sick when I couldn't reach you. Lorcan, talk to me. What's going on with you? Is it drugs?'

'You're always looking out for me.' He poured another drink. 'I appreciate that, I really do. Not like the old bastard.'

'That's not fair. Dad was worried too.'

'But he wasn't going to ring or call to the apartment.'

'He was busy yesterday, some problem in the yard.'

'The yard. He has a fucking manager. He was probably more worried about what the fucking neighbours were thinking.' Lorcan glanced through the tall windows to the mock-Georgian house facing theirs. 'Did they come in a squad car?'

'Yes.'

He laughed, a hollow bark that fooled neither of them.

'Please, darling, just talk to me.'

'I'm fucked, Caoimhe. I owe money to a guy and I've no way of paying it back.'

'What?'

'You heard.'

'How much? Maybe I can—'

'Eighty thousand euros.'

Caoimhe gasped. 'Oh, Jesus.'

'Yeah, Jesus.'

'But, how do you owe so much? Dad gives you an allowance.'

Lorcan looked at her. 'An allowance? Is that what you call it? Like I'm a fucking teenager.'

'If you don't like it, get a bloody job.'

'Like you have, you mean?'

She snatched her arm back, stung. 'I work.'

'No, you dick around with a hobby and call it work. Dad still picks up your bills – he bought you your studio. What has he ever done for me?'

'You shithead. He bought you your apartment! Your car! He's given you anything you asked for and all he wants is for you to work with him. And, for the record, he doesn't just pay my bills. It's not the same thing at all. He's like a patron.'

'Oh, I bet he loves that. Patron to the fucking arts.'

'Why are you being like this?'

He wished she'd leave him alone. He wanted to go upstairs and look for his father's chequebook.

'Who is this person you owe money to?'

'You wouldn't know him. I doubt he runs in arty-farty circles.'

She thought about that for a second. 'Would Dad?'

'He might.'

'Well, maybe we can get him to talk to this guy, work something out—'

'Forget it.'

'But he can help you.'

'I said no. You heard him the last time.'

She let her hands drop to her sides, helpless. He watched her. She was four years his senior and the closest he had ever had to a mother. Well, he'd had a mother once, but she'd left him too. He hated seeing Caoimhe upset. He hated knowing he was the cause of it. He hated her for making him feel guilty.

He put the glass down and walked away. 'Stay out of my business, Caoimhe. I'll sort it out myself. I mean it. This goes no further.'

'But what will you do?'

'Something.' He grabbed his jacket off the banister, went out and slammed the door.

11

'He's probably done a runner, and if he hasn't, it was probably her old lad.' John had given up on his DIY and joined Sarah upstairs.

'You think her father killed him?'

'He's probably chopped lover boy up into a thousand pieces and buried him under the patio.'

'John, come on. Be serious, will you?'

'That's what I'd do if some no-hope slime-hole knocked up my teenage daughter.'

'I don't think that's the case here.'

'You don't think he's a no-hope slime-hole?'

'I don't think he's been chopped up by Stacy's father.'

'He should have been. If she was my daughter—'

'Assuming her father hasn't chopped him to pieces, why would he run Orie off a few weeks before the baby was due?'

'Sarah, think about it. Young guy, good-looking, girlfriend about to drop a sprog any second. It doesn't take much to work out what's happened here. I feel sorry for the kid, but it's one of the oldest stories in the book.'

'You think he's done a runner.'

'Don't you?'

Sarah looked at the photo Stacy had brought again. In it, Orie and Stacy were sitting in a bar somewhere. A considerably less pregnant Stacy had her arm thrown around Orie's neck and was grinning like a mad woman at the camera. Orie had lifted his pint partway to his face, almost as though he was trying to shield himself from the photographer. He was a dark-eyed man, with curly dark hair and prominent cheekbones that reminded Sarah slightly of Victor. A good-looking bastard, Sarah thought, irresistible to impressionable young girls. There was a tattoo of a shark on his right forearm – the beast wore a leer and a red bandana.

'Shit,' John said. 'Son of a bitch.'

'What in God's name are you doing?'

John held up his hand. 'Trying to get a splinter out.'

Sarah opened her handbag and rummaged around. She found a safety pin and a pair of tweezers. She pushed her chair back and walked over to him. 'Give me your lighter.'

'Here, I'll do it myself.'

'Stop being such a baby. Give me your lighter.'

John handed it over. She sterilised the tip of the pin with the flame and raised John's hand to the light.

'Did you get the press finished?'

'Not quite.' John winced. 'It's – Ow! Careful there – a work in progress.'

'It's a flat-pack press.'

'It's a bloody piece of crap, specifically designed to be almost impossible to make. Ow! Jesus, Nurse Ratched!'

'I nearly have it.'

'You break it, you own it, or at least you can buy it a pint.'

Sarah didn't reply. She twisted the safety pin once more and used her thumbs to ease the splinter free. 'There you go, all done.'

'Thanks.'

Sarah returned to her desk and dropped the safety pin and the tweezers back into her bag. John wiggled his fingers. 'So, what do you want to do?' he asked.

'She's young and thinks she's a tough cookie, but it's all for show. I get the feeling she's got a whole lot of her heart pinned on this guy.'

'Shit, at seventeen? She's only a kid herself.'

'She's a heavily pregnant kid. I think she's afraid he's hot-footing it around with some other girl. You should've seen her – it would have broken your heart.'

'Why the hell do these young ones let themselves get knocked up in the first place? Haven't they ever heard of birth control?'

'Jesus Christ, John, people make mistakes.'

'I know, but—'

'No buts. She made a mistake and she's fucking dealing with it.'

John looked at Sarah in surprise. She didn't normally curse. 'OK, no need to bite my head off. What do you want to do first?'

'I'm going to ring the carriage office and see if I can get a name and address for the partner of the car.'

'Guppy?'

'Gappy.'

'Well, if you're going to do that, I'll check out this Orie's pad, see if he's turned up. Then I might swing by her parents, see if they can throw any light on why your man decided now was the time to vanish. I'll ask to see the garden too. If there's a new deck or patio down, we've got ourselves a winner.'

'I'll talk to his boss at the cab office. If he was planning a runner maybe he cleared some time off in advance.'

'OK.' John stood up. 'Hey, there's something I've been meaning to ask you.'

'What?'

'Did you and Rodney have words?'

'No. Why do you ask?'

'I dunno. He's been acting strange. You should go and see him. He's really down.'

'He's got a broken leg and he's on a mountain of painkillers. Plus he's off the hooch, unless you've been sneaking it in.'

'Not guilty.'

'Well, then, of course he's not exactly himself right now.'

'I get that. But I'm worried. There's something definitely eating at him. I wonder did he have more serious concussion than we thought. It's weird he can't remember anything about the attacker. No good description, nothing concrete.'

Sarah shrugged. 'Shock, probably. Sometimes that's how people react to it.'

'Maybe. Speaking of the crippled, how's Jackie doing?'

'She's fine.'

'Between you, Rodney and Jackie, that was some couple of days, wasn't it?'

'Mmm.'

'Talk about bad luck coming in threes.'

Sarah opened her drawer. 'You going to stand there all day waffling?'

'No, ma'am.' John grabbed his coat. 'You don't want to talk, we won't talk.' He waited for her to look up, but she didn't. He gave up after a few seconds and left, a little dejected.

Sarah slid the drawer shut and propped her chin on a hand. Keep it together.

She took two painkillers, then dialled Directory Enquiries. She asked for the number of the carriage office and slugged down some water as she waited for the reply. Her free hand began to tremble and she laid it flat on the desk. Normal. Just keep things normal for a little while longer.

Two minutes later, she learned that Orie Kavlar was not a registered taxi-driver and the carriage office knew nothing about him. But the Toyota at least was a registered hackney cab. The owner was one Derek O'Connell.

Sarah gathered her car keys, her phone and her notebook. Time to hit the road. Panic fluttered as she left the office. She forced it away and hurtled down the stairs as fast as her legs could carry her.

12

'And then she asked if I'd go with her to see if anyone had handed it in, right? And I said, "Don't be fucking stupid, it's gone", right? And then she said that if she didn't find it her sister was going to kill her, right? Next thing you know she starts roaring crying and I was scarlet, right? And she's going on about how, like, her sister paid so much money for it, right? And I was nearly laughing 'cause, like, I know it was a knockoff 'cause I've seen them selling the exact same bag down in the market and you can tell it's not the same gear. I mean, it looks the same and all, but it's not and, like, the lining always gives it away, and anyway, she just kept crying and I was like . . .'

Stacy stifled a yawn and eased herself further back on the bed, trying to look interested in Melissa's story, even if she couldn't bring herself to feel it. Who cared about stupid bags? Who cared about Melissa's stupid big-chinned cousin? If she hadn't taken the bag it wouldn't have got lost so it served her right.

They were in their friend Chloe's house, up in Chloe's

bedroom. Stacy was sorry she had come over, but Melissa had insisted on meeting up with her, and while initially she had been happy to have something to take her mind off Orie, now that she was here she just wanted to be on her own.

She moved again. However the baby was lying, she was making Stacy's legs go numb. She tried again to focus on Melissa's voice but her mind wandered. She hadn't liked the way Chloe's mum had said hello to her downstairs, making such a big deal out of stepping aside to let her in, offering her tea, asking after her mum with such sympathy that Stacy had almost turned tail and walked out. It was different when it was her and Orie: then she felt sure, confident. When it was just her, everything seemed that much darker, lonelier. She didn't feel as though she belonged anywhere, not even here with her friends.

As Melissa prattled on, Stacy laid her hand on her stomach. Her baby . . . It didn't seem real – whenever she thought about the little person curled inside her she felt weird. She had told no one, not her mum or her friends, that she was carrying a girl. She wanted to keep it to herself for as long as possible, although she didn't know why. But it was her secret, hers alone. She had told the detective she hadn't thought of any names, but that was a lie. She was going to call the baby Jasmine, like the flower. Jasmine. It made her smile to think of her baby with her own name. Jasmine was part of her, part of Orie, and yet she would be a separate person, with her own face and hands and hair. She would grow up and have thoughts and opinions and just . . . be.

She hoped Orie wouldn't be disappointed that he was going to have a daughter. She sometimes felt bad about keeping it secret, especially because he had talked about going to the park and teaching his son football. He'd still love a girl, wouldn't he?

Stacy sneaked a glance at her mobile for the umpteenth time

but the screen remained frustratingly blank, meaning there was still no message and no call from him.

Where was he? Why couldn't he just pick up a phone and call her, even if it was only for a second?

'Stacy!'

'Huh?'

'I said, are you coming on Friday night or what?'

'Friday?'

Melissa rolled her eyes at Chloe, who laughed right on cue. Stacy hated the way Chloe did that.

'Friday – we're going to Spirit. Remember?'

'I'm not coming.'

'But it's Jenny McCarthy's birthday.'

'So? Don't be stupid, Melissa – the size of me, I'd look like a right scobie.'

'You should at least come to the pub for an hour or two beforehand.'

'Lissa, I have nothing to wear because nothing fits me any more. I can't drink. What's the point?'

'Speaking of wearing stuff,' Chloe said, 'I've still got to go into River Island and see if they have that dress in my size.'

'The red one?' Melissa asked.

'Yeah, the one I saw in Dundrum. Remember they didn't have it in my size?'

'Oh, yeah. Has it got, like, a back?'

'Scooped. I'm going to have a Mystic spray tan the day before.'

'Where you getting it done?'

'Super Tan, down off Nassau Street.'

'Oh, right. Don't let Dotty do it. I was, like, streaky as hell last time.'

'I remember. Honestly, I was half thinking of just doing it myself. What do you think of the St Tropez?'

'Gets streaky if you don't put it on right, and you have to, like, exfoliate and all that shit first, then scrub it all off. You're better getting it done for you.'

'Yeah, you're probably right. Don't want to be an Oompa-Loompa.'

'Nah, leave that to Jenny.'

'Melissa!'

Stacy leaned her head against the wall. She longed to be able to wear real clothes again. Just looking at the girls lately had filled her with jealousy and resentment. She was so huge, so round and swollen. She glanced at Melissa. Her friend wore low-rider jeans and a skinny-rib vest. Would she ever fit into clothes like that again? What about her stretch marks?

She hated the way she looked. Hated it. Her boobs were covered with blue veins and her fingers were so swollen she couldn't even wear her rings any more. She knew Orie was going off her even if he said he wasn't. They hadn't had sex in weeks.

Maybe that was why he'd gone. She felt tears building and blinked rapidly.

'You all right, Stacy?' Chloe said. Chubby cute Chloe, with her bob and kind eyes.

What did they say about her when she wasn't there? she wondered. Did they pity her? Did they think she was a total loser? 'I'm grand, just a bit tired.'

'Hormones,' Melissa said. 'Is it, Stacy?'

Chloe smiled, then picked up a copy of *Glamour* and flicked through it idly. 'Here, did you see what Posh has done to her hair?'

But Melissa wouldn't be sidetracked. 'What's going on with you? You've been acting funny all day.'

'It's nothing.'

'Is it him?'

Stacy raised her chin. Melissa was her best friend and had

been since primary school, but lately she had been getting on her nerves. She hated the way Melissa would never use Orie's name. 'No.'

'Yeah, right! Why do you even bother, Stacy? I can see you're, like, all upset about something. What's he done now? Did you ask him about that girl?'

'Melissa, shut up.'

'What girl?' Chloe said, Posh and the magazine forgotten. 'What girl, Liss?'

'It's nothing.' Stacy glowered at her friend.

'I saw him and some wan in Eddie Rocket's on Dame Street the other week,' Melissa said, 'sitting in a booth acting all . . . friendly.'

'It wasn't what you thought,' Stacy said.

'Yeah, and it was.' Melissa stood up and checked herself in the long mirror between the wardrobe doors. She tutted and smoothed her hair, even though it was as flat as a board.

'Who was she?' Chloe asked.

'Some blonde yoke with mad long hair.'

Chloe glanced at Stacy. Stacy felt her gaze but couldn't bring herself to meet her eye. She wished Melissa would just shut her fat mouth.

'Well, maybe he was having a bite to eat,' Chloe suggested.

'He was in his hole. You should have seen the look on his face when he saw me. He couldn't have got out of there fast enough, and I could tell yer wan hadn't a clue what was going on. Listen, don't take my word for it. Ask PJ – he was with me.'

'Melissa, come on,' Chloe said softly.

Melissa turned and put her hands on her hips. 'Come on what? Stacy's got a right to know, hasn't she?'

Stacy lowered her head. A dart of pain in her side made her wince. She started to gather her things.

'Stacy, where are you going?' Chloe asked.

'I've got to get home.'

'Wait, we'll walk down town with you.'

'No, it's all right.'

'Stacy—'

'I said it's all right.' She dragged herself off the bed and made for the door. 'I'll call you later.'

'OK,' Chloe said.

'Yeah, Stace I'll give you a shout later on,' Melissa added. 'Will you be home?'

'Where else would I be?'

13

Forty minutes later, Sarah was on the North Circular Road. She parked her battered Fiesta and locked it, even though it hardly seemed worthwhile any more. It was so decrepit no self-respecting car thief would touch it with a barge pole. She dreaded the NCT coming up. Although, she reminded herself, she probably wouldn't have to worry about that any more.

She checked her notes again. She was definitely at the right address. She was surprised to see that the building housing Ace Cabs was even more dilapidated than theirs. Obviously the Celtic Tiger was selective where it set down.

She read the labels by the bells beside the broken front door, found one with a drawing of a taxi in the slat and pressed the button.

'Yeah?' a gruff voice answered.

'Hi, I'm looking for Ace Cabs.'

'We don't have any available cars at the minute.'

'I'm not here for a taxi. I need to talk to one of your drivers.'

'There's no drivers either. It's call-out.'

'Look, can I come in?'

'Door's open.'

She pushed it and stepped into a hall cluttered with junk mail and air that stank of old takeaways and stale smoke. She was wondering if she was supposed to guess where the cab office was when a man peered over the banisters. 'Up here.'

He disappeared from view. Sarah climbed the stairs. On the next floor she found one door open to the front of the building. She stepped into the office of Ace Cabs. Well, 'office' was a stretch. It was a small shabby room, with only one other door, which Sarah guessed led into a toilet. It was sparsely furnished, with a desk, a few plastic chairs, a phone and a cork noticeboard well pinned with notes, ads and rotas. The double-height window was filthy. There were dead bluebottles on the ledge and a questionable stain on the carpet by her feet.

The man sat behind the desk. There was a tabloid newspaper open in front of him, a notepad and four mobile phones sitting in chargers. He was sickly-looking, with washed-out skin, bushy eyebrows and a grey handlebar moustache yellowed with nicotine. He wore glasses and a brown cardigan over a checked flannel shirt. Sarah guessed him to be in his fifties, but he could have been any age, really.

'Well?' he said, looking her up and down. 'What are you?'

Succinct. That she didn't mind. 'A private investigator.'

'Yeah? I thought it might be something about dole. I keep telling them. If the drivers don't tell me they're signing on, how am I supposed to know?'

'It's not about the dole. What's your name?'

'Dave Coleman.'

'Is this your business, Mr Coleman?'

'Yes.'

'I'm looking for Orie Kavlar. I believe he works here.'

He squinted at her. 'I don't want to know nothing about any trouble.'

'Me neither. I never said anything about trouble.'

He took his glasses off and began to clean them, even though they were probably the cleanest thing in the room. 'Orie Kavlar doesn't work here.'

Sarah smiled. 'I really hope I don't have to come here every single day looking for him. That would be a real pain. Maybe I'll ask my friend from the carriage office to keep an eye open for him. I've got his taxi number. I hope he's not driving illegally or anything. I don't like to cause trouble. Especially if it's not necessary.'

Coleman put his glasses back on and regarded Sarah once again, only this time with a bit less of a sneer. 'Hold your horses. He used to be a part-time driver for one of the hackney guys.'

'Used to?'

'Are you sure you're not with the social?'

'I already told you, I'm a private investigator.' Sarah cocked an eyebrow. 'I don't give a damn what you do here, and I don't care if Orie's on the books, off the books or under that desk. I just want to find him.'

'What's he supposed to have done?'

'He's missing.'

'Missing?' Coleman's face still didn't register anything other than mild disinterest. 'Since when?'

'Saturday.'

'So why are you here?'

'I was told he pulled a double shift here on Saturday.'

'You were told wrong.'

Sarah took out her notebook and jotted that down. She wasn't sure she believed Coleman, but why would he bother lying? 'So, when was the last time Orie worked here?'

'I don't know – months back.'

'Try to narrow it down some.'

'I reckon Orie hasn't been pulling shifts here since early in the year. So maybe eight months ago.'

'Can you check?'

'I don't keep any official record for unofficial drivers.'

'Was Orie sacked or did he quit?'

'Quit.'

'Why?'

'Dunno.'

'Who did he cab-share with?'

'A guy by the name of Derek O'Connell.'

'That would be Gappy, right?'

Coleman bared his teeth in what passed for a smile. 'Funny, I knew you'd happen to have that name on you.'

'And is he working today?'

'Yeah.'

'Can you call him in?'

'What – now?'

'Now would be good.'

Coleman sighed heavily. 'He won't like that.'

'I'm sure he'll get over it.'

He picked up one of the mobiles and made the call. When he hung up he seemed pissed off. Sarah felt she could guess why. Even from where she was standing she'd heard O'Connell's angry outburst.

'He's on his way,' Coleman said, 'but he'll be about twenty-five minutes. He was out in Santry.'

'I don't mind waiting.'

Coleman's shoulder slouched another inch. 'Suit yourself. You might as well take a seat so.'

Sarah sat in one of the plastic chairs. 'What's Orie like?'

'I don't know much about him.'

'But you never had any problems with him?'

'No.'

'How long did he work for you?'

'He didn't work for me. I keep telling you, he cab-shared. What the drivers do with their cars is their own business.'

Sarah sighed. This guy was too much. 'You don't seem too shocked that he's missing.'

'He's a Polack. Those lads are hard-working but they come and they go.'

'Polish?' Sarah frowned. 'I thought he was from Slovakia.'

'Poland he told me.'

'Did you ask for any ID before he started working for you – sorry, for your driver?'

'I think I got a photocopy of his passport.'

'Can I see it?'

He opened a drawer in his desk and pulled out a blue folder. He opened it and flicked through some papers, selected one and drew it out. 'This doesn't mean anything. He still didn't work for me.'

'You can take that record off now.'

'Just so's we're clear.'

'Right.' Sarah took the page from him. It was a pretty poor-quality copy and slightly blurred, but Sarah could see it was definitely Orie Kavlar in the passport photo. Or rather Orie Owsiak, if what was printed under his face was true. According to the passport, he was Polish. Maybe Stacy had got her countries mixed up, but Orie's name too?

'Why does it say Owsiak?'

'That's his name, isn't it? I told you no Orie Kavlar worked here.'

'Can I have a copy of this?'

'Keep it, I don't need it,' Coleman said. 'How do you know he's missing? It's only Monday now.'

'His girlfriend.'

Coleman gave Sarah another sly smile. 'Girlfriend, eh? Which one?'

'Excuse me?'

'I said which one? Orie's always had a good couple of those knocking around.'

Sarah thought of Stacy's frightened, swollen face, her forceful belief in her and Orie's love. She was surprised to feel a dull anger build inside her. And was surprised that she was surprised.

'Regular ladies' man, that Orie, not that he needed to do much chasing – he could charm the birds out of the trees.'

'I'm sure he's a real catch.'

'Used to have young ones calling here looking for him all the time. Had to tell him to cool his jets in the end. I'm running a business.'

'Really?' Sarah offered Coleman an unpleasant smile of her own. 'And here I was thinking he didn't work for you.'

Coleman's grin faded. 'I'm just saying that if he was here—'

'Any of these ladies in particular catch your attention?'

'There was a little blondie one. She was something, all right. Had a set on her like you wouldn't believe. Looked like a young Sam Fox.'

'Did she have a name?'

'Vanessa.' Coleman grinned. 'She had one of those little voices, all breathy.'

Sarah said nothing to that. She studied Orie's photo again. Coleman's smirk was making her feel sick.

14

Stacy sat at the kitchen table with a cup of tea before her. Her mother, Pauline, was drying the dishes, and clattering them down with as much force as she could muster without smashing them.

'I can't believe you'd do something like that! Detectives? Are you out of your mind or what?'

'Stop going on about it, will you, Ma?'

'And for that upstart! Wasting Nana's money on that little, little . . . shite!'

Stacy was startled. Her mother rarely cursed. 'Will you stop shouting? I'm right here.'

'Some yoke who's probably off with God knows what young one—'

'Ma!'

'Well, I'm not helping you. And your da won't help you. We don't work our fingers to the bone to throw our money away like that.'

'I didn't ask for your help.' Stacy could feel her face burning. 'Will Da go really mad?'

'Of course he will! What did you expect? We told you this would happen, didn't we? We told you he'd do something like this but you wouldn't listen. Young ones, you always think you know everything. Well, now look!'

Stacy tried to shift her weight. Her stomach felt rock hard and her back was killing her.

'I'm telling you Stacy, he's not worth it. You need to call them detectives and cancel.'

'He's worth it to me.' Stacy hauled herself up and made her way towards the kitchen door. 'Something's going on with Orie, and I want to know what it is.'

'There's nothing going on! He got what he wanted and now he's run off.'

'Stop saying that! Orie loves me. We're going to get a place together – you'll be sorry then.'

'A place? Are you mad?' Pauline laughed. 'You can barely look after yourself. What the hell makes you think you can look after a baby on your own?'

'I won't be on my own. Orie—'

'Jesus, Stacy, will you grow up? Orie's gone.'

Stacy burst into tears and ran out of the room.

Across town, Lorcan was also feeling the pressure. He paced back and forth across the carpet of the small office like a caged tiger. Although he had showered and changed, he felt like shit, and he could tell from Neil's carefully composed salesman smile that he probably looked as good as he felt. 'Look, I hear what you're saying, but I need to make this sale, Neil. I'm having a serious cash-flow problem.'

'I don't know what to tell you. It's not like the past few years. People are tightening their belts across the board.' Neil Dawson of Dawson Motors spread his hands in front of him. 'It's a tough time to sell cars.'

Lorcan felt a rush of blood to his head. He and Neil had been classmates back in the day, and it rankled that he had to appear so needy. 'But it's a beaut, everyone says so.'

'So is every car I have on my forecourt, Lorcan. They're all beauts, all sitting there, ugly chicks at Wesley College. Come on, Lorcan, you know how it is.'

'No, I don't. How is it?'

'Look.' Neil pinched his trouser legs higher and sat on the corner of his desk. He was, Lorcan noticed, wearing blue and white striped socks. 'If you're serious about selling, you have to be realistic about the price.'

'But I've taken nearly two grand off already. Fuck it, Neil, you told me this car would hold terrific resale value when I bought it from you earlier in the year.'

'And it will. Lorcan, I understand your frustration, I really do, and I'd like to help but my hands are completely tied.'

'I fucking bought it here. You should at least consider buying it back.'

'Aha, yes! Look out there.' Neil waved in the direction of the plate-glass window. 'I've more cars than I know what to do with. It's a bad time – everyone's scared the Tiger has roared its last. People are cutting back, and the bonuses are tighter this year. You don't need me to tell you what it's like. Have you considered placing an ad in *Auto Trader?*'

'I have it in every paper and magazine out there and still nothing. Just some bunch of time-wasters the first week and that's it.'

'It's tough, a tough time,' Neil said, agreeing with his earlier pronouncement. 'I'm not sure the body kit will help sell it either.'

'What?'

'Would you consider . . . toning the car down a bit?'

'Are you having a laugh? That kit makes the car. You should see the heads turn when I'm driving it.'

'I know, but it does limit the market in terms of who might buy it.'

'The kit stays on.'

'OK.' Neil's head bobbed up and down. 'Of course.'

'What about if I take another grand off the asking price?'

'Sure, it can't hurt.'

'It's hurting me. It's daylight robbery.'

'OK, tell you what I'll do. I'll call my dad and ask him put out a few feelers. He must know every car dealer in the country.'

Lorcan was barely listening. He thought of Orie's scared face, of Slim's warning. He knew the fat man would follow through if he didn't get the money on time, and the last thing he wanted was a visit from Ga-Ga. He needed to get his hands on hard cash. If he had some, he could double it – maybe even triple it – at the casino. Everyone knew you needed to spend money to make it. That was the way it worked. That was the cold, hard reality.

He shouldn't even be in this situation. If Mink hadn't fucked him over he'd be laughing. Every time Lorcan thought of Jimmy McKellen or Mink, he pictured them laughing – laughing at him, laughing at screwing him over. Laughing at sucker-punching him. It killed him to know Mink could just cast him aside, after all his talk, all his back-slapping bullshit in the casino.

Well, he wasn't a pushover, no way, and in an even fight he'd crush McKellen. He would have liked to send that message to Mink. He balled his fists, thinking of what might have happened if he hadn't shown up to the Chinese game.

Mink owed him big time. And Mink was going to pay. He'd get his money together somehow.

'Lorcan?'

'What?'

'Are you OK?' Neil offered his most loathsome practised smile.

'Yeah, why wouldn't I be?'

'Well, unless there's anything else, I have another appointment before lunch . . .'

Lorcan hated Neil Dawson. He hated everything Neil stood for. Another fucking lackey, that's all Neil was, and here he was, giving Lorcan the big freeze. 'Just make sure your old man knows how important it is to get a buyer. Tell him I don't mind driving anywhere in the country to deliver.'

'Of course.' Neil stood up. He offered his hand while at the same time shepherding Lorcan towards the door. Lorcan allowed himself to be moved. Truth was, as much as he disliked Neil, he needed the slick little bastard.

He strode out past the receptionists. He noticed that they were studiously avoiding his eye. Was the stench of desperation about him that obvious? He ground his teeth and kept moving, head up, back straight. Stupid bitches – why should he give a shit about what they thought? Orange-faced, false-nailed skanks in too-tight shirts and high heels. If he wanted a woman he could get a woman – a real woman – with a click of his fingers.

But he couldn't shake the feeling that they were judging him, maybe even pitying him, and it infuriated him.

Times shouldn't be so tough, not for people like him, not for the movers and shakers. Not for a young man willing to do what it took to get to the top of his game. He had read many books on making it to the top, and he knew what it took. All you had to do was look at any self-made man – Alan Sugar or Donald Trump. Even Mink, for God's sake. They all took risks, they all thought outside the box. Like him.

They were the men he idolised, not idiots like his father, a man who had once lived by the seat of his pants but was now content to fumble through each day, toothless and boring. Living a hazy, dull existence. Where was the fun in that? What was the point in breaking your back day after day?

He was a risk-taker, and risk-takers needed flexibility. It sickened him to be at the mercy of people like Neil, with his smarmy smirks and clammy hands. It sickened him to listen to people like his old man shite on about work and responsibility as if everything was about the bloody timber yard.

He had seen how the other half lived. He had tasted it. He had sat at a roulette table with a beautiful girl draped over each arm, had heard the applause when he brazened out a hand. It was ambrosia to him. When he was winning, people had treated him like a king. They called him sir, offered him complimentary drinks. It was such a rush. He had taken his risks, rolled the dice and made serious money, not the dribbling of a wage slave. Money that Neil, with his cheap aftershave and Louis Copeland suit, could only dream of. Earlier in the year he had made almost more money in one night than guys his age could earn in a year. Only complete losers worked like slaves when it was there for the taking.

He would be a winner again. He would be that man, he would live that dream. To be the best you had to think like the best.

He slipped a Timbaland CD on and ramped up the sound. As the heavy bass hit, Lorcan Wallace pulled away from the kerb, filled with anger and loathing at how the universe was treating him.

15

John parked the Manta on the footpath outside Orie's building, a three-storey Georgian house that seemed to contain – according to the doorbells – an incredible fifteen separate flats. He reckoned whoever owned the place must have divided every room into two units.

He trotted down a flight of rusty litter-strewn steps. Orie's bedsit was directly in front of him, but he could carry on under the steps to a second on the other side of the building. The difference between the two areas couldn't have been more than twenty feet, but while the area outside Orie's door was filthy and scattered with cigarette butts, the other was pristine, and a box filled with bright pink geraniums sat on the window ledge.

Unsurprisingly, John found no one home at Orie's place. He tried to peer through the window but the curtains were almost drawn.

He checked his watch and counted how many pairs of legs

passed by along the street above. At least four every minute. It was too early in the day to try a break-in.

Time, he decided, to call to Stacy's parents' house, see if he could get their view on their daughter's lover suddenly upping sticks and scarpering. Although he had been joking about the patio, it wouldn't be uncommon for the man in a family to suggest to an interloper that his continued health might best be maintained with a little distance.

Stacy Power's parents had opinions, all right, lots and lots of them. And now that they had a captive audience in their small, neat, over-furnished sitting room they weren't holding anything back.

'Tell her you're not going to work for her,' Tommy Power said, glaring at John in a way that made him wish he had picked a chair closer to the door. That way, if Stacy's father decided to kill him by tearing his head off his shoulders he might have some hope of high-tailing it. It didn't seem right to make it too easy for the big man.

'I didn't take the case,' John said. 'Your daughter spoke to my partner, and she took it.'

'Wasting her money on that fucker! It's not right.'

'I understand—'

'Oh, do you now? You understand how I'm feeling?' Tommy leaned his considerable bulk forward until he was practically hanging off the sofa. He was a big man all round, with shoulders like basketballs and forearms like steel pistons.

John glanced at the door again, measuring the distance. He guessed four feet.

'You want to know what Orie is? He's a bloody dirt-bag, that's what he is,' Tommy said, his face darkening. 'And I'll tell you something else. I don't care where the bollocks is. I hope he's lying dead in a ditch somewhere.'

'Tommy!' Pauline, Stacy's mother, wrung her hands. She glanced at John. 'Look, you don't understand. That fella has her mind poisoned. He filled her head with all sorts of nonsense. She wouldn't hear anything against him. Stacy was always a good girl, never a moment's trouble till that fella showed up. She had her weekend job and she was doing well in school. Now she's out all hours of the day and night and doesn't call to tell me if she's coming home or not. I'm out of my mind with worry half the time.'

John nodded as tears welled in the woman's eyes. She was heavy-set, like her husband, but soft, while Tommy looked as if he'd been hewn from a rock. She wore a ruby velour tracksuit that was straining to contain her. Rolls of fat spilled over the waistband of the trousers – what Sarah called a muffin top. Her hair was short and mousy with a few highlights. But she had a kind, gentle face, and John didn't like to see any woman cry.

'I understand how you feel, but your daughter has hired us to try to locate him.'

'And you're happy enough taking her money off her, is that it?'

If John had thought Tommy looked scary before, he learned now that the man could inspire a whole other level of terror.

'She took that money from her post-office savings account,' Tommy said, as though John had offered to violate his wife, 'and that money was for the baby.'

John licked his lips. 'Well, I—'

'It was for the buggy and a cot. Her nana gave her that money for the baby. Do you know how long it took my mother to put that money aside and she on a pension?'

'Mr Power, I really didn't know—'

'Do we look rich to you?'

'I—'

'I get up every morning at half three and I drive a bread van. Pauline works part-time in Dunnes, and we get by – we get by.'

John nodded.

'That dirty shite!' Tommy stood up so suddenly that John flinched. 'He has her driven demented. Going off with a young one, getting her pregnant – what sort of a man does that? He's too old for her, and she's not even eighteen. He's a filthy pervert. She had her whole life ahead of her, and she goes and lets that dirty bastard get her pregnant.'

'Tommy—'

'He didn't even want a job. I offered to get him one in the depot and he turned me down. And now she's spending her nana's money looking for the bastard! I told her he was bad news – I told her from the start, didn't I, Mam?'

'Tommy, love, will you sit down?'

Tommy sat, but he still looked murderous.

'I warned her,' Pauline continued. 'I warned her he would do this, running off, and she about to give birth.'

'Cowardly shite!' Tommy slapped his hand on the arm of the sofa. 'I should have wrung his neck when I had the chance.'

'Oh, Tommy, come on now.' Pauline placed a hand on his shoulder. 'You're only upsetting yourself.'

'Sounds like he has good reason to,' John said.

'Her whole life ahead of her.' Tommy curled a hand as big as a shovel in front of John's face. John swallowed nervously. But Tommy dropped his hand, his expression one of tired defeat. 'But sure what can I do?' He looked at a photo of Stacy on the mantelpiece. In it, his daughter was wearing her school uniform and braces. It had probably been taken when she was about fourteen. 'What's done is done. Stacy's going to have that baby soon, and what's done is done.'

'Maybe it's just as well he's gone,' Pauline said, patting his hand. 'We don't need him. Stacy has us, love, and we're here for her and the baby. She's better off without the likes of him hanging around.'

'She could have been anything she wanted,' Tommy said, but now he spoke more to himself than to John. 'She was clever, did well in school . . . anything she wanted.'

'She still can,' Pauline said, but her tone was as defeated as her husband's.

John closed his notebook. He had written nothing in it since he had sat down. He knew neither of these people was behind Orie's disappearance and, frankly, the more he heard about Orie the less he liked him.

He didn't ask to check the patio.

Tommy wasn't the only one who'd have liked to get his hands on Orie. Derek 'Gappy' O'Connell was a short man, about thirty, out of shape, almost completely bald, and he had the biggest gap between his two front teeth Sarah had ever seen. He hadn't stopped bitching since he had set foot in Ace Cabs.

'This is gonna have to wait, I've got a regular pick-up after lunch, daily job. I can't be hanging around here talking.'

'You mentioned that,' Sarah said evenly, 'and the sooner you answer some of my questions the sooner we can be on our way. Fair enough?'

'Why couldn't it have waited until after me shift?'

'In a missing-person case, time is important.'

'Missing? Orie? Yeah, right.'

'You don't think it's possible Orie's missing? Your boss tells me he hasn't pulled a shift here for nearly eight months.'

'Yeah, so?'

'So when did you see him last?'

'When I pulled the fucker out of my Toyota by his ears.'

'You did what?'

'Yeah. He was supposed to be working, and then I found out he'd taken the taxi plate off my car and had driven it to fucking Holyhead.'

'Orie took your car out of the country? Why?'

'I dunno, do I? Stupid gobshite forgot and left the ferry docket in the glove compartment. Other than that I wouldn't have bleedin' known.'

'And then he quit.'

'Hey, it's my name on the papers. I was doing Orie a favour, letting him earn a few quid, like. Look, it's not like he even wanted to work. I offered him more shifts but he didn't want them.'

Sarah scribbled all this down.

'He's as crooked as fuck, that young lad – you should write that down too. Look, the stupid fucker probably went on a bender and forgot to call anyone.'

'Did Orie often go on benders?'

'He gambled a fair bit.'

'Is he a winner or a loser?'

'What do you think?' Gappy said. 'But he must have been making some money. Orie only worked when it suited him and that's the truth. Isn't that right, Dave?'

Coleman shrugged one shoulder and went back to his newspaper.

'He's a Pole,' Gappy continued, 'and that's all they do, drink, gamble, whatever. Fucking shovel-heads. Worse than us lot they are.'

'And yet you shared the cab with him.'

For the first time O'Connell looked uncomfortable. 'Well, I was going through a few things meself. I needed money to buy out the car and the licence to get started. Orie offered to help with the initial layout.'

'How did you two meet?'

O'Connell shifted from one foot to the other. 'He used to work the door of a place with another friend of mine.'

'Where?'

'A nightclub. Don't bother asking me about it – it's closed down.'

'He was a bouncer?'

'Look, I just knew him, OK? He used to do, maybe still does, security, nixers and shit. That place was closing and Orie needed a job, and my friend asked me would I be interested in a split on the cab business. Orie said he'd go in on the money and, like I say, I needed the leg up at the time. Orie was happy enough with the deal, and we were supposed to rotate shift every couple of weeks or so, no hassle. But it didn't work so we parted ways.'

'Tell me who Vanessa is.'

Gappy grinned and exchanged a glance Sarah didn't like with Coleman. 'She was one of Orie's special lady friends.'

'Do you have any idea where I might find her?'

'I don't know – she was a hairdresser, I think, worked up in Drumcondra somewhere.'

'You know the name of the salon?'

'Do I look like I know the names of ladies' hair salons?' He pointed at his shiny head.

'Can you describe her?'

''Bout twenty, short, got real blonde hair and . . .' He lifted both his hands and did the universal sign for large breasts. Behind him, Coleman – who had merely been pretending to read the newspaper throughout her questions – leered afresh.

'Did Orie ever mention a Stacy to you?'

'Don't think so.'

'I tell you what . . .' Sarah closed her notebook and took her wallet from her jeans. She passed Gappy her business card. 'If Orie does contact you for any reason, I want you to give me a call or, better yet, ask him to.'

Gappy took the card but he wasn't happy. 'I won't hear from him. I'd be the last person he'd be popping round to see. Let me tell you, love, that man's a law unto himself.'

'We have all sorts of cures for that, these days,' Sarah said. 'Give me a shout if you see him.'

'Yeah, all right, but I don't want any fucking trouble. If Orie's in some kind of shit, it's got nothing to do with me.'

'Right,' Sarah said. She nodded to Coleman. 'Same for you. If he gets in touch give me a call, or ask him to get in touch.' She let herself out, content in the knowledge that no matter what happened she'd probably never hear from either man again.

16

Mink was drinking his first coffee of the day and poring over the newspapers when he caught the story. He shook out the paper and reread the short report slowly. 'Fuck.'

It said that the body of an unidentified girl had been discovered in Stocks Lane, Sandyford, in the early hours of the morning by two walkers. Gardaí had yet to ascertain a cause of death, but foul play was suspected.

Mink read it once more and put down the paper. He picked up the phone on his desk and punched in a number.

'Hello?'

'Jimmy.'

'I'm reading it now.'

'The stupid bastard didn't even hide her properly.'

'I know.'

'I don't want an investigation. This stops now.'

Jimmy didn't reply. He knew better than to aggravate the situation.

'That kid, Orie, the one you couldn't convince to take a ride with you the other night, needs to be convinced next time. Do you understand me? I want him tied in with the girl. This needs to be cleaned up immediately!'

'I'm on it. But you've got to do something about Lorcan.'

'Don't worry about him.'

'Look, Mink, that's all well and good, but with him pumped up and talking about branching out, it's risky doing anything. I mean, you didn't see him – he was laying on the hard man thick as concrete.'

'I don't care if he was dancing a tango naked. That moron doesn't know what he's talking about. He doesn't know anything except how to suck his daddy's money teat. And I aim to remind him of that. Forget Lorcan, find Orie and take care of the problem. We can make it look like he was distraught over this girl. It's got to be handled quickly.'

'Lorcan will know it wasn't no suicide.'

'I told you, don't worry about him. I'll bring that pup to heel.'

Mink hung up. He didn't care what Jimmy thought. He didn't care what Lorcan thought. He didn't care what anyone thought. He only wanted to hear that Orie Kavlar was out of the picture, that the dead girl was not connected to himself in any way.

He poured himself another coffee and buzzed Poppy.

She arrived through the door of his office less than a minute later. Though she had an apartment not twenty minutes away, she always seemed to be on the premises. If Poppy ever slept, Mink often mused, it had to be in remarkably short bursts.

'Yes, boss?'

'The other night there was a girl who came in with the new delivery to the penthouse. She was crying.'

'Right.'

'Find out has she settled down yet, and if she has, I want you to send her down the country to one of the other places. Cork, maybe.'

'OK. And if she hasn't settled down?'

'Then we need to make sure she does. Give her whatever is necessary to help her adapt to her transition. You hearing me, Poppy?'

'Yes, sir.'

'I don't want that girl talking to anyone, so keep her away from the others and make sure she's good and calm at all times. No public transport. Organise a car to bring her down. Make sure she's put with someone from a different country, no speaky the language. Clear?'

'Yes, sir.'

'Good girl.'

'Everything all right?'

'It will be.'

Poppy nodded and closed the door behind her. She knew when not to pry.

Mink sipped his coffee. Idiots. Lorcan Wallace and his damned unpredictability. Why had he ever taken a chance on such a bloody idiot? Mink knew he deserved this trouble: hadn't he learned over the years to keep a tight rein on his workers? Lorcan Wallace was a jumped-up undeserving shit and, if it hadn't been for his old man, Mink would never have given him a job, not in a million years. But memories or nostalgia or just plain stupidity had overridden good sense for once and now he was paying for it. The kid had owed him money and it had amused him to hire him. It had amused him to know that Darren Wallace's son now worked for him.

What a fool he had been. Vanity had cost him. It always did.

There was nothing else to do. If he didn't want a war on his hands he needed help. He needed to talk to Darren Wallace about his son. He needed to make clear to Darren that he was not a man to be fucked with but that he understood young men liked to act as young men. Shit, hadn't he been one himself? Although, admittedly, he had as much in common with Lorcan Wallace now as he had had when he was a youth, which was nothing at all.

He folded the newspaper and tossed it into the bin. What the hell was up with Jimmy? He'd never known his man to be so slack. He was disappointed in him. He'd known Jimmy almost three years and had hired him on the QT after Jimmy was released from jail, having served time for dancing on the head of his closest competitor. Of course, Jimmy had kept a straight job too – that was vital when you did what Jimmy did. Threw the cops completely out of the loop.

He hoped sincerely that Jimmy McKellen wasn't coming to the end of his usefulness. If that girl didn't settle down she, too, would have to be got rid of. Of course, that would mean he was down two girls, and the clients liked fresh meat.

Jesus, he thought, buttering his toast, when it rained it bloody poured.

17

John's phone rang just as he was getting out of his car. He was back on Dorset Street.

'He's been lying to her,' Sarah's voice crackled. 'He doesn't work at the taxi company and hasn't for nearly eight months. The guy he was cab-sharing with, Gappy, turfed him after catching him taking the car out of the country.'

'What did he do that for?'

'I don't know, but when I run into him I'll ask him. Thing is, John, from what I gather, even when he was working he wasn't too keen on breaking a sweat. But he must have money coming from somewhere.'

'A man of mysterious means.'

John attempted to light a cigarette, turning his back to the wind. 'So where does he go in his free time?'

'I suppose he caters to his other interests. He's a regular little love machine by all accounts. Oh, and get this, he likes to gamble.' Sarah sighed. 'I'm starting to think you might be right about him skipping out on Stacy. The guys at the base had never heard him mention her, but they all seem to know his other lady friend, Vanessa.'

'He's got another?'

'Yep, though he might have more.'

'Maybe he skipped, maybe not.'

'Maybe? You've changed your tune.'

John finally got his cigarette lit and pocketed his lighter. 'It's just a hunch, nothing solid, but Stacy's old man tried to put the frighteners on Orie when he found out Stacy was pregnant. If you met Tommy you'd know that that would have been Orie's time to bolt if he was the type.'

'Do you think the parents had anything to do with his disappearance?'

'They're not going to shed any tears over it, but I don't think they're behind it. Anything else?'

'He lied about his surname.'

'It's not Kavlar?'

'Not according to his passport. His name's Orie Owsiak, and he also lied about his nationality. He's Polish.'

'Not from Slovakia, huh? What's with all the subterfuge?'

'Can't answer that either.'

John glanced at the house. The basement looked just as grotty as it had earlier. On the other hand, the street was a lot quieter. 'OK, here's what I'll do. I'll ask around at his building, see if I can find someone who knows him or has seen him. Maybe I can get an idea of his movements. Are you going back to the office?'

'I'm going to see if I can locate Vanessa. Maybe it's just a case that Orie's moved on.'

'You got a lead on her whereabouts?'

'She's a hairdresser and she's breathy, blonde, with big

bazookas. How hard can it be?' She laughed, but without a trace of humour.

John pocketed his mobile. He trotted back down the steps to Orie's entrance. The curtains were still partially drawn behind the filthy window, while pizza adverts and other assorted junk mail had been stuck halfway through the letterbox. No sign of anyone having been into the place since he had been there earlier. John glanced around and looked under the main steps to the second basement apartment on the opposite side. He hoped whoever lived there was at work.

He turned his attention to Orie's front door. The lower Chubb was rusty and disused. That left the top lock. A Yale. John smiled.

Two minutes later, he was standing in Orie's Kavlar's bedsit. He left the curtains drawn and flipped the light switch.

It was small and dingy. The air smelled of mould and damp. To the left of the window, a kitchenette area was shielded from the rest of the room by a length of plywood. Opposite that was a wardrobe and an unmade double bed shoved against the far wall. There was a boarded-up fireplace, and the newest thing in the room was a television that looked five or six years old. Everything else had probably been dragged out of a skip.

There was a second door in the corner of the room, with a key in the lock. John walked over to it and unlocked it, noting as he did so a second key dangling from a peg on the wall beside a washbag containing soap, toothpaste and a toothbrush. John opened the door. It led to a small hall with two other doors. One had 'BATHROOM' printed on it. He tried the key from the wall in the lock. Yep. it unlocked the bathroom door. There was nothing in there except the fittings and the tiles. It smelled strongly of Jeyes fluid.

John returned to the bedsit and locked the door again. 'OK, Orie, let's be having you.'

He set to work. The milk in the fridge was not sour, but the bread on the shelf was hard. It didn't look as if anyone had been there in a couple of days. He checked the wardrobe; there were clothes hanging inside. Next he checked the bed. The sheets were grubby and he tried not to handle them as he lifted the mattress. There was nothing under the bed but a battered pair of runners and an empty suitcase.

John searched slowly and methodically. After ten minutes, he struck gold. In a cereal box on a shelf over the two-ring hob he found three passports, one belonging to a woman from the Dominican Republic; the remaining two bore Orie's face. In the first he was Polish and called Orie Owsiak; in the second he was from Slovakia and was Orie Kavlar. There was also a black notebook and two thousand euro in cash, tied up in an elastic band.

The money worried John. Whatever about the passports, why would Orie do a runner and leave it behind? Who was the woman? And why did he have her passport? And why did he have two passports in different names and nationalities?

John was pondering those questions when he heard feet on the metal steps and, seconds later, knocks on the door, loud and fast.

John pocketed the money and the passports and moved quickly across the room. He switched off the light. He stood behind the door, scarcely breathing.

'Orie?' It was a woman's voice. 'Orie, I know you're in there. Open the door, Orie. I need to talk with you.'

John opened the door. 'How you doing?'

'Oh!' She took a step back. She was five foot six, and John guessed her age at early twenties. She had shoulder-length auburn hair and eyes the colour of a summer meadow. She wore a fitted brown leather jacket with a fur trim, grey-green trousers and leather boots. Her jewellery was simple and understated, and she wore little make-up.

'I'm very sorry.'

'For what?'

'I am looking for Mr Kavlar.' Her voice was low and husky. 'I thought I might catch him at home.' She glanced over John's shoulder. 'This is his home, right?'

'It is, but you're going to have to join the club looking for him,' John said. 'Are you a friend of his?'

'I wouldn't have said I was a friend.'

'Can I ask your name?'

Her nostril flared slightly and her mouth twitched. 'You can, but don't you think you should tell me yours first?'

'I'm John Quigley.' John fished out his wallet and handed her a card. 'I'm a private detective. I've been hired to find Mr Kavlar.'

She turned his card over in her hands. She had long, elegant fingers. 'Is he missing?'

'Yes.'

'Since when?'

'Hard to say just yet. Last anyone heard of him was Saturday evening.'

'It's a bit early to consider him missing, no?'

'Well, he's not answering his phone and his girlfriend is worried.'

She nodded now, but she was no longer smiling and her eyes were serious.

'So go on, it's your turn to volunteer some information. How about a name?'

'My name is really not important.'

'I'll bet it's a pretty one.'

Despite herself, she smiled, and John couldn't help but smile back at her. He always liked it when beautiful women smiled at him.

'What's makes you say that, Mr Quigley?'

'It would have to be to go with your face.'

'Oh, God, that's just too much.' She laughed. 'Do you practise those lines?'

'Not at all. You say you're not friends, so how do you know Orie?'

'Why would that concern you?'

'Everything concerns me at the moment, Miss No Name. I'm concerned because a man might vanish but leave all his clothes and a fair chunk of money behind. I'm concerned because he hasn't contacted his heavily pregnant girlfriend, driving her out of her mind with worry. I'm concerned that he hasn't called her since Saturday. I'm concerned that he's not replying to any of the messages left for him.'

'I can't help you, but if you're that concerned you should probably call the police, no?'

'Are you another of his lady pals? I hear he likes the ladies.'

She tilted her head and regarded him coolly with those beautiful eyes. 'Well, it's been interesting. Goodbye, Mr Quigley. I hope you find relief from your concern.'

'Let me walk you out.'

'There's no need.'

She trotted back up the metal steps. John followed. He rather enjoyed the way she moved.

'I don't need any more chaperoning. My car is here.'

'OK. If I see Orie do you want me to give him a message?'

She ignored him and climbed into a top-of-the-line BMW jeep. It was parked behind his car on the footpath, with its hazards on. So she hadn't planned to stay long. She revved the engine, spun the wheel and zoomed off down the street. As soon as she had disappeared from view, John jotted down the model and registration number.

He walked back to Orie's bedsit and completed his search. It didn't take long.

After he'd locked up he crossed under the step of the main building to the door of the flat opposite Orie's. He knocked softly, and after a moment a small, dark-skinned man answered and peered out over a chain. He was small, about sixty, with enormous bags under his eyes. 'Yes?'

John passed him his card and waited while the man studied it carefully. The smell of fried onions drifting from the interior of the flat made his mouth water. 'I'm looking for your neighbour, Orie. Do you know him?'

'Yes, to see here.'

'Have you seen him lately?'

The man shook his head slowly and offered John his card back.

'Hang on to it,' John said. 'Can you remember the last time you saw him?'

The man shrugged. 'There is trouble?'

'What makes you say that?'

He shrugged again.

'Not that I'm aware of,' John said. 'But I want to talk to him all the same. Can you do me a favour? See the number on there?' John pointed to his card. 'That's my mobile. Can you give Orie that number if he comes back? Tell him I have something for him.'

The man nodded once.

'And if you happen to notice anyone else lurking about maybe you'd give me a shout.'

The man frowned, but pulled the card all the way through the door.

'Cheers, take it easy.'

John stepped back and waited for the man to close his door. Then he hurried up the steps and made a call to Detective Sergeant Stevie Magher. 'Stevie, old pal, how's she cutting?'

'Ah, Jaysus, what now?' Stevie's soft Limerick accent did not make him sound any less disgusted to hear from John. It was an act, of course – at least, John hoped it was. Ever since John had helped save Stevie's career from the lies of a less than injured scumbag on the make, the garda did whatever he could to help his friend. Well, within reason. 'Nothing major. I just want you to run a number for me.'

'Do I have to remind you I'm not your—'

'Secretary, yeah, yeah. You need a new line.'

'I need a fucking break from you.'

'How's Ailbhe?'

'Good.'

'Give her a kiss for me.'

'Tell you what, I'll give her a kiss from me. Who knows where your mouth's been?'

'Oh, my, Stevie, that's just so cutting,' John said, falsetto. 'I thought you and I had an understanding. Where's the love? Where's the professional respect? Where's the day's golfing you keep saying we're going to have?'

Stevie sighed. 'Give me the number.'

'Thanks.'

'But you owe me.'

'Right.'

'Go on, then, shoot.'

18

Sarah checked the address and pulled across the road. She parked in front of a branch of Xtravision and stepped out of the car. 'Bingo.' Rebels hair salon was located over the video shop and a Spar supermarket. She hoped the Vanessa who worked here was the same Vanessa she'd heard about at the cab office. It had taken eight phone calls to locate her. Who could have known there'd be so many hairdressers in Drumcondra?

She pushed open the street door and climbed a flight of wooden stairs. She passed large, old-fashioned posters featuring old-fashioned haircuts, adverts for acrylic nails and spray tans. At the top she opened another glass door and stepped into a long, cluttered hair salon. It looked busy. The air was thick with hairspray, perfume and chatter.

'Hiya.' A girl with a magenta bob looked up from the reception desk. She slid a magazine off a much-scribbled-on appointment book. 'Who are you with?'

'I don't have an appointment, I'm looking for Vanessa.'

The receptionist glanced at the book. 'Do you have an appointment for colour?'

'I just want a word with Vanessa.' Sarah took out her card and handed it to her.

The receptionist read it, then glanced up at Sarah in surprise. 'She's pretty busy right now. You'll have to call back.'

'I won't take up much of her time.' Sarah squeezed out a smile. 'Which one is she?'

'The blonde by the last mirror.'

Sarah saw a girl, dressed from head to toe in black. She was small and a little chubby, but Coleman had been right: she was busty and very pretty. Her hair was the colour of pale gold and hung almost to her buttocks in rippling waves. She looked animated and friendly, and as she separated sections of hair onto tinfoil, she chatted cheerfully to her client.

'Can you tell her I want to speak to her?'

'Yeah, hold on a sec.' The receptionist got up, walked across the salon and whispered to Vanessa, who nodded.

The girl returned. 'She says take a seat and she'll be with you in a few minutes. Do you want coffee or a glass of water?'

'No, I'm fine, thank you.'

Sarah sat down on a scuffed leather sofa and shuffled idly through a stack of weekly glossy magazines. She wondered who cared about whether Brad Pitt got a tattoo or Jade Goody got married. After a few more pages, she decided one thing was certain: she didn't. She replaced the magazine and studied the salon instead.

She marvelled at the hum and buzz of the place. There were four stylists other than Vanessa, three women and a man, while a small, dark-eyed girl swept away the hair. The chatter was constant. What on earth did people find to talk about? Despite her two older sisters, Sarah had never felt comfortable in an all-female environment. Not in school, not in work and not now.

She didn't enjoy small talk, and had never acquired the skill for it. Her own hairdresser was Spanish and apart from 'Good morning' or 'Good afternoon' and 'How much do you want off the ends?' they said barely a word to each other. Both were happy with this arrangement.

But Sarah couldn't remember a time when she had fitted into the sisterhood, if such a thing existed. She couldn't see what was so important about having perfect nails and perfect make-up. She couldn't have cared less about clothes, only that they fitted well and were functional. She found high heels uncomfortable and impractical and said so regularly to Helen, who wore nothing but skyscrapers. She didn't watch television, she didn't blog, she didn't go to get waxed and bleached and spray-tanned. She didn't enjoy celebrity gossip. She didn't watch *The X Factor* or soap operas. She didn't go out on the pull. She didn't . . . well, she didn't do anything, really.

She knew she wasn't alone in that, of course, but she didn't do anything about meeting like-minded people either. Sometimes she felt that being a woman was a stupid act. To be a success at pulling it off she would have had to conform to certain ideals and characteristics.

She didn't fit in anywhere.

Maybe that was the problem. Maybe she was the problem. Maybe if she had tried harder to fit in she wouldn't be in the mess she was now.

Vanessa moved her client to a different seat and crossed the room to Sarah. 'Hiya.'

'Hi. My name's Sarah Kenny.'

'Vanessa Shaw.' She gave Sarah's hand a brief shake.

Vanessa was in her early twenties, with almond-shaped eyes. She was so short that Sarah felt like a giant as she towered over her.

They sat down.

'Mia says you're a detective?'

'Yes, private.'

'Well, that's interesting.'

Her voice was soft, babyish, the kind that voice people put on when they wanted to appear sexy. Sarah noticed she finished her sentences with a questioning inflection, like so many kids did nowadays. The mid-Atlantic tone, her sister Jackie called it. OC wannabe bollocks, her sister Helen said.

'I'm looking for Orie Owsiak. I believe you know him.'

'Orie?' Vanessa's eyes darted to the floor and up again. Sarah prepared for a lie or two to be lobbed her way. 'I don't think I know the name.'

That didn't take long, Sarah thought. 'You don't know him? Shit, that's a real shame.' She stood, as though about to leave. 'I'm sorry for wasting your time.'

'Wait – why are you looking for this guy anyway?'

'He's been reported missing and I'm trying to track him down.'

'Orie's missing?'

'Yes. Are you saying you remember him now, Vanessa?'

'Wait, I don't know, I just . . . What makes you think he's missing?'

'So you do know him.'

She hesitated, but only for a moment. 'Orie? OK, maybe I know him a little.'

'Why did you lie?'

'Well.' Vanessa blushed crimson. 'I didn't, you know, want, eh, to, em . . . Look, Orie's really private – I didn't want to talk about him behind his back.' She cleared her throat. 'So what's going on? Who hired you?'

Sarah skipped over the question. Vanessa didn't strike her as particularly deceitful. Maybe the girl knew about Stacy, maybe not. 'When was the last time you saw Orie?'

'I spoke to him on Saturday.'

'Evening?'

She shook her head. 'No, earlier, I was on my lunch break, so I'd say about one o'clock.'

Sarah wrote that down. Orie had obviously come straight here from Stacy's side. What a prince he was turning out to be. 'Have you spoken to him since then?'

'No. He was working this weekend, that's why I haven't spoken to him. Orie's a really hard worker. He works all the time.'

'What's your relationship with him?'

'What do you mean?'

'Are you going out with him? Are you his friend, girlfriend, what?'

Sarah's heart sank when Vanessa flushed.

'Well, yeah.'

'How long have you known him?'

'Oh, I guess nearly a year.'

Sarah thought about poor swollen Stacy and her puffy feet. Her already low opinion of Orie slithered below the base line. 'How did you meet?'

'At an internet café.'

'Did he—'

'Look, I don't want to seem rude or anything but I can't answer any more of your questions until you tell me what this is all about. You're scaring me. What makes you think something's happened to Orie?'

Sarah decided to change tack. 'How did he seem when you spoke to him on Saturday?'

'What do you mean?'

'Well, was he acting funny? Was he upset about anything?'

'No, he was his usual self, messing about, sweet.' She frowned. 'Why won't you answer my question? Has something happened that you're not telling me?'

'I don't know,' Sarah said. 'All I know is no one's been able to contact him since Saturday.'

'Have you called his work?'

'The taxi company?'

'Orie hasn't worked there for ages. At weekends he's with a security firm.'

'Can you give me its name?'

'I don't know . . .' Vanessa pulled a face. 'Global Security or something like that? He gets sent to all sorts of different places.' She turned in her chair so that now she faced Sarah directly. 'If you haven't even spoken to them, what makes you think Orie's missing? Did Wayne say he was missing?'

'Who's Wayne?'

'His landlord.'

'Oh, right. My partner was at the bedsit earlier, but he didn't speak to a landlord.'

Vanessa cocked her head, puzzled. 'What bedsit?'

'On Dorset Street.'

'Orie doesn't live in a bedsit. He rents a room in a house over in Fairview.'

Sarah felt like Alice after she had stepped through the looking glass. 'OK, can you give me the address?'

But now Vanessa's dander was up. 'Not until you tell me what's going on. Have you even got the right person? Orie? Owsiak? Why did you think Orie lived in Dorset Street?'

'His boss at the taxi company gave me that address.'

'But why would he do that?'

'Maybe that's where Orie lived when he first joined or something.'

'Oh,' Vanessa said, clearly unconvinced. 'I don't think that's right. The reason Orie was sharing a house was because he couldn't afford a bedsit.'

'Even with all the work he does?'

'He sends money home every month, He's got family in Poland, three younger sisters and a sick father. His mother is dead, and after his father got sick Orie took on the job of looking after them.'

'I see, quite the humanitarian.'

'He's amazing. He really cares about them.'

'So . . . the address?'

Reluctantly, Vanessa told her, and Sarah wrote it down.

'Have you been there much?'

'No, not really. It's a weird house and, honestly, Wayne's a bit of a creep. Plus I'm allergic to cats.'

'Cats?'

'Yeah, Wayne has millions of them. It's disgusting. I can tell Orie's really embarrassed by it. But it's cheap. There's a few guys rent rooms there. I don't really know them, but I think most of them are foreign too.'

'Polish?'

'I don't know.' Vanessa sighed. 'I think so. Like Orie.'

'I'm surprised you haven't considered getting a place together.'

Vanessa grinned. 'We're nowhere near that. I can't see Orie going for it either. I think he's a bit old-fashioned that way.'

'Oh, yeah?' Sarah smiled stiffly. 'Does he have any family here at all?'

'Just his cousin, Sally.'

'Sally.'

'Only he's a man,' Vanessa added glumly. 'Weird, I know. Sounds like a girl's name.'

'Do you know where I might find Sally?'

'No – he's a strange guy, doesn't talk much. Not in the least bit friendly. I saw him in the Porter House a few weeks after Orie introduced us and I said, "Hi," and he totally blanked me.'

'Maybe he's shy too.' Sarah said, trying not to roll her eyes as she wrote that down.

'Do you know why Orie might take it upon himself to lie low for a few days?'

'No, but maybe his dad took a turn for the worse and he had to leave suddenly.'

'Wouldn't he have called to let you know?'

'I suppose. Why won't you tell me who hired you?'

'I can't divulge that information.'

'But why? You're freaking me out here.'

Every head in the salon turned their way and Sarah almost shushed her. She probably would have done if she hadn't noticed the necklace dangling between Vanessa's breasts. It was identical to the one she had seen Stacy playing with back in the office.

'That's a nice necklace you're wearing.'

Vanessa glanced down and clasped the pale-blue pendant. 'Orie gave it to me.'

'It's unusual, can't be many of them about.'

'There aren't. It was his mother's.'

Sarah closed her notebook. 'Hang on to my card. Will you call me if he gets in touch?'

Vanessa nodded, but she looked frightened. 'I don't understand. Who told you he was missing? Who hired you to look for him? Was it Gappy? Or Wayne?'

There was a limit to how much lying Sarah was prepared to do. The girl was asking her a straightforward question. Although she didn't want to hurt her, she was not duty-bound to protect the Lothario's reputation. 'Has Orie ever mentioned a girl called Stacy to you?' she asked.

Vanessa had heard of her all right. Her upper lip curled and her eyes narrowed. 'Stacy Power's his ex. What's this got to do with her?'

'What makes you think she's his ex?'

'It was her who called you?' Vanessa stood and put her hands on her hips. 'Are you kidding me? I can't believe she called you. Oh, my God, Orie's so right! She's bloody obsessed.'

'She's worried about him.'

'She's got no right to be worried about him. What has anything about Orie got to do with her? They ended nearly a year ago!'

'That's not what she says.'

'She's a liar, then. I know she's been ringing him up, harassing him. She's jealous because Orie's moved on, she's—'

'She's pregnant.'

If Sarah had reached out and slapped Vanessa the reaction might have been the same. First the colour drained from the girl's face, and when she opened her mouth to speak no sound came out. Finally she managed to whisper, 'She's what?'

'Pregnant. She says Orie's the father.'

'Well . . . he can't be.' Vanessa shook her head. 'No, no, you've got this all wrong. Orie and me, she's jealous, that's all . . . she probably wants him back.'

'Because he's such a good catch?'

'You don't even know Orie. That Stacy, she'll say anything. I mean, Orie told me about her and . . . She's probably just saying she's pregnant for attention, or to split us up or something. The stupid cow's probably not pregnant at all.'

'She was in my office earlier today, and I can assure you she is. She's about to give birth any day now.'

'Oh . . . God.'

Sarah wondered if she should just stamp on the girl's heart and be done with it. She noticed a sudden lull in the salon and became uncomfortably aware that everyone in the room seemed to be keeping one ear cocked to the drama unfolding.

'Vanessa, listen.' She put a hand on the younger woman's shoulder, but Vanessa pulled back as though Sarah's touch had scalded her.

'No, you listen. I don't care if she is pregnant. She's lying about him. Orie told me they broke up. He told me they were finished. He told me!'

'I don't know what to say about that. But she's not faking the pregnancy, and I don't think she was faking worry.'

Vanessa burst into tears and collapsed into the chair, emitting loud, racking sobs.

Within seconds a group of concerned hairdressers had descended on them, like crows on a freshly split bin bag. 'What's happened, love?'

'Jesus—'

'Here, what's wrong, Vanessa?'

'Get her some water.'

'What's going on?'

'Give her some space.'

'Ah, here, come on now.'

The receptionist elbowed Sarah neatly out of the way.

Christ, Sarah thought, wincing at Vanessa's wailing. She hadn't thought such a pitch even possible. She got up and slipped out of the door.

A few minutes later she was on her way to Fairview, home number two of the mysterious Orie Kavlar or Owsiak.

19

John left the Manta in a private car park on Pleasant Street. He paid a chunk of money monthly for the space but it was worth it. More than one disgruntled arsehole had put his windows in, and it worked out cheaper if he kept his baby behind bars. He was walking back towards the office when Stevie returned his call.

'Jaysus, Johnny-boy, if I took a shit you'd be the first fly on the scene.'

'I was never one for the cryptic wordplay, Stevie.'

'I've got a name and an address for you.'

John pulled out his notebook and a pen. 'Shoot.'

'First things first. What's the deal with this guy you're asking about?'

'Guy?'

'Yeah, guy.'

'I told you, it might be connected with a case I'm working on. That's all.'

'The car belongs to one Caoimhe Wallace.'

'Caoimhe, eh? What's she done that smacks of trouble?'

'Nothing. But Darren Wallace, her old man, is no daisy. He's got a bit of form, like, in case you're interested.'

'Oh, I'm always interested in form, Stevie, you know that.'

'He's got plenty of previous, mostly handling and petty theft. He did a short stretch in the Mount for GBH in seventy-eight, then ten years for his part in an armed robbery back in eighty-three. He's thought to have been behind a few post-office numbers in the eighties but nothing stuck until the armed robbery. He got a bit carried away and smacked around a jeweller who wouldn't open a safe quick enough. Got saddled with an ABH charge on top of everything else. Left his blood at the scene, the tosser, when he cut his hands on the jeweller's broken teeth.'

'Sounds like a right charmer.'

'Must be a slow learner, too. He was up before the courts again in 2004 on another ABH charge.'

'Bit of a gap.'

'After he got out in the early nineties he said he'd seen the light. He's straight now – he claims – and this one didn't stick. He decked a reporter for snooping around in his business, asking questions about his son. Despite a pretty solid case for the defence, he skated. Witnesses were confused and forgetful by the time it went to court, and the one witness with a good memory seemed to remember things very differently from the journalist. He walked that one.'

'Can't argue with that. Decking reporters should be written into the Constitution. Why was the reporter interested in the son?'

'From what I can gather, the lad's a bit of a chip off the old block. His name is Lorcan Wallace, and he's another prize. Nearly beat a young lad to death a few years ago outside a nightclub. Witnesses said it was self-defence, that he was jumped. Course he was well represented and got a suspended sentence. Like I say, he hasn't been in trouble since. At least, nothing that's been brought to our attention.'

'What age was he when the nightclub incident happened?'

'He'd just turned eighteen.'

'Nice. They sound just like the Waltons. Have you got a name for the journalist?'

'Paul Buswell.'

John laughed. 'That jug-eared fuck? I can't think of a person who needs a slap more. He's the guy who wrote a story on one of my first cases – when that cop Dillon hired me to find out who was playing hide the sausage with his wife. Remember?'

'Remember?! Who could bloody forget?'

'So, tell me this and tell me no more, where does the good and gentle Darren hang his hat of an evening?'

'Fortuna House, out in Castleknock.'

'Fortuna? Isn't that a cigarette?'

'I couldn't tell you.'

'And does the fair Caoimhe share the same address?'

'That she does.'

'Pity. I'll have to make it a clandestine operation so.'

'I don't want to know. The less I know the better I sleep at night. By all accounts Wallace is straight now. He owns Wallace and Son, timber merchants, out in Cherry Orchard. He's surface clean at any rate.'

'I owe you one, man.'

'I'm glad you said that, boy.'

'Shit, why?'

'I'm doing a job next Saturday. You can come and give me a hand.'

'What sort of job?'

'Just a job. I won't tell you now. Sure it's better to enjoy the suspense.'

'I don't like the sound of that.'

'Pity about you. You in or not?'

'All right. I suppose I do owe you.'

'That you do, John. I'll swing by to pick you up about seven.'

'In the morning?'

'Make sure you're up and ready to hit the road. You can even bring that wolf of yours if you want.'

Stevie rang off before John had a chance to protest. He slipped his phone back into his pocket and wondered what the hell he'd just agreed to do.

He was still worrying, albeit while enjoying a chilli-laced burger in Bobo's on Wexford Street, when Sarah called him. He licked a dribble of ketchup off his hand as he answered his phone. ''Lo?'

'Guess where I am?'

'Scotland?'

'I'm outside Orie Kavlar's house.'

'I can save you some time. I've already been through that place with a pretty fine-tooth comb. Picked up some goodies, too.'

'Not the bedsit, his other house on Haverty Road.'

'He's got a house?'

'According to girlfriend number two, Vanessa Shaw, he rents a room here.'

'Where the hell does this guy get the time or the energy? Multiple girls, homes, jobs. He's turning out to be quite the Playboy of the Western World.'

'He's turning out to be a lying scummy toe-rag. What goodies did you pick up?'

'A chunk of cash, two grand to be exact, and some passports. Two with his separate identities and one for a girl called Ayla Diaz, a charming young maiden from the Dominican Republic no less.'

'Who the hell is she? Another girlfriend?'

'That's the question.'

'Jesus. This guy is some piece of work.'

'He's certainly something. I've got a notebook here belonging to him too, but I can't make head or tail of the entries. Couple of dates and numbers here, though. I'll be sure to ring them.'

'Right. Look, there's no one here at the moment, so I'm going to hang around for a while, see if anyone shows up.'

'Later.'

John finished his food and paid. He thought of the girl who had called to Orie's again. He thought about the way her eyes had lit up when she laughed. He opened his notebook and checked the address Stevie had given him. What was the connection between Caoimhe Wallace and Orie, and why was she so eager to talk to him?

Only one way to find out.

John reclaimed the Manta, rolled down the window and put on an Otis Redding cassette. He drove across Kevin Street at a leisurely pace, with a cigarette dangling from his lips and his belly full. By the time he had reached Cunningham Road he was singing along to 'Nothing Can Change This Love' at the top of his lungs.

20

The Wallace family home was obviously expensive, but what it lacked in style it more than made up for in ostentation. Fortuna House was a mock-Georgian pile, like something a Premiership footballer might consider classy. John looked at the other homes in the small private estate. Certainly nobody else seemed to be digging Roman columns and balustrades, or mock-Victorian garden lamps, or black and gold fleur-de-lis-topped electronic gates with a big gold W.

He parked in the road and shut off the engine, climbed out and pressed the electronic intercom. No one answered and there were no cars parked on the black-cobbled drive.

Still, if Sarah was house-sitting in Fairview, it wouldn't kill him to do the same for a while. He could take the time to read Orie's notebook properly and smoke in peace.

He hadn't been there five minutes when the BMW jeep rolled down the street and the gates opened.

It hadn't even stopped before John was out of the Manta and bounding through the gates.

'Well, hello there!' He beamed as he opened the driver's door for Caoimhe Wallace. 'Twice in one day! Must be Fate.'

'Mr Quigley, what brings you here?'

She had expressed no surprise that he should turn up where she lived, and John liked that. He also liked the way her mouth twitched as she gathered up some shopping bags from the passenger seat and climbed out.

'Oh, it seemed like a nice day for a drive,' he said.

'Really?'

She pushed a huge pair of sunglasses on top of her head, and as she closed the door behind her John inhaled her perfume. Whatever it was, it made his skin tingle. 'And I was hoping to ask a beautiful woman her name.'

'You came a long way for that.' She looked him straight in the eye and laughed. 'And I'm guessing you already have a fair idea, right?'

'True. I was hoping to run Orie Kavlar's name by you again, see if maybe you remember a bit more about him.'

'I can't tell you any more than I told you this morning. So it looks like you had a wasted journey.'

'Why were you at Orie's house today?'

'How old do I look to you?'

'Oh, I'm not falling for that one. I have an older sister so I know never to guess anything about a woman's age.'

'Try.'

'I'm afraid I'd insult you.'

'I don't get insulted easily.'

'OK.' John looked her over. 'I'm going to go with twenty-one or -two.'

'I'm twenty-four. Which, as far as I know, is old enough to go where I want, when I want without having to explain myself to anyone.'

'Do you have any idea why Orie might be missing?'

'I have no ideas when it comes to that man.'

John tilted his head. There was a whole lot this woman wasn't telling him, he knew. But knowing a person wasn't a crime. Neither was not telling a detective your business.

'We weren't romantically involved if that's what you're thinking.' She wasn't smiling now. 'And that's all I have to say about him.'

A souped-up Honda pulled into the drive behind her jeep. An overstyled young blond man with a sallow complexion climbed out and gave John an unfriendly once-over.

'Hey, Caoimhe? Everything all right?'

'All right, bud.'

John nodded to him.

'Who's this guy?'

John bristled at his rudeness. 'I'm John Quigley, so nice to meet you. Hell of a personality you're sporting there, champ.'

'Lorcan, can you excuse us, please? We're talking.'

The chip off the old block, John realised.

The young man gave him another hard look. John winked at him. This caused every muscle in the younger man's jaw to bunch and twitch.

'Caoimhe, I need a word.'

'I'll be with you in a minute.' She said it firmly, but John picked up on the tension between them.

Lorcan slammed his car door and bleeped the alarm in an over-arm movement. Then he trotted up the steps and let himself into the house.

Jerk, thought John.

'My brother,' Caoimhe said.

'Intense sort of fellow, isn't he? Who does he remind me of?'

'I have no idea.'

John clicked his fingers. 'The big fella who fought with Rocky Balboa. What the hell is his name?'

'Rocky?'

'Yeah, you know, from the Rocky films.'

'Oh,' she said. 'I don't know. I've never watched any of them.'

John gawped at her. 'You're taking the piss. You've never seen Rocky? Any of them?'

'Nope, not a one.'

'What age are you again?'

'Old enough to know what I like watching and what I don't.'

'You can't dismiss the Rocky films like that. The first one was gold. Pure gold.'

'Right.' She glanced at the house. 'Well, as much as it was a delight to see you again, I'd better head on in.'

John stepped back. 'You know what? You should give me your number.'

'My number?'

'Sure, in case Orie doesn't turn up and I need to talk to you again.'

'I told you, I don't know anything.'

'Yeah, but it saves me having to come to your house if I need to talk to you.'

'Why would you need to?'

'Funny thing, in my line of business, Miss Wallace, people tell me all sorts of things.'

She looked at him, exasperated. 'You think I'm lying?'

'Not really, but who can say?'

She pulled her handbag off her shoulder and opened it. She removed a case and took from it a heavy embossed card. 'My number, and the address of my studio should you need to call.'

John read it. 'You're a sculptor?'

'Yes. I sculpt things, and that's what we're called.'

He grinned. 'I'll bet you're very dextrous with your hands.'

'Oh, God, you're too much.' But she smiled when she said it, and, once again, John found himself beaming at her like a gormless fool. This was ridiculous – what the hell was wrong with him?

She gathered up her bags and walked up the path to the steps.

'Dolph Lundgren!'

She turned round. 'Excuse me?"

'The actor. Big Swedish guy. That's who your brother reminds me of.'

'I'll be sure to tell him. He loves action films.'

'Not action, boxing.'

'Isn't that action?'

'Er, yeah, I suppose it is.'

Lorcan must have been watching for her to finish talking because he opened the door as she reached it, and she disappeared inside without a backward glance.

John returned to his car with her perfume in his nostrils and a skip to his step. He figured Caoimhe was hiding something, but he believed it wasn't anything to do with Orie's disappearance, and she had seemed genuine when she'd said she wasn't involved with him. That pleased John, which confused him.

What was he so pleased about?

And what was the deal with Lorcan Wallace, his bad manners and worse attitude?

John felt his antennae vibrate.

Lorcan slammed the door. 'Who was that guy?'

Caoimhe flinched but recovered quickly. 'Don't bloody yell at me. What the hell's the matter with you?'

She began to walk towards the back of the house, but before she had taken two steps Lorcan leaped past her and blocked her way. He grabbed her by the upper arms so hard that she yelped in surprise and dropped her bags. 'Who was that guy you were talking to?'

'Let go of me.'

'Who was he? I didn't like the way he was looking at me.'

'Let go of me!'

He released her. She took a step back and rubbed her arms. 'He's a private detective.'

'A what?'

'A private detective. He was asking questions about Orie.'

Lorcan backed her into the wall. 'What kind of questions? Why would he be here? Why would he be asking you questions? Huh. Huh?'

'He said Orie's missing and he's been hired to find him.'

'But why was he here? Why was he talking to you?'

She lowered her shoulders. 'I went to Orie's today and he saw me there. I imagine he—'

'What?' Lorcan grabbed her again. 'What the fuck did you do that for? Why were you there?'

'Because I'm worried about you!' she shouted. 'I'm worried sick you're involved in something you shouldn't be. I wanted to ask Orie who you owed money to. Did you know Orie was missing? Why would he be missing? What's going on, Lorcan?'

'Who hired this fucking guy? Who put him on to us?'

'Us?'

'Me, then!'

'Put him on to you?'

Lorcan punched the wall beside her head so hard the plaster buckled and his knuckles bled. 'Answer me! Who hired him?'

'His girlfriend. Orie's girlfriend reported him missing.'

'His fucking girlfriend?' Lorcan's eyes were wild. 'I need that guy's name.'

'Lorcan, you're scaring me. You look terrible, like you

haven't slept in days. Are you doing drugs? Is that it? Is that why you owe so much money?'

'For fuck's sake.' Lorcan released her and stepped away disgustedly. 'You're just like Dad.'

She took a step towards him. 'Lorcan, please. Did you do something? You can talk to me. Whatever it is, you can tell me. I won't tell Dad – I won't tell anyone. You've got to let me help you. If it's drugs there are brilliant clinics, these days, private. Nobody has to know anything.'

'I already asked you for fucking help and you were no use to me then. What's the name of that detective?'

'What?'

'The name – the name! Give me the fucking name!'

'Quigley. John Quigley.' She clutched at him. ' Lorcan, listen to me, promise me you haven't done anything to Orie Kavlar. Please! Tell me you didn't do something stupid.'

'Stupid? Stupid? The only fucking stupid thing I ever did was think you gave a shit about me.' He flung her away from him and took off out of the door as Caoimhe slid down the wall onto the cold floor. All her life she had tried to look out for her little brother. She had tried to be the mother he'd never had, but he had fought her every step of the way. It broke her heart to see him like this. She believed he was abusing drugs and knew his gambling was out of control. He had done something terrible, she was sure. She could read him like a book.

She had to help him. She had to protect him.

She just wished she knew how.

21

Sarah was cold, bored stiff and her neck ached. To pass the time she counted the cobwebs covering the filthy windows of forty-three Haverty Road. When she was done with that she tried to identify every weed that grew in the neglected front garden, and then she decided to count how many different cats she spotted climbing on and off the window ledges. By her reckoning she had seen at least five already, howling and rubbing their cheeks against the flaking wood.

The house stuck out like a sore thumb on the well-maintained street, full of chic Victorian red-brick homes. It had to be a rental, she thought.

At half past two she called Helen's house and had a confusing chat with Mrs Higgens, Helen's aged and slightly deaf housekeeper who confused Sarah with Jackie and then Helen. Finally Sarah managed to convince her to get Belinda, her mother's nurse, to come to the phone. She could tell immediately from Belinda's tone that her mother was having a bad day. Belinda confirmed her worst fears. Her mother didn't want to eat and was tearful and uncooperative.

Sarah leaned her forehead against the window. 'I'm sorry.'

'That's OK, she's bound to have days like this.'

'Will you tell her I'll come round later?'

'Of course.'

Sarah thought for a moment. 'Do you think it's because she's not in her own home?'

'Sarah, really, I think she'd be unsettled no matter where she is.'

'I thought the new tablets were helping.'

'They do keep her calmer.' Belinda made a funny grunt. 'She and Mrs Higgens make quite a team.'

Sarah hung up and drummed her fingers on the steering wheel. She wished for the umpteenth time that she had more patience for stake-outs. How the hell did John manage to do it? He could have sat and waited until hell froze over.

She flicked between Today FM and Newstalk on the radio, but neither station held her interest for long. She was debating whether or not to call it a day when someone walked past pushing a purple lady's bicycle with a straw basket attached to the handlebars with twine. Sarah checked her watch: four-twenty.

The man was clearly no youngster, but he was dressed in what Sarah imagined a Californian surfer might wear. He wore baggy multi-printed trousers tucked into faded red Converse runners, a long-sleeved Grateful Dead T-shirt and a grubby sheepskin singlet over the top. He had long, matted grey hair, partly in dreads, partly not, and wore an earring in his nose. He also carried a leather satchel with 'Silver Fox Body Art' printed across the flap in faded lettering.

Sarah waited until he had let himself into the house before she got out of the car. She approached the front door softly and rang the bell.

Time passed. She rang it again, keeping her finger on it this time, long enough to annoy even the most reluctant occupant.

He opened it eventually, carrying a large black cat under his arm. Two tabbies trailed behind, winding round his legs, wailing plaintively. 'Yeah?'

He was older than Sarah had first guessed, well into his fifties, maybe even early sixties. His eyes were bloodshot, and his goatee was grey and yellow from cigarette smoke. She could hear music blaring from deep within the house. It sounded like Iron Maiden. 'Hi,' she said. 'I'm looking for Orie.'

'Eh, yeah, there's no one here.'

He was a Dub through and through, not Polish. Sarah raised an eyebrow. 'You are, aren't you?'

This seemed to throw him somewhat. 'Yeah, I know, but, um, who'd you ask for?'

'I told you, I'm looking for Orie Kavlar.' Sarah pulled her notebook from her pocket and flipped it open, tilting it up to the light for dramatic effect.

'There's nobody here by that name.'

'What about Orie Owsiak?'

'I – I don't, um, know—'

'You don't know anyone called Orie, is that what you're telling me? Because that's weird, seeing as how he gave this as his home address.'

The cat glared balefully at Sarah with its amber eyes while the man scratched at a rash on his scrawny neck and shuffled uncomfortably. Sarah wondered what he was smoking that made his eyes roll independently of each other.

'Well, sure, OK, he lives here. What's this, um, about anyway?'

'Has he lived here long?'

'Look, I'm not trying to be funny or nothing but, like, I don't think that's any of your business.'

'Not my business?' Sarah said, snapping her notebook closed.

'Well, you know—'

'What's your name?'

'Wayne.'

'Is this your house, Wayne?'

'Well, yes, it is.'

'I see. So that makes Orie your tenant. Right?'

'Um, I wouldn't exactly call—'

'And from what I gather he's not the only one.'

The cat gave a desperate squeak as Wayne tightened his grip on it. 'Look, I don't know what anyone's been saying but, you know, I've offered a bed to some friends from time to time, when they've been stuck and so on, but that's not a problem . . . or anything. I'm a generous man, you know. But I wouldn't say they were tenants. I mean if they wanted to, you know, offer to buy some food and stuff I'd be OK with that. It's not a formal arrangement or anything . . .'

Sarah let him waffle on. When, eventually, he dried up, she said, 'So you've issued him with a book of tenant's rights, with receipts for his rent and so on?'

'Um. Well, you see, I—'

Sarah pinched the bridge of her nose and sighed. 'I think I see what's going on. It's OK, Wayne, you're not in any trouble here – no real trouble anyway. Let's start again. I know you don't want to lie to me, I know you won't want me coming back here again and again, looking into your affairs. Now, my name is Sarah Kenny. I need to talk to Orie. I've been through his file so I know that this is the address he uses.'

'His file?' Wayne's Adam's apple bobbed up and down. 'What file?'

'Oh, come on now, Wayne, what file do you think I mean?'

She could see the pressure building. A dull red flush spread across Wayne's face as he swallowed repeatedly. The black cat squirmed.

Finally Wayne managed to put a name to his concerns. 'Are you, like, um, from the welfare?'

'Let's put it like this, Wayne. I'm not here for the good of my health.' She opened her wallet and flashed her private investigator's licence. As she had hoped, Wayne barely looked at it.

'Fuck, he told me he didn't sign on.' Wayne sagged against the door, and the black cat, entirely fed up with being squeezed, let out a long, mournful yowl. 'He swore he didn't.'

'Wayne, it's probably in your best interest to talk to me. This doesn't need to get any more official, believe me.'

'Huh?' Wayne looked confused. 'Official?'

'Well, you're collecting, too, aren't you?'

'Wait, I only get disability! I'm entitled to that.'

'Right.' Sarah looked very severe 'Do you really think it would take much for me to find out where you've been working? If I put a call in to Silver Fox Body Art, would they confirm or deny you do some work for them?'

Wayne looked up and down the street suspiciously. 'Did somebody report me? Um, well, I don't know who's been telling you all this stuff. I mean, it's unreal, just fucking unreal, you know. It's – it's not a real job, it's only . . . um, I was just helping a friend out for the day and anyway it's not – I mean I can't work long hours or anything. You can ask anybody. I get blinding headaches.' He pressed the back of his hand against his forehead. 'I'm getting one now.'

'Wayne, come on, you're on disability, you're working, and you're pulling in God knows what in rent. But the truth is I don't really care. You're not my case so I'm prepared to overlook you. However, I do need to talk to you about Orie.'

Wayne nodded furiously. 'Sure, sure, I understand. You got to believe me, I didn't know he was on the dole. I didn't know anything.'

Sarah smiled. 'Good, so can I come in?'

Wayne stepped back and kicked the door wide with his heel. 'Yeah, s'pose so.'

Sarah stepped inside and closed the door. She followed Wayne down a narrow hallway into the filthiest kitchen she had ever laid eyes on. The air was stuffy and stank of the cat-litter trays that were lined up by the back door. There were at least another five adult cats in the room, some sleeping on piles of newspaper or jumbled clothes. A gang of unruly kittens played and scampered around Wayne's feet. A fat joint lay in the ashtray on the worktop beside a pan of bread. It had gone out and, even as she watched, Wayne spirited it away.

'You have quite a lot of cats,' she remarked.

Wayne dropped the black one and turned down the radio. 'Hum?'

'Cats – you have a lot.'

'Oh, yeah. I inherited most of 'em.'

'How many do you have?'

'Fifteen adults, and about nine kittens. There might be a new batch on the way.' He pointed with his thumb to a massively swollen female sprawled in front of a gas heater.

'What do you do with them all?'

'I get homes for them, although this time of year is weird, with all that don't-get-an-animal-for-Christmas vibe.'

'You ever consider neutering and spaying?'

'Expensive, man.' Wayne turned back to the bread. 'I was just about to make a sandwich before you called. Do you want tea or something? I've got mint, green, dandelion—'

'I'm fine.' Sarah took out her notebook and looked for somewhere to sit. She chose the only chair that wasn't covered with clothing, cats or newspapers. She balanced her notebook on her knee and kept her elbows close to her body. The oilcloth on the table was covered with stains and cat hair and looked sticky.

'When did Orie move in?'

'Um, just before December, I think.'

Sarah wrote that down. 'And how did that come about?'

'Huh?'

'How did you meet? Did you know Orie beforehand?'

'Ah, no. See, my father owned this house, and then he died. So there was all this, um, space, see, and I had to pay the bills and it's hard on just . . . well, you know how it is. So I put up an ad on the noticeboard in a local supermarket, and Orie answered it. He came, liked the place and just rented a room.'

'You didn't do any background checks on him or anything? Place of employment, things like that?'

'Well, he paid the first three months in advance.'

'Did you ask for identification?'

'He gave me a copy of his passport.'

'Could I see that, please?'

'Now?'

'Yes.'

'Hold on a second.' Wayne put down his sandwich and went out.

Sarah heard him crashing about in a room off the hall. While she waited, she played with a small tabby kitten with four white socks and a white bib. She hid her finger behind the leg of chair, smiling when he pounced and retreated. She had played this game with another kitten years ago. Ziggy had been his name. Vic had killed him because she had been late home from work one evening.

She rubbed the kitten's head and watched as he scampered off to his brothers and sisters.

Finally Wayne came back, wiping dust off his T-shirt. 'Phew,

I don't know how things get so cluttered. Here you go.' He passed Sarah a tattered piece of paper.

It was another photocopy of the passport Orie had given to the taxi company. So that was two for Polish, only one for Slovakian. 'Thanks.' She handed it back to Wayne and thought for a minute. 'So Orie came to live here. Was he your first tenant?'

'Yes.'

'And then you got some more. Tell me something, did Orie help you out with that?'

Wayne squinted at her. 'He knew a few people who needed a place to bunk down from time to time, but, like I said earlier, there was no formal arrangement or anything. More like doing a favour for a friend.'

Sarah got it. The men were sub-letting too, cash, no names, no questions asked. Maybe Wayne wasn't as dumb as he liked to pretend. With full rents, rent allowance, disability benefit and a cash-in-hand job she reckoned he had to be making a pretty tidy sum.

'When was the last time you saw Orie?'

'Dunno. Last week maybe.'

'You remember what day exactly?'

'I dunno.'

'Think.'

'Could have been Monday or Tuesday.'

'Does he spend a lot of time here?'

'No. He's hardly ever around.'

'You don't find that odd?'

'No, why would I?' He waved the butter knife in the air. The cats circled and wound figures of eight round his legs, miaowing and clawing at his trousers. 'I mean, that's why it works, man. Everyone's got their own space.'

'Can I see his room?'

Wayne looked quizzically at her over his shoulder. 'Why? Anyway he keeps it locked.'

'OK. What about work?'

'He's with some security crowd.'

'Can you give me a name?'

'I don't know it.'

'Oh, come on. He's been living here a year almost and you're telling me you don't know who he works for?'

'He pays his rent in cash and we don't discuss stuff like that. I'm telling you, Orie keeps himself to himself. I mean, he does weird hours so I always thought it was some shift shit, but he never actually came right out and said who he worked for, and I don't hassle him about his business.'

Sarah didn't believe a word he was saying. 'How did he seem to you the last time you saw him?'

'What do you mean?'

'When you saw him last, how was he? Did he seem different?'

'Different?'

'I don't know – upset about anything. Did he mention going back to Poland? Any difficulties he might be having?'

'Um, I'm not trying to be funny or nothing, but how come you want to know about those kind of things?'

'I'm just curious,' Sarah said, but now she could see that Wayne, even with his room-temperature IQ, was getting twitchy. It was time to wrap it up.

'I thought you'd be more interested in his work and shit. I thought you'd be asking them types of questions, not how he seemed. Seemed? How the fuck would I know how he seemed?'

'It was just a question.' Sarah closed her notebook and stood up. 'Well, thanks for your time.'

Wayne had turned and now he was watching her closely. He didn't, Sarah thought, look quite so soft and hippie-like. 'I think I should have taken a closer look at that identification,' he said.

'Here.' Sarah pulled out her wallet, found a card and passed it to him.

Wayne read it, and as he did so his Adam's apple began to bob again. 'This says you're a private investigator.'

'I know.'

'You told me you here with the welfare.'

'No, I didn't. I told you my name. You assumed I was with the welfare.'

'You tricked me into thinking you were welfare.' Wayne stepped closer to her. 'That's fucking bogus, man, fucking outrageous. You've been asking all these questions. For what? That's what I want to know. What's going on?'

'Those questions are relevant to my investigation.'

'What investigation? You lied and scared me half to death and I've got a right to know why. Who are you working for? Who sent you here?'

'I'm sorry, I'm really not at liberty to say.' Sarah slipped her notebook into her pocket and took a step towards the door.

But as she did so Wayne grabbed her wrist and jerked her round. 'I want to know who sent you here. I want to know what's going on!'

'Let go of my arm, Wayne,' Sarah said. 'I won't ask you again.'

'You come into my home under false pretences, threaten me and make me tell you things . . . You'd better answer me or I'll—'

Sarah didn't hesitate for a second. She kicked Wayne as hard as she could in the shin. He shrieked and released her. As he bent towards his legs, Sarah took the opportunity to shove him as hard as she could. She caught him completely off balance, sending him crashing into his presses. He collapsed onto the floor.

The kittens disappeared under the kitchen table.

Wayne lay gasping and clutching his shin. 'There's no need for violence!' he yelled. 'What's the matter with you?'

'I warned you. I told you to let go of me.'

'I wasn't going to hurt you.'

'I warned you.'

'Get out of my house!'

Sarah turned and walked down the hall. She went out of the door without looking back.

Moments later, she got into her car. She put the keys into the ignition and put her seatbelt on. But she did not drive away. She had to wait for her hands to stop shaking. She had to wait for the bile to make its way back to the pit of her stomach.

Stupid, stupid, stupid. She tapped out the word on the steering wheel. Stupid, letting yourself get trapped in a house with a strange man. Stupid, not being on guard just because he looked like a dopey eejit. Stupid not to be vigilant. Stupid.

It had grown dark while she was inside talking to Wayne. She was glad of the cover. No one would notice how much she shook or the clenching of her jaw.

Stupid.

She leaned her head back against the seat and closed her eyes.

Breathe, she thought. Breathe, goddamn it, just breathe.

22

Detective Sergeant Ray Devlin wondered if he could smell the alcohol seeping from his pores. He was suffering from a monster hangover. His brain felt as if it was in a vice and there was a sandpit at the back of his eyes. Despite the Nurofen and three cups of coffee he'd had since he'd come on shift, the pain remained. Maybe he should try food next.

He opened the autopsy report and read it. Furlong's notes were concise and easy to follow. The Jane Doe on the wasteland had died from asphyxiation; her toxicology screen was negative as was her blood alcohol. Furlong placed her death at no more than twenty-four hours before the body had been located. He couldn't be more precise than that. Lividity suggested she had been killed elsewhere, then dumped.

Devlin scanned down the page. She had shown signs of dehydration and her stomach contents were virtually nil. So, wherever she had come from, she hadn't had much access to food or water.

So where had she come from?

Also, although her T-shirt and jeans had been generic, her bra and knickers were a matching set from a company that was not sold in Ireland. She had a tattoo of a hawk at the base of her spine, and her ears had been pierced twice in each lobe. Furlong had found traces of diesel, sawdust, oil and cement dust in her hair. There were also traces of blood – her own.

Devlin read on: 'The brain was congested and mildly swollen and the heart (385 g) was dilated and mildly hypertrophied in association with a narrow aortic valve ring (measured as 5.4 cm). Cranial ossification was incomplete. Three of the five sacrum bones were not fused.' Foley had estimated that Jane Doe had been between fourteen and eighteen years old.

'Poor girl was only a kid,' Devlin muttered.

There was evidence of petechial haemorrhage in her eyes and behind her ears, which Furlong found consistent with his view that the girl had been suffocated, and faint bruising to the sides of her mouth. There were wood scrapings under her nails, some of which were broken, but there were no defensive wounds.

She had not fought back, and she had not been drugged, which led to Furlong's next hypothesis. He had concluded that Jane Doe was already unconscious when she had been suffocated, and she had definitely been dead when the rats had attacked her hands. He had made a note that Jane Doe's cheeks, lips and tongue had been badly bitten when she was alive, leading him to conclude that she had thrown a fit at some point on the night she had died. This, along with the fact that there was no trace of drugs or alcohol in her system, meant she might have suffered a seizure, possibly as a result of epilepsy. Older and more recent scarring found on Jane Doe's frontal lobe certainly backed that hypothesis.

Devlin read on, but there was little else in the report to enlighten him. They had the how, but not the who or the why.

The lab had photographed her, and he had earlier released her image to the press and had sent her fingerprints out across the wires, but so far no one had reported her missing or had come forward to claim her body.

She was a mystery girl.

Devlin closed the report and looked back over the statements he had collected from the two reluctant lovebirds that night, but he'd read and reread them several times and no new insight leaped out at him. He leaned back in his chair and groaned as he stretched.

'Did you have a rough night, Ray?' an amused voice said. 'I hear I missed a right party.'

He looked up. Lovely Reba, the sergeant with the beautiful smile and gorgeous curly red hair, was walking across the carpet to him.

Ray and Reba . . . it had a lovely ring to it, he thought. 'Oh, sure, you know yourself.'

'I heard it was some shindig. That Brady is a lunatic for the drink. Mind you, he wouldn't be the only one from what I hear.'

Devlin wondered just how much Reba had heard. Did she know he'd got so wasted he'd passed out in Brady's front garden? Or that Brady and a few others had drawn all over his face, then duct-taped him in his underpants to the garden bench and forgotten about him? Or that it hadn't been until a passing milkman found him the next morning that he'd been freed? When he'd staggered, frozen stiff and furious, into the house he'd upended a kettle of freezing water on the sleeping Brady, causing a minor rumpus. It had taken four of Dublin City's finest to separate the two men.

Devlin groaned again.

'Honest to God, do you lot ever grow up?'

Oh, she'd heard all right.

Reba collected some paperwork from a drawer and closed it. 'What are you working on?'

'The body on the wasteland, the young girl.'

'Tough case?'

'Strange one. No one's reported her missing, and no one's claimed the body or responded to the photo release. It's like this girl just dropped out of the sky.'

Reba nodded. 'Well, good luck with it.'

'Thanks. What are you up to?'

'I got a call-up. I'll be moving into Harcourt Terrace for a few weeks. Inspector Stafford wants me working with Cassidy.'

'On Operation Shield?' Devlin sat straighter in his chair, hardly able to believe his ears. It was the biggest operation the squad had ever mounted. Officers from four different units were involved in an effort to break a cocaine-smuggling ring linked to a notorious family in West Dublin. He had put in a request to be part of it two months before and hadn't heard anything back.

'We're being briefed later today.'

'I see. When did you hear?'

'Late last week.' She looked down. 'I'm sorry, Ray. I know you wanted in on it.'

Late last week – when his own inspector had fobbed him off with overtime. The bastard had known Operation Shield was about to start, and here he was hobbled with a near impossible case.

'Did Stafford say anything about me?'

'Just asked how you were.'

'What did you tell him?'

'That you seemed to be settling in OK out here in the sticks. He laughed.'

'I'll bet he did. Well, good luck. And remember, they're a pack of sharks in there.'

'Thanks, I'm sure I'll be OK.' Reba smiled. 'And good luck with your Jane Doe.'

Devlin waited for her to leave before he allowed himself to express his true feelings. He booted the metal bin by his desk across the room and said, 'That fat son of a fucking two-faced caterpillar-browed bollocks.' But it didn't make him feel any better.

He stuffed the reports into his desk, grabbed his car keys and stood up. He had to get out of there before he did something he regretted. It was time to revisit the crime scene.

He drove along by the Dodder river, still fuming and muttering under his breath. By the time he'd reached the turn-off for the small lane where his Jane Doe had been discovered he was in the blackest pit of despair.

Why did Stafford hate him so much? Was it something he'd said? Something he'd done? OK, he wasn't the best officer in the squad but, damn it, he worked hard – well, he worked the same as everyone else. And yet his ex-commanding officer seemed to thwart him at every step.

He reached the car park at the edge of the woods and parked. The day had started brightly enough, but now ominous black clouds were gathering over the mountains, and a bitter wind was rising. Devlin fastened his coat and climbed over the gate, which now had a brand new lock and chain on it. He walked along the path to where the girl's body had been dumped.

The woods were silent, and as he stepped over the mulch and pine needles, he couldn't help but feel sad at the fate of this young woman, her life cut so tragically short. He reached the dumping ground and cast his eyes around. A lot of the bags of rubbish had been taken away as evidence, but basically it was much as he had found it that night.

He paced along the edge where the mud was thinner, keeping an eye open for . . . what? What did he think he was going to find that the crime-scene team hadn't already?

He didn't know, but as he paced in a gradually tightening

circle it dawned on him that he had nothing concrete, and since that was so he might as well start dealing in the probable.

Whoever had abandoned the girl had been confident they wouldn't be spotted, which meant it had probably been dark. Rigor was waning, so she had been there probably since the Friday. Unless the killer or killers had dropped her off by helicopter, they had probably driven here, and if they had, they must have come off Stocks Lane.

Stocks Lane.

It was probable that that was where he needed to start.

23

Stacy Power walked down Synge Street, her frayed bag dangling from her left hand. She was smoking and her feet were dragging. She had been to every place she could think of looking for Orie, and nobody had seen or heard from him. She had left so many messages for him that his voicemail was full.

She was completely out of ideas.

She was angry and hurt. Everyone was against her, absolutely everyone, her folks, her friends. Her father had hit the roof when he'd heard about the money and the detective agency – she'd never seen him so furious. And then, to make matters worse, when she'd called Melissa to cry to her about it, Melissa had been on his side! Why was she so horrible about Orie? She was Stacy's best friend, and yet sometimes she acted like a total bitch.

But she was right about one thing. Why had Orie been with that girl in the first place?

And if it was as innocent as Orie had claimed, why had he

looked so guilty when she had told him Melissa had seen him? Why had he been so angry, so defensive? He had sworn to her it wasn't what she thought, but how could she believe him? She wanted to, but somehow she just couldn't bring herself to buy his version.

Orie. She had never had a real boyfriend before him. He was the first – and the first man she had slept with. She loved him so much it hurt. She loved everything about him, his laugh, the way he said her name, the way he looked when he was sleeping. He owned her heart.

And he was breaking it.

She felt tired – no, tired wouldn't, couldn't, begin to cover it. She felt physically drained; her back ached so badly it felt like someone had taken a bat to her spine.

She wished the baby would hurry up and come. She stopped to catch her breath. She couldn't possibly get any bigger, could she? She was already covered with stretch marks, and no amount of cocoa butter seemed to make any difference to them. And no matter how she lay in bed at night she couldn't get comfortable. Not that she'd been able to sleep with Orie missing.

She shouldn't have fought with him, shouldn't have slapped him. She should have waited before she'd gone round to his place, hurling accusations like a lunatic. What on earth had she been thinking? Why had she listened to Melissa? What if Melissa had been lying? Maybe that was it. Maybe Melissa had been making shit up, trying to come between them. Maybe she should call JP, see what he said. Although that would be a waste of time – JP always backed Melissa up. Maybe she should—

'Ow.' She gasped and pressed her hand to her side. She had a stitch or something – she'd been getting pains like this one all day. Every now and then it fluttered up into a sharp pang that left her wincing. Braxton Hicks, the nurse had called them. She'd said that it was nothing to be alarmed about.

'Oh.' She'd got another. She threw away the cigarette and bent forward, trying to stretch her muscles. After a few moments the pain seemed to ease, and she could breathe easier again. She straightened slowly and let out a long sigh, feeling sweat break out on the back of her neck. People were staring at her. Suddenly she couldn't face going home, couldn't face her mother's concerned eyes, listening to another of her lectures. It was all too much. She just wanted to be left alone – she just wanted Orie back, with his assurance that everything would be all right.

She wished she could shake off the feeling of dread, but she couldn't. She had carried it deep within her since she had heard his message. Maybe he'd come back, maybe it had all been a big misunderstanding – things happened sometimes. Maybe something had happened to his family, and he'd had no option but to go, just hadn't been able to get in touch. Did they even have landlines in Slovakia? Why didn't she know? Why didn't she know anything about the father of her child?

She turned the corner onto Aungier Street and dithered over whether or not to catch a taxi. In the end she decided to save her money and walk. She slung her bag over her shoulder, hitched up her tracksuit bottoms and set off.

She'd leave a note this time, beg him to get in touch. Maybe he'd be back by now: she'd knock and he'd throw open the door, a cheeky grin on his face. She'd be mad, he'd call her 'baby' and tell her he was sorry for scaring her like that. He'd bring her in and give her a back rub. He'd make her tea and laugh at all the fuss.

Her spirits lifted slightly, and as she hurried down the road, all memories of the pain faded.

But her determination was short-lived. By the time she made it to Dorset Street she felt light-headed and she had a really bad stitch in her side. She ignored it as best she could and hurried down the metal steps to Orie's door. Her heart sank when she saw the same junk mail peeking out of the letterbox. The curtains were still drawn. Nevertheless, she hammered on the door. 'Orie! Orie, it's me, love. It's Stacy.' She waited, her ear pressed against the bubble glass. She heard nothing, not that she'd expected to. She felt tears build. What had happened to him? Where was he? Where was he?

'Orie—'

And now she couldn't stop the tears falling. She had never felt so scared in all her life. Another ribbon of pain shot through her. This one was so bad she almost sank to her knees.

'Hey.'

She blinked and tried to clear the tears from her eyes. She heard shoes ring off the metal steps. 'Orie?'

But it wasn't Orie: it was the blond guy, Orie's friend, the angry one. She had seen him with Orie once or twice before. What was his name? Lorcan? Maybe he knew something.

Before she could ask, Lorcan grabbed her and flung her hard against the wall. 'Orie, where is he? Is he in there?'

'What? No. I—'

Lorcan banged on the door with his fist. 'Orie, get out here.'

'He's not there.'

'Shut up. Orie!'

'I'm telling you he's not fucking there. Let go of me.'

Lorcan's eyes turned to her. 'You're the stupid bitch who called in the detective, aren't you? Why did you do that?'

'Let me go. You're hurting me.'

'Why did you get fucking detectives into our business? Answer me, you stupid bitch.'

Stacy tried to yank herself free but she couldn't. She glanced towards the neighbour's door.

Lorcan swatted her across the face, not hard but enough to shock her and make her gasp. 'I asked you a question.'

'I was worried something had happened. He wouldn't not call me.'

Lorcan searched her face, his eyes wild. 'Or maybe nothing's happened and he's just not fucking interested in some skank.'

'Shut up.'

'"Where are you going, Orie? Why don't I know your friends, Orie? How come we never go anywhere, Orie?"' Lorcan mimicked, squishing his face up. 'You think any man wants to hear that shit?'

Stacy looked at him in utter disbelief. Tears spilled down her cheeks.

'You're going to call that detective and cancel him.'

'Why won't you tell me where he is?' she whispered. 'I want to talk to him.'

'Never mind where he is. Are you listening to me? You're going to call the detective and say you made a mistake. You don't want him looking for Orie. Right? Where's your phone?'

He snatched her bag out of her hand and, when she tried to grab it back, he shoved her in the chest, hard, sending her sprawling on the dirty concrete.

Lorcan opened her bag and upended it. He kicked her make-up and other bits and pieces out of the way and picked up her mobile phone. He thrust it into her hand. 'Here. Ring him.'

'No.' Stacy shook her head. 'Tell me where Orie is. I want to talk to him.'

'Ring the fucking detective.'

'I'm not ringing anyone until I know he's all right.'

'You stupid bitch.'

Stacy could do nothing but put her hands over her face to protect herself as Lorcan kicked her meagre belongings across the ground. He ground the heel of his shoe into Stacy's mobile, his face purple with rage. 'He doesn't want you! He doesn't want anything to do with you! You're a fucking mistake. You're nothing to him! If you hadn't gone and got yourself knocked up, he'd have dumped your arse months ago. Wait until he hears how you got outsiders involved in his business. Our business!'

Stacy tried to curl into a ball, but now the pain she had felt earlier exploded down her right side. She tried to cry out but couldn't get enough air into her lungs to do so. She needed to get away from this lunatic.

She rolled onto her hands and knees and tried to crawl away. The pain was unbearable. She shook her head and her vision cleared. She could see the door to the neighbour's flat opening. She started to crawl towards it.

'Where the fuck do you think you're going?' Lorcan bent down and grabbed her hair, dragging her face close to his. The smell of his aftershave nearly made Stacy gag.

'You think I won't hurt you? You think I wouldn't cut that kid right out of you?'

'Please . . .' Stacy managed. 'Please don't hurt me.'

'Do you think because you're knocked up you're safe? I don't give a shit about you or your bastard. You're going to ring that detective and you're going to tell him you made a mistake.'

'I – I'll call. Please stop. You're hurting me.'

He yanked her head back so hard that Stacy felt some of her hair rip free at the roots. She looked into his blue eyes and saw nothing but anger. There was no mercy, not a trace of human kindness. He was enjoying himself.

'Please, you have to believe me. I will – I'll call, I promise.'

'Hey.'

Her eyes darted to the right. The little man who lived next door to Orie stepped out. Stacy was amazed to see he was brandishing what looked like a large Samurai sword. 'Please. Help me!'

Lorcan looked up. 'Go back inside and mind your own fucking business, Grandpa. This doesn't concern you.'

'Let the girl go.' The man took another step forward, moving lightly on the balls of his feet. He raised the sword over his head and swung it slowly in an incredibly graceful move.

Lorcan released Stacy's hair and stood up. He splayed his hands in front of himself in a placatory gesture. 'Hey, relax, man, there's no need for—'

The old man swung again. This time the tip of the sword missed the end of Lorcan's nose by a millimetre.

'Fuck!' Lorcan stumbled backwards. 'Are you fucking crazy? You could have taken my fucking head off.'

'Let the girl go.'

'Yeah, relax, she's OK.' Lorcan turned his gaze to Stacy. She could tell from his face that he wanted nothing more than to finish what he had started.

'Leave,' the old man said. 'Now.'

'I'm going, I'm going. Keep your hair on.' Lorcan backed away another step. 'I know where you live,' he said softly. 'And you'd better fucking call off that detective bullshit. I mean it.' He jerked the front of his jacket down, turned and walked up the steps, coolly and slowly.

The old man watched him go. Only when he was absolutely sure Lorcan was gone did he lower the sword and come to Stacy's side. He held out his hand to her. Stacy tried to scramble to her feet, but she hadn't an ounce of strength left in her legs.

'You are hurt?'

Stacy shook her head. 'No, I'm . . . I think I'm OK.' She pushed her hair back from her face. How many times had she laughed at this little man and his quirky ways? How many times had Orie been rude to him or imitated his accent? How often had she played her music late into the night, ignoring his thumps on the walls? The tears started again. 'I'm really sorry, mister.'

The old man patted her shoulder. 'Come. Come on.' He slipped his arm under hers and helped her to her feet.

Stacy limped to his front door and gripped the jamb while he picked up her belongings and brought them to her. 'Thanks, mister.' She looked forlornly at her smashed phone. It was beyond repair. Without it she suddenly felt very vulnerable and alone.'That's some sword, mister. You one of them martial-arts freaks?'

'This?' The old man grinned and raised the fearsome weapon. He pressed his thumb against the blade and lifted his hand to show her the imprint it had made against his flesh. 'Not sharp, only ornament.'

'Yeah?' Stacy smiled. 'Better than three flying ducks.'

The old man tilted his head quizzically.

'You know, like people have on their walls.' Stacy wiped at her tears with the heel of her hand. 'Never mind, it doesn't matter. I'd better go.'

'You are OK?'

'I'll be grand. Listen, thanks again. You were really . . . really something.' She sniffed and drew herself upright. He swung her bag over her shoulder and she made her way gingerly to the steps.

She reached the street and wondered again if she should get a cab home. She didn't want her mother to see her in such a state, but where else could she go? Nowhere. The realisation hit her hard, and she fought back the tears as she managed to hail a taxi.

24

'So this girl you followed—'

'Caoimhe,' John said. 'And I didn't follow her. I got Stevie to run the registration number.'

'She turns out to be the daughter of Darren Wallace, who turns out to be a scumbag extraordinaire—'

'Ex – he's a retired scumbag, these days. Now he's a noble worker, same as you and me, only with lots and lots of cash and a fancy house. Exactly not like us.'

'And she is a sister to Lorcan Wallace, another man with a record for beating people half to death. This girl was at Orie's house earlier?'

'Correct. And she seemed pretty keen to talk to him.'

'Is she another of his girlfriends, do you think?'

John stirred his Pot Noodle with a pen and replaced the plastic lid. 'She says she's not and I'm inclined to believe her. She's definitely hiding something, but I think she's on the level about that.'

'What makes you so sure?'

'She's a bit out of his league.'

'Oh, is she now?'

'Plus she's twenty-four. Judging by his other conquests I'd say she's probably too old for him.'

'But we shouldn't rule her out, right? She could be involved with him romantically.'

'I suppose, but I don't think so.'

Sarah's head was slightly fuzzy. After she'd left Wayne's she had gone directly to her house and had taken two of her mother's Xanax tablets to calm her nerves. Only sheer determination had made her return to the office. But fuzzy or not, she knew John: the goofy look on his face meant only one thing, that this Caoimhe was a looker and he liked her.

'Think about it for a minute. Maybe she's one of his surplus girlfriends and maybe the Wallace clan didn't like her fraternising with Orie. What does she do?'

'She's a sculptor. She has a studio over in Herbert Park.'

'If she isn't a girlfriend, what the hell is her link to an immigrant two-timing work-shy shit like Orie?'

'She refused to say.'

'Are they friends or something?'

'Maybe he modelled for her.'

'Come on.'

'I got the impression she didn't think much of him.'

'Hmm.' Sarah tapped her pen on the desk. 'OK, so let's think about this for a minute. Darren Wallace has a record for assault, and so has his son. We know Orie doesn't let himself get run off too easily. Maybe this Caoimhe was playing belly-slaps with Orie and maybe the family didn't like it and decided to take matters into their own hands. Maybe Orie didn't take kindly to them telling him what to do, maybe there was an altercation and things got out of hand. For all you know, Caoimhe' – to her horror she had whined the name – 'might have discovered Orie was playing the field on her and chopped him into a thousand pieces. She might only have been there at his place to cover her tracks.'

'Sarah, she was knocking at the door and calling his name. I think I might have noticed if she'd been wielding a chainsaw. I'd also have noticed if she was carrying a black sack and a bucket of bleach. Shit, I'd even have noticed blood or body parts lying around. She had a Hermès bag with her but not a chainsaw.'

'How the hell do you know what an Hermès bag is, let alone what it looks like?'

'Cynthia used to have one.'

Cynthia was John's old girlfriend. She had been young, blonde and as a shallow as a puddle in May. Sarah's nose wrinkled involuntarily.

'So, let me see what we have here,' John continued. 'As far as we know, Orie's got two addresses, two confirmed identities and two girlfriends.'

'Right. Stacy, Vanessa and probably that Caoimhe one, too.'

'She says she's not. OK, now this guy Orie—'

'Oh, well, if she says she's not then we might as well forget about her.'

'—seems to have a ready supply of cash, but—'

'I mean she turns up at his place, she has criminal connections—'

'—I didn't find any mention of dole and he doesn't seem to be collecting rent allowance.'

'It would be stupid not to consider—'

'So the question is, how is Orie supporting his lifestyle—'

'People lie, John, they lie about everything.'

'—if he doesn't seem to have a full-time job?' John looked at his partner.

'Could you please stop biting my head off? I know people lie. I'm too long in the tooth not to.'

'Just don't underestimate her.'

'I won't.'

'Good.'

John shovelled a spoonful of Pot Noodle into his mouth and winced as it burned his tongue. 'Did the landlord have anything else to say?'

'Wayne? Not really, but you can be sure none of his tenants has ever received a rent book or a receipt.'

'So, which do we think is the true Orie? Polish or Slovakian?'

'He used the Polish passport to get work and obtain a room, I'm going to lean towards that.'

'So why the lie to Stacy about where he's from?'

'I don't know. But those guys at the cab company didn't even know Stacy existed. Poor bloody kid, she's going to be devastated.'

'What now, then?'

'I guess we check out the Global Security crowd, see if maybe we can track him down that way. Or at the very least find out when or where he worked over the weekend.'

'Assuming he did work.'

'Right.'

Sarah's mobile rang. She glanced at the screen. It was Helen. She hesitated before answering. 'Hi, Helen.'

'Sarah, good. I wasn't sure if I'd catch you.'

'Well, I'm caught. Did Belinda tell you I was going to call later?'

'I haven't spoken to her. I'm calling about Jackie.'

Jackie was their sister, younger than Helen, older than Sarah, kinder than either of them put together. She was a secondary-school art teacher and a gifted painter in her own right. She was the mediator of the family, the pacifist, and Sarah loved her fiercely.

It had been Jackie whom Victor had run off the road, Jackie

who might have been killed but who had suffered a broken arm and concussion. And the worst thing of all: the crash had forced her to postpone her first exhibition. It was Jackie and the price Jackie had been forced to pay for Sarah's choices that kept Sarah awake in the twilight hours.

Sarah felt a jolt of fear. 'What is it? Is she OK?'

'She's fine. But I need a favour.'

Sarah was relieved and surprised. Helen never needed favours, or if she ever did she never saw fit to mention it. Sarah assumed Helen thought asking for favours was a sign of weakness. Jackie always claimed, laughingly, that Helen would rather smell of wet dog than give off that aura.

'Fire away.'

'I was talking to Barry earlier about Jackie's postponed exhibition.'

'Oh, yes?' Barry Swan was Jackie's fiancé, a fey, womanly sort of man whom Sarah found hard to tolerate, let alone be civil to, although even she had to admit her sister loved him to distraction.

'She's a bit down about missing it.'

'I know that. She's trying to put a brave face on it but I can tell she's very disappointed.'

'We were just saying that it seemed such a horrible shame for her to miss out completely, but I've checked and, unfortunately, the gallery is booked out until well after April.'

'Right.'

'I've rung around a few other suitable spaces but there's nothing else available for months. So then I had a brilliant idea. Why not have it at the house?'

'What house?'

'Mine. I was thinking we could stage a sort of private gathering, rather like an old-fashioned salon evening. We could open up the two reception rooms and clear them of furniture, take the mirrors and pictures down and hang fabric as a backdrop – I'm thinking pale silk or organza, something like that. We could have the bigger canvases in the dining area and the smaller ones in the living room. We could even have a hostess bar with wine and finger food and set it up in the central divide, nothing too formal but enough so that people can mingle and view freely. What do you think?'

'Well—'

'We'd keep it a surprise, of course. Barry knows who to invite. Honestly, it would give Jackie such a lift. What do you think?'

'When were you thinking of holding it?'

'Friday.'

'This Friday?'

'Yes, why not? Barry's already drawn up a list of guests, and Rose from the gallery has offered to call her buyers. I can put an ad in the paper today, so why not Friday? Two of the main buyers are only available this week – Christ knows when they'll be around again. It might be months.'

Sarah closed her eyes and pinched the bridge of her nose until her eyes watered. When Helen got the bit between her teeth there was no stopping her. She thought of Helen's large, sterile house, the childless home she shared with Paul, her husband, the Great Surgeon, as Sarah and Jackie had christened him. It was perfect for an opening, perfect for a show. 'I think the house is a terrific idea, I really do, and very kind of you, but do you really think a surprise is the best way to go about it? You know Jackie, she'll want her pictures hung a certain way and the music to be just so and—'

'Right, so she'll get worked up to ninety, and we can't have that. That's where I thought you could come in.'

'Me? What do I know about art?'

'That's just it, Sarah. You know how Jackie's mind works better than anyone – who better to organise that end of it? As I said, Barry and Rose are dealing with the guests, and I'll take care of the venue and the catering.'

Sarah was almost too stunned to speak. Who was this woman and what had she done with the real Helen? Miss Perfectionist? 'OK,' she managed. 'I'd be happy to help. What do you need me to do?

'Brilliant. Well, this is what we were thinking . . .'

John opened the Yellow Pages and scanned the pages of security ads while Sarah's phone conversation drifted into 'uh-huh,' and 'aha'.

Only Helen, John thought wryly, could reduce Sarah to a tongue-tied adolescent. Immediately, his mind was drawn back to the last face-to-face conversation he'd had with Helen a few weeks ago. She had more or less accused him of not caring for Sarah at all, happy to lay her sister's troubles at John's feet. He had been feeling vulnerable and scalded at the time, having just returned from the Katie Jones case to discover Sarah had been hospitalised. How he hadn't given Helen a toe up the arse he'd never know.

He found Global Security and scribbled the address into his pad. Then he checked the numbers against those in the back of Orie's notebook.

Of course, in a way, he understood Helen's hostility. She had never forgiven him for cheating on Sarah all those years ago when they were teenagers, and she held John solely responsible for Sarah moving to England. It seemed to infuriate her that Sarah had given him a second chance.

He glanced at Sarah now. She was resting her chin in her hand, eyes closed, as Helen talked on. Women, John thought as he gathered up his car keys and jacket, he would never understand women. They were a foreign language that he couldn't even begin to master.

'I'm going to check this place out.'

'Which?'

'Global Security.'

'Need me to come?'

'Nah, it's over on James Street. If I'm not back before you go, just lock up. I'll call you later.'

25

Darren Wallace wasn't tall but he was built like a brick outhouse and, at fifty-five, he showed no signs of ageing, other than a few wrinkles and the grey streaks in his hair.

He was not an easy man to like and he knew it. He worked hard and he expected hard work in return. He was driven, gruff and impatient, with a quick temper and low tolerance for stupidity. And right at that second he was dealing with stupidity.

'I don't give a flying shit,' he snapped into the phone. 'You tell Williams a deal is a deal. It was high-quality Canadian maple, delivered on time and stored right. If them floors were buckled it was because they were laid wrong, nothing to do with the wood. You know and I know floors need room to expand once they're laid. Who knows what kind of cowboy he had laying them? Now I want my fucking money, and if he doesn't come up with it this week I am going to see to it personally that he and his profit margins are only going to have a distant relationship. I have lads here need paying. Are you getting this loud and fucking clear, Pat?'

He strode the length of his timber yard as he listened to the garbled excuses, his face flushed with temper. Some of his employees glanced at him, then quickly found something else to do in another part of the yard.

'I don't give a bollocks who pulled out of what fucking sale. That wood was delivered and them houses floored. If I have to, I'll drive up there and rip every one of them bleeding floorboards up myself tonight. Let him open his fucking showhouse then. I'll blacken him, Pat, and you can tell him I said that. You tell him I want paying and I won't wait after this week. All right? Right.'

He snapped his phone shut, surprised to find he was almost out of the main gates and into the lane leading out to the motorway. It had always been a habit of his to walk and talk, especially if his dander was up. And lately he'd seemed to be permanently aggrieved. He stalked back across the yard.

As he entered his office, he checked the wall clock. Five twenty, nearly knocking-off time, and still no sign of Lorcan. Not that he'd really expected the lad to turn up.

Lorcan showed about as much interest in the yard as he did in any other form of an honest day's work, which was none at all.

He gazed down at the photo on the desk of his late wife. Lucy had died from ovarian cancer when Lorcan was eight and Caoimhe twelve, leaving him with no choice but to raise two young children on his own. Her untimely death had forced Darren to take stock and look long and hard at what he was doing. It had forced him to step up and take responsibility, maybe for the first time in his life. He had looked at those two children on the day of his wife's funeral and he had vowed to go straight. He couldn't risk any more time inside, couldn't leave them to fend for themselves or at the mercy of relatives, not after everything they had already been through.

He had done his best, calling in favours, clearing the decks, starting his own timber-import business with a loan here and there, all of which he had paid back. The Celtic Tiger and the building boom had taken care of the rest. Now he was a wealthy man, owner of a respectable business. Was he happy?

Was he hell.

Lorcan was a worry and no mistake. Darren loved his son, of that he had no doubt – at least, that was what he told himself. But he found him increasingly hard to get through to, hard to comprehend. No matter what he did or said he couldn't reach him.

From the day Lucy had passed away, Lorcan had been trouble – hell, long before it, if he was honest, getting kicked out of one school after another, causing fights and disruption. No matter how much trouble the lad got himself into, he couldn't control that hair-trigger temper of his. He suffered one punishment after another but nothing stopped him going off on one.

After Lucy died, Darren had tried everything to get through to the troubled lad, football, hurling, boxing, but nothing seemed to work. The only thing Lorcan ever expressed any interest in was kickboxing. And even that had come at a major price, such as when his son had used his freshly honed skills to half kill a young fella outside a nightclub. Now that had been a real eye-opener. And it had cost Darren a great deal to stop the kid's family pressing charges.

Of course, Lorcan had always sworn blind he had been defending himself and, OK, the witnesses – if you could call them that – seemed to back his story, but Darren was no fool. He had seen the hostility in his son's eyes when challenged as clearly as the triumph when he had learned the charges were to be dropped. He had not reacted like an innocent man: there had been no relief, no gratitude, just a bristling sense of entitlement.

Darren knew his son was straying down a dangerous path. He'd been on it himself half his life. But no matter what he did, no matter how he tried to interest the lad in the business, Lorcan resisted.

Maybe he'd had too much handed to him too soon. Lorcan didn't want to work, didn't want to get up early, didn't like to get his hands dirty. All he wanted was his PlayStation or to sit at his computer day and night.

It was hard to admit, but Darren suspected Lorcan thought hard graft was beneath him. He'd rather spend all night out on the tiles, gambling with degenerates and whores, than work.

Not that he'd been much different at Lorcan's age – but, still, he wished his son would show some interest in working with him. Or any sort of interest in anything, some sign of get-up-and-go. He was twenty years old, and he acted as if he was fifteen.

And why hadn't he got a girlfriend? Or any kind of friends at all? Apart from that greasy sleaze Orie, Darren had never seen his son interact with anyone his own age. He never hung round with any of the lads he'd gone to school with. Why didn't he want to go out for a few pints or a round of golf or any other normal, healthy activities? If Lucy had lived, things might have been different. After all, what had he known about raising kids? It wasn't like anyone ever gave you a handbook or a set of instructions. He had done his best, and of that he could be sure, but the boy had never been like others of his age.

Darren sat back in his chair and crossed his hands over his stomach. Maybe he was being too hard on himself. Caoimhe had had much the same upbringing as her brother and she had turned out OK.

Darren smiled when he thought of her. Caoimhe was a fire-cracker and no mistake. She took after her mother, artistic, impetuous, fiery, but quick to throw her arms around you too. The Loreto nuns had done a fine job – she had perfect manners and a funny snotty accent he found charming. She was the image of her mother when Lucy was that age, although Lucy had never been quite so striking.

She was the opposite of Lorcan in so many ways. She was open, confident, trusting, determined to succeed. When she had first told him she wanted to be a sculptor Darren had groaned inwardly, imagining another fly-by-night notion. He had counselled her to get a real job, some training, a trade, anything. But she had stood her ground, applying for and getting into DIT. There she had flourished, coming out with some impressive comments and praise from her tutors.

Darren had set her up in her studio, buying the little flat and charging her a nominal rent, but even then he had considered the sculpture more of a hobby than anything else.

But she had persevered and had even sold a couple of pieces recently. Her single-minded devotion to her art had impressed the hell out of him.

If only Lorcan would take a leaf out of his sister's book, but he seemed to resent his sister's foothold in the world, her abilities. He had once accused Darren of favouring her over him, and it was all Darren could do not to agree.

Why shouldn't he have a soft spot for his own daughter? Caoimhe didn't speak to Darren as though she despised him, she didn't draw away from him when he reached for her. She had his work ethic, and she was happy – or, at least, she seemed so. She had her work. She had interests, friends, a life. She seemed normal, content.

Lucy had been the calm one, the rock of the family. It always stung him that she had never lived long enough to see what he had made of himself, how he had turned his life round. Lucy had never doubted it was possible. She had always kept complete faith in him, even when he was banged up, even when she saw him being carted away in the back of a squad car, while her house was turned upside down by the cops. No matter what, she had never wavered in her support of him.

It was cruel that she had been taken. Her death burned Darren at strange times. And the older he got, the more he felt her loss. He'd see or hear something and wish, more than anything else, he could just call and tell her, hear her raspy laugh.

Nobody asked about her any more either. He knew it was because so much time had passed, and he understood. But it still bothered him. It was as if she had winked out of existence, as if she had never truly been there at all. But she had: he had held her in his arms, he had kissed her soft lips, he had rubbed the papery skin on her hand when she was dying.

Maybe that was love at its most basic – maybe you never did get over the loss of your one true love. Maybe you just managed in their absence. And he was managing.

He had kept his promise to his dying wife. He had looked after their two children, had raised them, educated them, set them on the right path, or tried to.

He glanced at his watch again. Ten to six. There was no point in lying to himself any longer. Lorcan wasn't going to show.

Through his office window he could see men climbing down from machinery, slapping dust from their overalls. He knew some of the lads would go for a quick pint before they headed on home. They often asked him if he'd like to join them, even though he was their boss. He knew why. He was one of them, a grafter, happy to put his back and sweat into it. Had they ever asked Lorcan? Somehow he doubted it.

Darren began to gather up his things, setting the answering machine, loading his papers into his briefcase. He was always the last to leave and first to arrive in the morning. The men respected that. Sure, he could be a hard taskmaster: he expected things done, and he expected them done right. But he was no harder on them than he was on himself.

You had to be hard to be respected.

He needed respect. He had worked to earn it. Sometimes he felt as if that was all he had left in the world.

He locked up his office and was about to climb into his car when a silver Avensis pulled into the yard and parked. Darren looked around. Most of the men had gone home.

He stiffened as the driver's door opened and a meticulously groomed man with suspiciously dark hair stepped out.

'Can I help you there?'

'I hope so. And, in return, maybe I can help you.'

'Oh, yeah?'

'It's about Lorcan.'

'What about him?'

Mink smiled and walked across the yard.

26

Darren poured Mink a Jameson and one for himself. 'Well, let's hear it.'

'To your good health.'

Darren raised his glass but didn't drink.

'You don't remember me, do you?' Mink said.

'Should I?'

'Perhaps you remember my associate, Jimmy McKellen?'

'Haven't seen him in years – last I heard he was inside.'

'He's out now.'

'Yeah?'

'He works for me.'

'Can't imagine Jimmy would be much of a croupier.'

Mink smiled. He should have known Darren had placed him. 'No, he does lack a certain finesse.'

'So, what's this about Lorcan?'

'Your son's a fine young man, Darren, but like all young men he can be a touch impetuous.' Mink unbuttoned his coat and crossed one ankle over a knee.

'How much does he owe?'

'Ah, well, not a whole lot, really. Not any more. Not to me at any rate.'

'He's winning, is he?'

'No. But in lieu of money he offered his services to me and I helped him out.'

Darren said nothing, but Mink could sense him tensing.

'Nothing terrible, really. He and his friend Orie made a few collections for me.'

'What sort of collections?'

'Girls, mostly.'

Darren took a sip of his drink. Mink noticed him glance at a photo on his desk.

'Let's hear the rest of it, I'm sure you didn't come out all this way just to tell me that.'

'Well, no. You see, there was a minor mishap on the last collection.'

'A mishap?'

'One of the girls died en route.'

Darren looked at him steadily. 'Are you expecting me to pay you or some shit?'

'Nothing like that. You misunderstand. The girl is dead, that can't be helped. No, the problem is your son – or, rather, your son's friend.'

'Orie.'

'Right. Jimmy had Orie dispose of the body and, not being a native, he disposed of her rather badly. She's been found.'

'So?'

'So now there's an investigation.'

'Jesus Christ.'

'Naturally I've taken a decision to lie low for a while, but . . .' Mink paused and looked into his glass dramatically.

Darren had no time for theatrics. 'Get on with it, for fuck's sake.'

'Lorcan doesn't agree with that decision. It now seems he and Orie have decided to set up in business together, importing ladies into the country. My impression is that your son owes quite a substantial amount of money elsewhere so naturally he's unhappy with me and he feels he can do a better job on his own. Unfortunately, as you and I both know, Darren, the young can be foolhardy.'

'Why are you telling me any of this?'

'Well, it strikes me that Lorcan is impressionable. Clearly Orie's been whispering in his ear, abusing his friendship, so to speak. If Lorcan does owe money, he probably feels vulnerable, and this Orie fellow is likely to be using that against him. I feel that without Orie egging young Lorcan on, suggesting risky and riskier behaviour, Lorcan would understand how serious it would be for all of us if we were to be connected to this dead girl. Orie doesn't give a damn about your son, Darren, he cares only for money. Lorcan, of course, can't see this. And I can't get through to him.'

Darren took a sip of his drink and set his glass on the desk. 'You talk a lot of bollocks,' he said quietly, 'so let me see if I can whittle it down. What you're telling me is you've got a fucking mess on your hands and you want my help to clean it up.'

'Well, technically your son and his friend created the mess. I'm not sure it can be cleaned up entirely but, yes, certainly if we all work together it can be tidied away.'

'So what do you need me for?'

'Lorcan is very fond of Orie, perhaps too fond of him.'

Darren bristled. 'What are you getting at?'

'Nothing untoward,' Mink replied swiftly, 'but Orie has too

much sway over Lorcan. I admire loyalty, and those two are like Velcro. But Orie is bad news for your son and while Lorcan won't listen to me right now I thought perhaps you might be the man to help convince him that his loyalties should rest . . . elsewhere.'

'What the hell makes you think my son will listen to a word I say?'

'I'm sure you'll find a way to get through to him. You are, after all, the boy's father.'

'And if I reel him in for a while you'll tie up the dead girl and Orie nice and tight, right?'

Mink beamed at him. 'I certainly will.'

'I'll see what I can do.'

'I appreciate it.'

'And I'd appreciate you not giving my son any more errands to run.'

'Indeed.'

Darren cracked his knuckles. 'I'd also appreciate it if you took yourself out of my office.'

Mink put his glass down and stood up. 'It was a pleasure to meet you in the flesh at last.'

He stuck out his hand and, after a moment's hesitation, Darren shook it.

27

The Global Securities office was a tiny one-roomed space, situated on the first floor of a rundown building on James Street. To be exact, Global Securities consisted of one desk, two chairs and a wall of filing cabinets.

It also had Kwenzo Howard. And it was Kwenzo's bone-crushing handshake from which John was currently trying to recover.

Kwenzo was very tall and very smiley. He wore black trousers, highly polished black shoes and a sharply pressed black shirt with an emblem on the breast, two white wings and the words 'Global Security' in white.

'He does not work here,' Kwenzo said, barely glancing at the passport John had slid across the table towards him.

'That doesn't surprise me.'

'He has not worked here in many months.' Kwenzo smiled so broadly that John wondered if it meant something very different in whatever language he spoke when he wasn't dealing with private detectives.

John took Orie's passport back and pocketed it. 'What did he do for you?'

'Initially he worked security.'

'Where?'

'Wherever he was needed.'

'I'm confused. What are we talking about here? Nightclubs? Shops?'

'Yes, all of those.'

'When was the last time he worked for you?'

'I would have to look it up.'

'I'm in no hurry.'

This caused Kwenzo Howard's mouth to stretch even further. 'What is it Orie has done to deserve your attention, Mr Quigley?'

'Call me John. As far as I know he hasn't done anything but tell a bunch of lies to his girlfriend. But he's missing and I'm trying to locate him.'

'Missing? Perhaps Orie has decided to return to his native land.'

'I don't suppose you know where that would be, do you?'

'I believe he is Polish.'

'That's possible. So, can you dig up his work record for me?'

Kwenzo sat forward in his chair and rested his elbows on the desk. The smile shortened a touch, but didn't vanish. 'Do you know why Orie no longer works for me?'

'Nope.'

'When I came to your country I had nothing more to my name than the clothes I stood up in. I was a victim of war, poverty and economic malfeasance.'

'Sorry to hear it.'

Kwenzo inclined his head. 'I left my home and my family to

strike out. I came to Europe and finally to Ireland in 2001.' He lifted his hands to either side of him. 'This office is mine. This business is mine. I built it with nothing more than these bare hands.'

John looked around him at the shabby office. 'Right.'

'I am a builder, John. I want only to build and here in Ireland I was given a chance at life. So I said to myself, "Kwenzo, this is your time, this is your chance to build, this is the land of opportunity." God, in His mercy, had shown me a way forward. God told me to take my destiny in my hands. So I took that chance and I began to build my new life. I help others build their new lives. I give back to the community and I help people build. I show them that if they trust in God they, too, can make a better life.'

John shifted uncomfortably in his chair. He wasn't sure what was making him squirm – the constant smiling or the God talk. It had been a long time since he had been in the presence of a true believer and clearly Kwenzo Howard was truly believing something.

'Are we talking about actual building here or is this metaphorical building?'

'It is spiritual building. I am a member of the Life Way Congregational Church. When people come to me, they are in crisis. They are fearful. They have come from places you cannot even imagine. Lived through violence and war you would not comprehend. They need security. They crave it, almost more than sustenance. I help people find security. I give them peace of mind. I help them on their path.'

'No offence, but what in the name of all that's holy are you talking about?'

'Security.' Kwenzo beamed at John. 'People need it and I provide it. I see to it that anyone who contacts me sleeps well at night. I also provide gainful employment. I try to help fellow travellers. What I do is help them find the road to freedom. Economic freedom. Freedom from uncertainty.'

'So you hire immigrants as security? Or you provide security for immigrants?'

'Both. The Lord helps those who will help themselves. I provide peace of mind for people like myself, people who have made the leap, who have moved here and who are trying to create a new life for their families. People know when they see my people that no trouble will affect them, no violence will be visited upon them. Like the Archangel Gabriel,' here he tapped the wings on his shirt, 'I am the Lord's servant. The shepherd to watch over the flock.'

'I see,' John said. 'Do you have many people working for you?'

'A few – enough to provide peace and tranquillity for those who need it most.'

'You ever have to crack a few heads to instil peace and harmony?'

Kwenzo's smile broadened again. 'Sometimes the Lord's work can be a challenge.'

John laughed. 'So, tell me this, did you help Orie on to this path of spiritual enlightenment?'

'Ah!' Kwenzo wagged a long, slender finger. 'To help a man, that man must first seek redemption. Then, and only then, he can open his heart and mind to the way of Our Lord Jesus Christ. He must open his heart so that he will hear when the Lord speaks to him.'

'Orie wasn't interested in the Lord's way, I take it.'

'Orie is in shadow.'

'I see.' John lowered his head for a moment, gathering his thoughts before he had another pop at making sense of Kwenzo. Was this guy for real, or was he just pulling his leg and John was too much of a dullard to see it? He seemed sincere, but he also seemed a bit mad, so maybe it would be better to stick to absolutes. 'When exactly did Orie start to work for you?'

Kwenzo's eyes never left John's face. 'He came to me in the spring. He asked my help. I gave it freely.'

'What did he need assistance with?'

'He was in turmoil. He had given in to the ways of Mammon. Seduced by all that glitters. Sucked into a world he had no grasp of. He needed to be shown the way. To accept the light.'

'So, what did you do?'

'I offered him spiritual guidance.'

'OK.'

'And a job.'

'Good. What happened?'

'He abused my faith in him. He stole, he lied, he abused those who needed his services most. He is a fallen man, John. I tried to help, but he refused to stay on the path. I had no option but to release him.'

'Release him?'

Kwenzo sighed. 'Even the most vigilant shepherd cannot watch over the entire flock all the time. We do not stop our search for the lost lamb, and we rejoice when the lost return to the flock. I pray daily that Orie will return, but I cannot seek him out.'

'Well, I need to seek him out. And if you've any idea where I should start that would be terrific.'

'You should speak with this man.' Kwenzo took a pad from his desk and wrote out a name and an address.

'Who is he?' John said, taking the note and reading what Kwenzo had written.

'He is one who has taken the path of the light.'

'Right.' John tilted his head slightly. Soli? Sally? Was this the name Sarah had been given by the hairdresser? 'This dude wouldn't be Orie's cousin, would he?'

Kwenzo nodded. He reached across and tapped the page with his fingertip. 'A good man.'

'Not like Orie, then.'

'We all suffer the shame of sin.'

'But some get more of a lick at the bar than others, right?' John said, smiling.

Kwenzo beamed at him, and for one split second John could have sworn his whole face lit up with an inner light. Great, he thought. I'm losing it.

Kwenzo leaned back in his chair. 'If anyone can help you locate Orie, I believe Soli can. It is not for man to understand the way of Our Lord, only to seek Him out and reflect on His wisdom. I hope one day Orie realises this.'

'One last thing.' John got to his feet. 'The problem Orie needed assistance with. You got a name for it?'

'Orie liked to gamble.'

'That it?'

'It is never "it",' Kwenzo said, his tone now grave. 'To gamble you must be prepared to lose, to lose you must be prepared to pay. Sometimes the cost is very high. Orie would use anything or anyone to cover it.'

John handed Kwenzo his business card. 'I know you've got security and I'm pretty sure you've got the holy back-up too, but if you ever need any detecting done, you've got my number.'

Kwenzo lifted the card. 'An open door is a good door.'

They shook hands, and as John left the tiny office he was touched to hear Kwenzo Howard ask his God to keep John safe from harm.

28

John tried Stacy to see if Orie had shown but his call went straight to her voicemail. He tried Sarah next. 'It's me. Any word from our client?'

'No.'

'I'm guessing Romeo hasn't turned up.'

'Where are you?'

'Still on James Street.'

'How did you fare with the security firm?'

'Surreal. But same stick as Ace Cabs. Orie hasn't worked there for months either.'

'What the hell is he doing, then?'

'Whatever he's up to, he sure as shit doesn't want anyone knowing his business.'

'Can't be good so.'

'Nope. I got a line on Sally.'

'The cousin?'

'I'm going to check him out this evening, see if he's clapped eyes on Orie over the past day or so. Oh, and his name's Soli, not Sally.'

'That makes more sense. Give me a shout later and let me know what's happening. I've got to go. I'm pulling into Helen's drive.'

'Will do.'

John drove home to Ranelagh, back to the cottage he had owned since his parents had died. It was a quiet street, just off the main drag, where neighbours knew each other by name. Ranelagh had become gentrified during the property boom, and the tiny cottage was worth stupid money now. Not that it mattered: everywhere in Dublin was worth stupid money. What was the point in selling if you couldn't afford to buy?

He let himself in and opened the back door to his garden. He was greeted by Sumo, his half German shepherd, half wolfhound, who was so overjoyed to see him, he wagged his tail at least twice. John rubbed Sumo's massive head. He had rescued him from behind McDonald's on the Naas Road when the dog was nothing but a tiny bristling, growling pup with paws the size of plates. He had taken him home that night, washed and fed him and let him sleep on the end of his bed. The dog had grown into the tank he was now and was devoted to John. He would willingly have given his life to protect him but was hardly what anyone would have called a friendly pooch.

John felt bad for Sumo, spending so much time alone lately. He couldn't imagine Sumo was too impressed either, any more that he had been impressed with the new kennel John had constructed in the back garden. John poured dry food into his bowl and made up half a litre of Bovril to pour over it. Maybe Carrie, his sister, was right. Maybe he ought to look into getting a walker to take him out during the day. Trouble was, he'd have to get one Sumo wouldn't eat alive on sight . . .

He put the bowl down. 'I'm sorry, old fella. I've got to nip back out to see a guy. I'll take you out as soon as I get back, I promise.'

John patted the big dog's back and watched him attack his food with gusto. He wondered why Sumo hadn't defended Sarah on the night she was attacked and, for the umpteenth time, what sort of person would dare attack a person walking a hulking beast like Sumo. It was a mystery.

He patted the dog again, and hoped Sumo wouldn't take out on the furniture his frustration at being left alone again.

He drove into town, calling first to the address Kwenzo had given him, a tiny two-up-two-down cottage off Manor Street, but no one was at home. John checked his watch. It was possible Soli had left for work already.

He parked the Manta in the Jervis Street Centre and walked round to O'Connell Street. Soli worked security in the big arcade near the Ambassador, but according to the bored girl with the pierced eyebrow seated behind three-inch security glass at the coin desk, he didn't come on shift until eight o'clock. John had nearly an hour to kill.

Normally he didn't mind waiting – people-watching suited his temperament – but a damp, miserable fog had settled over the city, chilling the night air, and not even a flame-grilled Whopper and fries from Burger King could lift his spirits. It helped, though.

John didn't mind working extra hours, not really. The business needed the money and he knew how things stood with Sarah and her family. But – if he was totally honest – he wondered how much longer he could carry on doing the bulk of the donkey work, but part of being a private investigator was working awkward hours. Theirs was not a nine-to-five gig.

Even thinking that about Sarah made him feel bad. She did her best. It couldn't be easy with her mother ill like that. John's parents had been dead for a good few years, but he remembered how he had felt when it became obvious that he was going to lose them. It had been hard and no mistake.

Sarah was doing right by her mother – that was the sort of woman she was, loyal and responsible. It couldn't be easy, but she never complained. That was one of the things he admired about her most.

He finished his food, balled the paper and tossed it into a nearby bin.

He let his thoughts wander to less troubling things and, lo and behold, his mind went straight to Caoimhe Wallace.

She really was something, and John couldn't remember the last time he had felt so drawn to someone, well, other than Sarah. She was the sort of woman who could have electrified water with a glance. He was still thinking of the way her eyes lit up each time she laughed when a man in a security jacket let himself in through the front door of the arcade. 'Showtime,' John muttered.

He crossed the street and slipped in behind the man, who was now talking to the Chinese floor manager. John peered at a game to his right. It was one of those street-fighter games where massive flame-haired Hentai guys and gals kicked the shit out of each other and screamed, 'Hi-yah!' a lot. John pretended to be engrossed, but he needn't have bothered: neither man took any notice of him.

From where he stood, John could hear the floor manager telling Soli he had run three youths from the premises earlier and that he should keep his eyes peeled for some people called the Roach Kings. The floor manager said he didn't want any trouble, but Soli was to be firm in his refusals.

Trouble, John thought. Nobody ever invites it but still it turns up.

He waited for another few minutes, until the little Chinese manager ran out of puff and left. Then he said, 'Must be tough keeping an eye on everyone in a place like this. You wouldn't happen to be Soli, would you?'

The security man turned round and gave him the once-over.

John returned the favour. Soli wore his hair in a no-nonsense buzz-cut. He was older than John, but not by much, maybe pushing forty. He was short and stocky with a thick neck and flat grey eyes.

'And you are?' Soli asked.

John opened his wallet and passed him a card. He waited for the bouncer to read it.

'You might be able to help me out here, Soli. See, I'm looking for Orie, your cousin, and I was wondering if maybe you'd seen him over the past day or so.'

John would tell Sarah the next day that he wasn't certain what had happened next. One minute he was putting his wallet back into his pocket, the next he found himself sitting on O'Connell Street in the rain.

'What the fuck, man? Let go of me.'

Soli leaned over him, so close John could see every pore on his face. He grabbed the front of John's jacket and bunched it in his hands. 'I don't have money,' he said.

'Whoa, big man, keep your hair on.'

'You tell them. I work. I don't have money. You tell them.'

'I'm telling you, you've got the wrong end of the stick here.' John held up his hands. 'Look, I don't know what the hell you're going on about or who you're expecting, but I'm not here to cause trouble, I swear. Kwenzo sent me.'

Soli released John's jacket. 'Kwenzo?'

'Yeah, I was in with him earlier. He said you were one of his people.' John tapped the winged insignia on Soli's jacket.

'What do you want?'

'Can I get up?'

Soli hauled him to his feet. 'What do you want?' he repeated.

'I'm looking for Orie. He's been reported missing.'

'Hah.'

'Glad you find it funny, but his girlfriend's not laughing. If you know where he is I'd sure appreciate a heads-up.'

'I have no idea where he is.'

'He wouldn't be kipping in with you?'

'Kipping?'

'Sleeping.'

Soli's upper lip curled. 'No. He doesn't kip with me.'

John straightened his jacket. 'So, Orie owes money, huh? I heard he liked to gamble.'

Soli glanced back to the arcade where the manager now stood in the doorway, watching them anxiously. 'I can't help you. I have to work.'

'Before you go, where did Orie play?'

'Anywhere.'

'He have a favourite?'

Soli raised a finger to his manager and watched as he slunk back inside. 'He played with Chinese a lot.'

'Where?'

'Somewhere near bus place.'

'The bus station?'

'Yes. I don't know place. I don't gamble. I work.'

'Cheers, man.'

Soli stalked back inside.

John checked his watch. He had just enough time to pay a visit to the house on Haverty Road. With any luck, Orie had turned up and he could put this case to bed early.

29

Wayne was wearing multicoloured trousers, a multi-stained vest, mauve check slippers and a satin ladies' dressing gown thrown over the whole rig-out. He had opened the door less than six inches and peered out. 'What? There's no one here.'

After taking a long look at Wayne's cloudy yet suspicious eyes, John decided there was no point even trying to pull a fast one. 'My name's John Quigley.' He took a card from his pocket and passed it to him. 'I'm a private investigator with QuicK Investigation. I'm here looking for Orie Kavlar, but you probably know him as Orie Owsiak.'

'Forget it, man.' Wayne started to close the door.

John threw his hand against it. 'Wayne, I understand your reluctance to—'

'Reluctance!' Wayne waved a bony finger in his face. 'You can say that again. I don't want anything to do with this business. That crazy bird from your place nearly broke my leg. She lied about who she was and then she attacked me.'

John didn't know what to say to that, but as it turned out he didn't need to. Next thing he knew the door was wide open and the torrent of Wayne's injured feelings sprang forth.

It seemed to John that Wayne was enjoying having a captive audience on whom to vent his spleen. He showed no signs of flagging. Eventually, when the man paused to draw breath, he said, 'I get what you're telling me, Wayne, and it sounds very out of character.'

'She told me she was the social, man. But I knew she was bogus. She kept asking all these questions, weird questions, like how did Orie fucking feel, shit like that.'

'Oh?'

'If she wanted to know how long Orie's been here she coulda just asked, man, no need for violence. She was acting crazy. I've seen people with that.'

'With what?'

'With those crazed looks – it's in the aura. It was dark. Real dark. And you don't get that overnight.'

'No?'

'No way. That shit grows. It's organic.'

John tried not to laugh and instead managed to nod. 'Yeah, she definitely has some dark moods.'

'Oh, I know. You don't have to convince me. Look at my leg, man, look what she did to it.' Wayne stuck out one scrawny leg and hiked up his trousers.

John had to admit it was a hell of bruise he was sporting. 'Nasty.'

'She tricked me, man – she lied to me. Uncalled for. Violence is never the answer, you know. I've always been a pacifist. I believe in communication, you know?'

'Women.'

'Right! All she had to say was she was a detective, like you did, man, be straight, you know?'

'Sure, sure.'

'There's no need for this violence and stuff. I wasn't, um, doing anything. I just thought she was up to something.'

'Oh, I understand, especially in this day and age.'

'And she totally freaked out, you know, she freaked out.'

'I can see that.'

'Fuck that shit. I don't need it, you know? I don't need that kind of aggravation. It's bad for my heart. I'm on disability. Did she tell you that?'

'Nobody needs that kind of shit,' John said, laying the sympathy on with a trowel.

'Exactly, man, and when that Orie shows up he's fucking outa here. I mean it. This day's so bleak. I got attacked and then this other guy comes by and I'm thinking, Hey, now, whoa, this is messed up. This is some bad shit right here.'

John cocked his head. 'What guy?'

'I don't know.' Wayne's head bobbed up and down. 'Banging on the door and shouting.'

'Did you talk to him?'

'Nah, fuck that. I saw him from upstairs and there was no way I was opening the door to some shouting guy after the day I'd had. I don't know him, I don't want to know him, that's it.'

'What made you think he was looking for Orie? Don't you have other tenants?'

'I know he was looking for Orie 'cause he called Orie by name. He nearly broke my door down. But that's not my business. I told that crazy woman and now I'm telling you. I don't know a thing about Orie other than I just rented a room to him. I don't know his business, I don't know what the fuck Orie does. I don't know how he feels.'

'Why would you?'

'Exactly.' Wayne bent down and scooped up a ginger kitten

that was trying to escape through the front door. 'Right, that's it, that's exactly right. I mean, he just pays for his room, his board, man. It's not like we hang around and socialise or anything – we're not, um, friends.'

'I hear you.'

'Am I supposed to be keeping track of tenants now? I mean, what's that about?'

By now Wayne's sense of persecution was at its zenith. He glanced at the joint in his hand, but it had gone out. He tucked the kitten under his arm, relit it and took a drag so deep John's eyes watered. 'She attacked me, man, in my own home. Like, that's, um, assault.'

'Not sure it would stick if you put your hands on her first.'

'I didn't hurt her, man.'

'Wayne.' John cut him off before he launched into another litany. 'This man who called earlier, you didn't happen to get a good look at him, did you?'

'Huh?'

John tried not to sigh. 'The man who was banging on the door.'

Wayne's eyes reflected nothing for a moment. Then he snapped the fingers of his left hand. 'Oh, yeah, he was big. I wasn't opening no door, no way. Albin, that's one of the other guys who lives here, he was freaking out, man. After he was gone, he legged it.'

'Really? Why? What did he say?'

'Nothing, just started gibbering like a madman.' Wayne took another drag and rolled his eyes. 'These guys! They're here to work and shit, but you ask me, half of them are . . .' he put a nicotine-stained finger to his temple and twirled it.

'How many have you living here?'

Wayne looked at John shiftily. 'Well, um, I don't see how that concerns Orie.'

'No, you're right, fair enough. Can you tell me anything else you remember about the man?'

Wayne squinted. The kitten he was holding seemed to give up hope of escape and now dangled from his bony arm, gazing at John with huge blue eyes.

'Look, is Orie in trouble? I mean, I've got a right to know if I'm in danger here.'

'Why would you be in danger?'

Wayne leaned against the door. 'I dunno, but I'm getting a bad vibe. First your crazy lady partner attacks me, then some heavy comes to the door, and now you. And I haven't seen Orie in days, so yeah, I reckon some shit's up.' He took a last drag and tossed the butt into the weed-filled front garden. 'Come on, man, is there some shit going on I need to be aware of?'

'I don't know,' John said. 'But my spider senses are tingling.'

'Huh?'

'Look, I'll be straight with you, Wayne—'

'That's all I ask. That and no violence.'

'Orie's been missing since Saturday. Now, I don't know what he's got himself into that might require him to lie low, but I'm guessing he's involved in something he shouldn't be. I don't like the sound of this guy coming here. And I'm pretty sure you don't need more hassle—'

'Right, I don't.'

'So the sooner I locate Orie and get to the bottom of his disappearance the better. Now, is there anywhere you can think of, anywhere at all, that Orie might go to keep a low profile?'

'I dunno. It's not like we discuss shit, you know?'

'OK, can you give me a description of the man who called here earlier?'

Wayne thought about it. 'Yeah, all right. He was square.'

'Square?'

'Square, blocky. Square body, square head.'

'Age?'

''Bout the same as me, I suppose. I don't know.'

'OK. Good.' John took out his notebook and flipped it open. 'Did you notice the car he was in?'

'It wasn't a car. It was big, black – could have been some kind of van.'

'Like a Hiace?'

'Nah, squarer than that.'

'You didn't happen to take note of the numberplate, did you?'

'I didn't get that good a look, but it wasn't new. And the guy, he had a Nordy accent.'

'Brilliant. Anything else.'

Wayne shook his head. 'Nah, that's it. Like I say, it was dark and I wasn't exactly hanging out the window, you know what I mean?'

'I got you. So, he was Northern, square and driving a large van, but not a Hiace.'

'Yeah, does he sound like somebody to you?'

'No, not yet. Say, Wayne, I don't suppose there's any way I could take a quick look at Orie's room, is there?'

Wayne frowned. 'Man, I don't know. He'd freak out. That's his private zone.'

'I know, and I can appreciate how this would go against your ethics, but, Wayne, I've got a bad feeling something's happened to Orie.' John touched his stomach. 'And the sooner I find him the sooner I can set my mind at ease.'

Wayne dropped the kitten onto the floor behind him and tightened his robe around his bony shoulders. 'Well, see, the thing is, his room's locked, man, and I don't have a key or nothing.'

John beamed. 'What kind of lock is it?'

30

Sarah followed Helen through the dining room into the drawing room. They'd just finished a dinner of asparagus and mushroom risotto. Helen was eager to talk about Jackie's show.

'So, if we change the shades and use the spotlights we can highlight the bigger pictures, and in the centre divide I was thinking we could set up the canapés and drinks. That way people can help themselves and get settled but still see all of the paintings. It'll take the formality out of it.'

'Mmm, I see what you mean,' Sarah said. It was nearly nine o'clock and she was exhausted. She wished Helen would hurry up and get it over with. She wanted to sit with her mother for a while, maybe help get her ready for bed. The later it got, the foggier and more irritable her mother became.

'Good. Now, about the frames . . .' Helen strode on, her dark bob gleaming under the spotlight, high heels clicking on the parquet flooring. She was waving her hands towards the walls and Sarah knew she could already visualise the soirée and people's reactions to her hospitality.

'We can put the smaller paintings in here.'

Sarah followed her, one ear cocked to where their mother sat by the fire. Deirdre Kenny had seemed happy enough earlier in the evening, alert and calm, almost normal, in fact. She had accepted Helen's offer of a cup of tea and had even exchanged pleasantries with Paul, Helen's husband, over dessert. Then she had asked Helen what time her sister would be picking her up for her hair appointment. And, after that, she had asked Sarah how work was going and had she any news on the baby. When Sarah asked which baby she was referring to, her mother had blinked and turned away, as though even conversation was a trial.

It was weird the way she could drift away but seconds later swim back to the surface, as though the fog lifted and revealed the world to her as she had always known it. But now she was restless and Sarah recognised the tics that indicated distress. Her hands were constantly moving on her lap and she frowned or smiled at nothing.

How did she see things, Sarah wondered, how did she rearrange the thoughts and memories? Why could she remember things from forty years ago but not Belinda's name, or where the bathroom was? Was it as upsetting for her as it was for them? Was it painful? Did she know she was slipping away? Could she feel it?

'Sarah?'

'Mm?'

'I asked you a question. What do you think about the frames? Will they work with the lighting?'

Sarah forced herself to pay attention. 'I think for the bigger pieces the spots will work fine, but we should arrange the smaller ones in clusters of four, especially the dawn and dusk paintings. And I wouldn't use frames for those. I think they'll stand out better on clear Perspex.'

'Really?'

'Well, yes, because that's how Jackie always thought of them, as progressions, unfettered. If we arrange them correctly it will give the viewer a sense of continuation.'

'I see.' Helen's face betrayed her disapproval of that idea. She tapped an index finger against her lip. 'But won't clusters take from the impact of the pictures?'

'I don't think so. The bigger ones need to be seen alone, but I really think the smaller landscapes work better as a group – it would offer an interesting dynamic.'

'Well, we'll do a trial run and see. Maybe you're right.'

Sarah said nothing. She knew Helen didn't agree, but she could see that her eldest sister was trying not to come across as bossy and overbearing.

'How are you?' Helen said suddenly.

'Me?'

'Yes.'

'I'm fine.'

'You look like you've lost weight.'

'Oh. Well, maybe a pound or two.' Sarah touched her cheek. 'It was a bit sore to eat solids for a while but I'm more or less back to normal now.'

'Uh-huh, and are you sleeping? The shadows under your eyes are very pronounced.'

'I'm sleeping.'

'Because, if you're not, Paul can write you a prescription—'

'I'm sleeping fine, Helen.'

Helen's mouth drew into a thin line. She sat down on the arm of a calfskin-covered chair, which had probably cost more than Sarah's Fiesta. 'It's such a shame you can't remember anything more about that night. I was talking to Alan Shepherd the other day about it and he says it's not too late to file a report.'

'Who's Alan Shepherd?'

'Oh, he's a friend of Paul, a detective with Special Branch.'

'Jesus Christ, Helen! Special Branch? Wouldn't they have, I don't know, far more important things to worry about than a mugging?'

'Of course, but he's a friend and—'

'I'd prefer you not to discuss my business with anyone.'

'Your business?' And now Helen's dark eyes flashed. 'Oh, well, excuse me, but I thought you'd have been keen to find the person who beat your face to a pulp.'

Sarah swallowed. She had suddenly remembered the way her stomach had surged when Vic had struck her in the face. She felt the pain, the breathlessness, the way her shoulder had wrenched as she fought to free herself. She could feel the heat of Victor's blood on her hands, hear the rasp of his breath as he fought to fill his lungs with air.

'Helen.' Her voice sounded strained, far away. 'I was unlucky, I was stupid, careless, and I got mugged. It happens every day of the week in this city.'

'Does it? I don't know, Sarah, but you're awfully cagey about that night.'

'Cagey?'

'Yes. Cagey. And you know what? I think there's something you're not telling us. Jackie thinks the same.'

'What are you talking about?'

'You were acting weird when you dropped Mum off with me, like you knew something was going to happen.' Helen raised an eyebrow. 'How can you not remember anything about it? How come you were even down on the promenade that night?'

'The dog. I was minding Sumo for John, remember? I went

for a walk, Helen. I went for a walk like a bloody fool and I got mugged.'

'I still can't believe anyone would risk attacking you with that brute of a dog by your side.'

'Whoever it was could have been off his face on something.'

'I don't believe you.'

'I don't give a shit what you believe,' Sarah said, with more force than she'd intended. She took a deep breath and lowered her voice. 'I thought you wanted my help. I thought you asked me here to help with Jackie's show, not to give me the third degree.'

'See? I ask if you remember anything about that night and you automatically go on the defensive. You know who you sound like right now?'

'Who?'

'Dad.'

'What?'

'Dad. You sound just like him. He couldn't cope with anyone asking him anything either, always ready to deflect questions with an attack. God forbid that anyone should try to help him or talk sense to him. You're just like him.'

'Please stop, Helen,' Sarah said.

Their father had died seven years before, killed coming back from the pub, having accepted a lift from an equally drunk mate driving a motorbike. He had been a charming, difficult, domineering man, a street angel and a house devil. It was unsettling to be told she was like him.

Sarah glanced towards their mother, afraid she would over-hear them, but Deirdre appeared mesmerised by the flames, unaware of the rising tension. 'Helen, I don't want to fight with you.'

Helen stood and crossed the room in short fast strides. She reached out to her sister, but the movement was so sudden that

Sarah flinched. Helen was taken aback. She lowered her hands and looked at Sarah with real concern. 'Jesus, Sarah. I wouldn't hurt you.'

'I'm sorry.'

'I know I get on your last ever nerve, and I'm sorry if it seems like I'm having a go at you. But I'm worried about you. It's not just this latest attack, or your job. It's not even John Quigley. It's everything. I've been worried about you since you came back from England. Why won't you talk to me? Why won't you let me help you?'

'Help me? Help me do what exactly? What on earth makes you think I need your help, Helen?'

'You don't see it, do you?'

'What?'

'Everything is so transient with you. Your home, your job . . . You've no friends, no boyfriend. Sarah, you've barely settled and you've been back now – what? Three years? What's making you so unhappy?'

'I don't want to talk about this any more.'

'You know I love you, you've got to understand that I care about you. We all do, Jackie, Paul – God, even Barry's worried sick about you.'

'I'm fine. I appreciate your concern, I do, but really there's nothing to worry about.'

'I don't want anything to happen to you. We've all been through so much lately.'

'I know that.' She tried to make eye contact, but could not. She felt unsteady, claustrophobic. She shouldn't have come here – should have known better. She needed some air.

Helen took her wrist gently, forcing her to look up. Her owlish eyes, so dark they were almost black, searched Sarah's face. 'There's an opening at work. The HR head said he'd be happy to interview you if you—'

Sarah turned her head away. 'Helen, I have a job.'

'It would be nine to five, sick pay, good benefits.'

'I have a job.'

'Insurance, a pension.'

'Helen!'

Helen released her. For a moment neither sister said anything.

'I just wanted you to know that if you ever need me, I'm here, right?'

Sarah looked at her. 'Helen, if I ever needed anything, I wouldn't hesitate to call you.'

'Promise?'

'I promise you.'

Helen gave her one more lingering gaze before she stepped back. 'OK . . . So, how are we going to get Jackie's pictures here and hung without her noticing?'

Sarah blinked and took a breath. 'Helen, wait.'

'I suppose we—'

'There is something. I think you might have been right about Mum. I can't do it any more. I think . . . I think we should start maybe considering a – a – what did you call it before?'

'A care facility?'

Sarah nodded, no longer trusting her voice.

Helen tilted her head to the side. She didn't look surprised or angry or triumphant, only curious. 'I thought you were dead set against it.'

'I was, but these last few days without her have really opened my eyes to how exhausting it's been. I've been thinking, and what with work and . . . It's so hard now she doesn't . . . Helen, we're losing her anyway.'

'I know that.'

'I can't keep her any more. It's not safe.'

'Paul said this might happen. He was worried you'd taken on too much. We both were.'

Sarah doubted Paul cared much for anyone other than himself, but she had nothing more to say on the subject, except hollow, useless words.

She glanced out to the drawing room. Deirdre was still sitting there, like a mother-shaped waxwork. Was she aware of what had just happened? Could she feel it? Would she comprehend that her youngest daughter had sold out on her? Was she, Sarah, going to turn her back on her after all her promises?

But everything had changed on the night she had plunged a knife into Vic. What did promises mean now? Would it be better if she kept her mother with her until the police came and arrested Sarah for Vic's death? Would it be better for Deirdre to see her daughter led from the house in handcuffs? To be left with Belinda or, worse, alone, confused and frightened down in the Garda station until one of her decent daughters came to her rescue? Who the hell would that suit?

'I just think it would be for the best.'

'Oh, honey, we don't have to talk about this now,' Helen said, her voice soft and so full of compassion that Sarah felt like crying. 'Look, I'll speak to Jackie and call you tomorrow. We'll discuss it then, all of us. I'll take a half-day – maybe we can have lunch here. It's been so long since we've done anything like that.'

'OK, sure.'

Helen beamed at her. 'Sarah, I know this is hard, but you're making the right decision. I don't know how you managed it for so long. You did your best, and nobody can take that from you.'

'Right. My best.'

Helen wrapped an arm round her sister's shoulders. 'And the facility is really top notch. I'd gone out to see it before we spoke about it last time. The grounds and the rooms are beautiful and the—'

'Helen, please, I don't want to discuss it any more today.'

'I understand.'

'Thanks.'

'OK, so if we group the paintings together, you think they'll have more impact?'

They carried on talking about Jackie's exhibition as Deirdre Kenny continued to watch the flames dance, unaware that her fate had been sealed.

31

Lorcan sensed something was wrong the moment he put his key in the door of his apartment. His suspicion was confirmed when he saw the light from his sitting room spilling out into the hall. But it was late, and he'd already had a couple of drinks. By the time 'What the—' had left his brain, he found himself wrenched off his feet. The next thing he knew he was sliding along his hall floor.

He tried to regain his feet even as he reached behind him for his taser. A huge hand clapped him on the back of the neck and he was tossed into the sitting room. He hit the floor so hard that he almost blacked out. Then he heard,'You stupid fucking gobshite.'

Lorcan managed to sit up. He shook his head to clear it and opened his eyes. 'Dad?'

'After all I've fucking done for you, and you go and do this.' Darren Wallace stepped over him and sat down on the edge of the sofa. Even in his shock Lorcan could tell the old man had a couple on him. Darren's face was flushed and his shirt was open to below his chest, tufts of grey hair sprouting free. A tumbler and a near empty bottle of Jack Daniel's sat on the coffee table. It had been nearly full when Lorcan had left the house earlier that day.

He tried to ease himself into a sitting position. His forehead hurt and something trickled down his cheek. He raised his fingers to it. Blood.

'You had to go and act the fucking big lad. You had to get involved in something stupid. Had to dig yourself into the shit with the rest of the scumbags.'

'Dad, I don't know—'

'Shut up. Just shut up.' Darren balled his right fist. 'I don't want to hear any more of your lies. I know about the girl, you gobshite. I know about the special deliveries you've been making for that piece of shit Dunlop.'

Lorcan had to think who Dunlop was. Then it hit him. He stared at his father in amazement. 'How?'

'Never mind how. What you want to mind is who. Who else knows about her?'

'Nobody.'

'Don't give me that shit. Jimmy McKellen knows. Where's the kid you run with?'

'What?'

'That greasy foreign kid you're always hanging around with. Where is he?'

'Orie?'

'Don't stall. Where is he?'

'I don't know.'

'When did you see him last?'

'Whenever.'

Darren was off the sofa and across the distance in a flash. He grabbed the front of his son's shirt and yanked him closer. 'When did you see him last?'

'Saturday night.'

'Where?'

'Here.'

'I want you to call him, get him to meet you.'

'Why?'

'Because this shit . . . needs to be tidied away.' Darren's mouth twisted the words out.

'Look, Orie won't say nothing to no one about—'

Darren banged Lorcan's head against the wall.

'Ow! Stop!'

'You listen to me, and listen to me good. You're going to contact that kid and you're going to get him to meet you. Tell him whatever the fuck you need to tell him to get him to meet—'

'Dad—'

'And you need to do it sooner rather than later.'

'No.'

'Do you think I'm gonna sit back and watch you slide into that life? Do you think I worked that fucking hard to sit back and watch you throw it all away?'

'Fuck you. Orie's my friend.'

'You don't get it, do you? It doesn't matter what he is, his number's up. This is your one chance. This is your get-out-of-jail-free card. The cops have her, do you understand? They're investigating her death. Do you think Mink or McKellen or anyone else will let their business go under because some fucking kids want to play at being gangsters? The longer that kid is out there running his mouth off the worse it's going to be for you. Mink coming to me is a fucking courtesy. My being here is costing me. You're lucky you're still alive.' Darren released him and went to the sofa. He sat down and stretched his arms out along the back. 'Where's all your stuff? Where's the plasma screen I got you for Christmas? Where's your stereo?'

Lorcan said nothing.

Darren looked at his son. 'You hocked it?'

'Yeah.'

'Why?'

'I needed the money.'

'You needed the money?' Darren sat forward. 'How the fuck did you need the money? You get two grand a month into your pocket. You've got no rent and no mortgage.'

'Yeah, I know.'

'So how come you needed the money?'

Lorcan shrugged.

'You're a fuck-up Lorcan, a Grade-A fuck-up. Your mother would be mortified if she saw the state of you. Why didn't you go to the Gardaí yesterday?'

'Huh?'

'About the clamping van. You were supposed to call Shankley and set up an appointment. I told them you'd be in to see them. You need to get that sorted.'

'Yeah, I will.'

'Go and see them – at least clear that shit up.'

Lorcan flushed. 'Are you finished?'

'Nah. This is what you're going to do. After we clean this mess up you're going to check yourself into a Gamblers Anonymous programme, you're going to spend the fucking time there and you're going to get your fucking head sorted. Then you're going to come out and you're going to work for me, down at the yard, nine to fucking five, same as me, same as everyone else there. How much money do you owe?'

'Eighty.'

'Grand?'

Lorcan nodded.

'How the fuck did you run a tab up like that?'

Lorcan shrugged again.

'Who's this tab with?'

'Slim Keane.'

'I should have known.' Darren blew out his cheeks. 'You've been spoiled, Lorcan. This is my fault. I've fucked up here but I'm going to see it's made right.' He got to his feet. 'Time for you to pull yourself together. Get on the blower, organise a meet with that kid, get him to come here or to the yard. Whichever. Don't say nothing to no one about it, and don't breathe a word about it to Mink or Slim. When you've got him on the hook, call me and I'll take it from there.'

'What are you going to do? Turn him over to Mink?'

'Don't worry about that. Just make it happen.' Darren grabbed his car keys and walked out of the apartment.

Lorcan picked himself up slowly and made his way to the bathroom. He gazed at himself in the bathroom mirror. His face was cut. Mink had gone to his father behind his back, like he was a fucking kid. He clenched his fists, thinking of how that conversation must have gone. He imagined every word his father must have used on learning his son had been involved in such a total mess.

Mink had fucked him over. Mink wanted Orie dead, and his old man was going to let it happen. Instead of standing tall, he was going to let some jumped-up nonce like Mink tell him what to do. Back in the old days his father would have kicked Mink out of the yard on his face. Mink wouldn't have dared touch him – or Orie, if his old man had said Orie wasn't to be touched.

He washed the blood from his head carefully. The wound wasn't deep but it was jagged; there would be a scar. He dried it and covered it with a plaster.

He went to his bedroom and lay down without bothering to undress or turn on a light.

He listened to the sounds of the city below him, and as he did, he formed a plan all of his own.

32

Darren stumbled out of his son's apartment block and rested briefly against the wall.

He couldn't believe he'd struck Lorcan. He hadn't hit the boy for years, and after the last time he'd sworn never to do it again. But fear and desperation had fuelled his arm. Ever since Mink had driven into his yard it was all he could do not to shake with the relief and fear that coursed through his body.

He couldn't believe how badly Lorcan had messed up. How had he not seen it? How had he not known his son had dug himself such a vast hole?

He closed his eyes. What if Mink hadn't come to him? He'd been out of the game a long time. Mink might have decided to deal with the mess by taking care of Orie *and* Lorcan. Would he have been any the wiser if that had happened? No, he might have blamed any number of people – Slim, maybe, or any other reprobate his son mingled with. He might have pointed the finger all over town, but it wouldn't have brought the boy back.

No, he'd been lucky Mink had seen fit to go about this as he had. It gave him some time.

Eighty fucking grand. What the hell had Lorcan been playing at?

He pushed himself away from the wall. He knew Lorcan didn't fully grasp the danger he was in. He had seen it in his son's eyes. He was of that age, thought he was invincible.

Jesus.

He looked at his watch. It was almost two a.m. He wondered if Slim would see a visitor so late. Only one way to find out. He hailed a cab.

It had been a long time since he had been in Fade Street. Things had changed, and nothing had changed. It was still that funny mix of storerooms and private homes, but now there were hairdressers, a tanning salon and a top-end French restaurant.

He rang the bell and waited. A moment later, a huge man opened the door. 'Who are you?'

Darren stuck his hands into his coat pockets. 'I need to speak to Slim.'

'Nobody by that name here.'

'Tell him Darren Wallace wants to see him.'

'I already told you—'

'Just fucking tell him.'

The big man closed the door in his face.

Darren waited, watching the plumes of his breath on the cold night air. After a minute, the door opened again. 'Go on up.'

He squeezed past the behemoth and made his way up the narrow steps. At the top a second behemoth held open a reinforced metal door. Darren stepped into Slim's office.

Slim wore an oversized fleece jumpsuit. He didn't get out of his chair to greet him, but it really didn't look as if he got up much at all any more. American football played on the widescreen TV, with the sound turned down low.

The upstairs behemoth stood directly behind him. Darren reckoned Slim had an idea he might be there in anger.

'I never thought I'd see the day when you'd be gracing us with your presence. How you doing, Darren? It's been a long time.'

'How's your brother?'

'Institutionalised.'

'I went to see him a few months ago.'

'I heard you brought him French bread and cigarettes. He appreciated it.'

'Benny always liked his bread. He once said he could live off bread and cheese if he had to.'

Slim folded his hand over his massive stomach. 'You here to chat about old times, Darren? I can break out the whiskey if you are.'

'No more for me today. I've already had a skinful.'

'Then what can I do for you?'

'I'm here to talk about Lorcan.'

'I see.'

Darren caught the look Slim shot his bodyguard and felt the big man behind him tense.

'No drama, I hear he owes you eighty grand.'

'Near enough.'

'What the fuck, Slim? Why didn't you put in a call to me?'

'Darren,' Slim said, in his quiet yet strangely menacing way, 'far be it from me to tell you how to raise your boy, but raise him you have. And when a grown man enters into a contract with another grown man, calls to his daddy aren't exactly what he might appreciate.'

'But eighty grand?'

Slim spread his hands. 'The boy runs with an expensive

crowd. He has expensive habits. I'm sure you don't need me to tell you that.'

'Cut him loose. I'll take on his debt.'

Slim looked surprised. 'You're a good man. That boy's lucky to have you.'

'That boy's an idiot.'

'Even more reason for him to be glad he has you.'

'There's something else I want to talk about.'

Slim looked over his shoulder. 'Dolan, get Mr Wallace a seat and a drink, please.'

Dolan went out, got a chair and poured him a glass of Jameson. Darren sank into the chair and, despite himself, took a sip gratefully.

'What do you want to talk about?' Slim said, accepting a drink from Dolan too.

'You know everyone, right, and everyone knows you?'

'Everyone who needs to know me.'

'I want you to put the feelers out. I'm trying to find someone.'

'Do you have a name?'

'Orie – Orie Kavlar.'

33

The following morning was wet and cold. Dark, oppressive clouds hung low over the Dublin rooftops and shrieking gulls wheeled over the streets, terrorising the city crows and pigeons. The air was heavy with angry car horns and irritable damp pedestrians.

John was late getting to the office. He was tired and slightly hung-over. He had got home after ten from Wayne's and had then gone out with an energetic Sumo. On the way home, he had received a call from his friend Andy and accepted an invitation to an impromptu Wii golf tournament at his house, Andy's missus being away for the week in Lourdes. John had almost declined, but Andy had mentioned there would be beer. What choice had he?

So, it was a battered and delicate John who tossed his notebook onto Sarah's desk. She glanced up at her partner, taking in his bloodshot eyes and pale, unshaven face. 'Rough night?'

'Andy.'

'Ah. Did you talk to our client today?'

'No, did you?'

'I haven't been able to get hold of her.'

'Well, assuming we're still on her dime you should probably read those.'

Sarah ignored the notebook and lifted her coffee cup to her lips. Her own night hadn't been much better and she had no friend to blame it on. John's scrawling handwriting was almost illegible to her at the best of times. 'I'll have a look in a second. Just give me the bare bones first. Did you get to talk to the cousin?'

'I did.' John dropped into his chair and rubbed his face with his hands. 'He's a straight-up guy and not exactly quick to sing Orie's praises. I doubt Orie's even welcome at his house, let alone kipping down there. Plus I get the feeling he'd prefer not to have to deal with any of his cousin's shit.'

'Did he say that?

'It wasn't so much what he said as the way he turfed me out on my ear when I mentioned Orie's name.'

'He turfed you?'

'Tossed, then – would that suit better?'

'Seriously?'

'One minute I was looking for my card, the next I was looking at concrete. Luckily, I managed to mention Kwenzo Howard before he made mincemeat of me. Soli's not a guy I'd like to have playing on my kidneys.'

'Tell me again what this Kwenzo bloke had to say.'

'I don't know why I even bother taking notes if you're not going read them.' John rocked back in his chair to reach for the Nurofen he kept in his drawer. He popped two out onto his desk.

'Can I have some?' Sarah asked.

John tossed her the packet and waited until she had two in her palm. They took their tablets with a gulp of coffee.

'OK.' Sarah grimaced. 'So, what do you know?'

'Kwenzo's a bit of a looper, but he's a sincere looper. He's part of some church and he hires immigrants to work at his security firm and they cover mainly immigrant places.'

'Man knows his market.'

'He said Orie worked for him back in the spring but he had to release him because he abused the place and his patrons.'

'How?'

'He wouldn't say, but think about it. This guy deals with immigrants and people who are looking for asylum. Who do we think Orie might abuse?'

'I get what you're driving at. Orie see who's coming in and coming out, who's vulnerable, who's desperate. He has two passports of his own and we know he's got a passport belonging to a woman from the Dominican Republic. You think he's making forgeries?'

'I'm worried he might be involved in more than that.' John reached into the pocket of his jacket and removed another set of passports, three in all.

'Can I see those?'

'I thought you were more interested in coffee.'

Sarah smiled. 'OK, John, you da man.'

'That's what I like to hear.' John passed them to her and threw his feet up on to his desk. 'Validation.'

Sarah flipped through them quickly. 'All these women come from outside the EU.'

'Yep.'

'So what's Orie doing with them? They don't look like forgeries either.'

'And where are their owners now? I didn't find any social-security paperwork in either home, and Orie pays Wayne in

222

cash, which I suspect suits Wayne just fine. He has lump sums of cash – there was at least three grand in Wayne's gaff – with the money from the bedsit that's five, a tidy sum for a man who claims he can't afford a buggy.'

'It certainly is.' Sarah opened the first passport and looked at the photo.

'He's making money somewhere. I'm beginning to think Wayne knows more than he's letting on. I'm guessing the reason he gets so cagey about his tenants is because he knows the score with Orie. I wouldn't be surprised if Orie helped get one or two people settled into digs there. Anyway, it's worth checking out. We've got the passports, which means we have photos.'

'Wow, poor old Stacy. She picked herself a real douche bag.' Sarah opened the last passport and frowned. It was for Irina Privalova. Age thirty-eight. Russian. 'I've seen this face.'

'What?'

'This girl, Irina. I've seen her face somewhere.'

'Where?'

Sarah pressed her fingers against her temples. 'Shit.'

'Think, Sarah.'

'I am bloody thinking.' She snapped her fingers. 'The hairdresser's! Where Vanessa worked. This woman was sweeping the floor there. That's where I saw her.'

'You sure?'

'Yep.'

'So, Orie got her a job and he's holding her passport. What does that say to you?'

'It says he's a bloody crook.'

'We need to talk to this woman.' John dropped his feet off the desk.

'Then let's roust her.'

'Hey, I have a question for you.'

'Shoot.'

'Why did you attack that man?'

'What?' Sarah felt the colour drain out of her face. 'What did you say?'

'Wayne. He said you went all Karate Kid on his spindly legs. He showed me the bruise. He said you knocked him down for nothing.'

'It wasn't for nothing. He provoked me.'

'Come on, Sarah, that guy would fall over if you blew on him hard enough.'

'That's easy for you to say. You weren't there so you didn't see how nuts he got.'

'Yeah, well, you're lucky he's not the type to press charges.'

Sarah yanked a pen out of her jar and opened her notebook with such ferocity that John couldn't help but frown. 'He's lucky it was only his leg I blackened.'

'Seriously, he could have had you up for assault.'

'He grabbed my arm first.'

'Sarah, look, I know you've been . . . stressed lately and it's understandable that you're defensive. You were attacked and I know you probably feel pretty vulnerable, but you can't just lash out like that.'

'He grabbed me and I retaliated. I had every right. You weren't there and I was.'

'I'm not trying to get at you—'

'No? It sure feels like it.'

'I only asked what happened. Why are you getting so angry?'

'I'm not angry. I just don't like being given the third degree.'

'The what?'

Sarah threw her hands into the air. 'I'm so fucking fed up of people trying to second-guess me all the time. There's nothing wrong with me. I'm fed up of being asked am I all right. I'm fed up of you looking at me like I might burst into tears any second. I'm fed up of feeling sore and tired. I'm fed up of not sleeping.

I'm fed up of being asked if I eat. I'm just fed up and I want to be left alone. OK?'

'OK, OK. Jesus, relax.'

'I kicked him because he put his damn hands on me. That's it, nothing more. If he hadn't touched me, nothing would have happened.'

John patted his shirt pocket. 'I'm going downstairs for a smoke. Let me know when you're ready to go.'

He got up and crossed the room, but before he left, Sarah called to him, 'John, wait.'

He paused with his hand on the door. 'What?'

'Nothing, I'm just . . . John, I'm sorry. I've a lot on my mind at the moment. I'm sorry I snapped at you. Really. You're right, it was an overreaction.'

'OK.' John walked out, closing the door gently behind him.

Sarah listened to his footstep on the stairs, feeling sick.

John was right. A few months before she would never have assaulted Wayne like that. She was unravelling, and no amount of pretence at normality would change that.

34

Mink opened his eyes and sat up. His mobile phone was ringing, the private number.

He glanced at the electric clock on his bureau. Ten past eight. 'Hello?'

'It's me.'

'McKellen, it's disturbingly early. Do you have any idea how late I retired last night?'

'I have a lead on the kid.'

'Really? The pregnant one gave him up?'

'I haven't even tried her yet. He's staying with someone out in Shankill. I'm on my way there now.'

'I see. Are you sure? How did you come by this information?'

'Because the wee shite called up the Chink house wanting to know if he could still sign in on a big game this weekend. He's at 49 Dangan Park, Shankill.'

'I see.' Mink pursed his lips. 'And Chippy just called you up like that?'

'Not me. Chippy called Slim Keane and Slim called Wallace.'

'And so the wheels turn. I can't believe he called about a game when he's supposed to be on the low.' Mink chuckled. 'The youth of today are idiots.'

'Yeah. So what do you want me to do? Bring him in?'

'Neutralise the problem, of course.'

'We're going to lose a good contact across the pond without him.'

'There are always contacts and always people looking to make a better life. Do you suppose Orie's an early riser?'

'I'll call you when it's taken care of.'

'Goodbye.'

Mink replaced the phone on the bureau and snuggled back under the covers. In less than a minute he was sound asleep.

Jimmy McKellen stopped at a petrol station and bought a copy of the *Star* and a breakfast roll. He glanced through the paper as he ate, relaxed and untroubled. He felt bad for the kid, he supposed. It wasn't Orie's fault that Lorcan was a rung higher on the ladder. It was just the way things played out sometimes. They had fucked up and now someone had to take the fall for it.

He finished his food and set off, timing his run so that he could be in the estate just after nine when most people would have gone to work.

At nine thirty, he drove up Dangan Park and counted the houses on the left. He spotted number 49, noticed a Punto parked in the driveway and carried on up the street and round the corner. He parked the Camper in the street running behind Dangan Park and checked his watch. He pulled on a peaked cap and took a clipboard off the passenger seat. He was wearing a blue jumpsuit, of the kind an electrician or plumber might wear. He climbed out of the cab of the truck, crossed a small green and in seconds he was back in Dangan Park and at the door of number 49.

He rang the bell.

A small busty blonde in a pink tracksuit opened the door. She was towelling her wet hair and her face was pink and free of make-up. 'Yes?'

'Hello there. My name is Sean Casey, I'm with Energy Ireland and we're doing a survey of homeowners with regard to energy usage. I was wondering if I could take a few moments of your time.'

'Oh, well, I don't really have—'

'I understand you're probably very busy.' He smiled. 'You must be so tired of people calling to your home for one reason or another, but before you decide, I just want to tell you that everyone who takes part in the survey will be entered into a draw for a two-week holiday in Orlando, Florida. You see, at Energy Ireland we're not just talking the talk, we're walking the walk.'

'Wait,' she pulled a disbelieving face, 'I could win a two-week holiday just by answering a few questions?'

'Sure, and if you sign up with Energy Ireland – not that you have to – you'll be astounded at how much money you'll save. In this cash-rich, time-poor world, Energy Ireland is committed to making the life of the hardworking individual easier, not harder, and unlike our competitors our company policy is specifically aimed at reducing household bills. Leaving you with more money in your pocket.'

He had snagged her. He could see it in her eyes.

'Well, what do I have to do?'

'Just answer a few simple questions and I'll enter your name in the draw. Simple as that.'

'What if I don't want to join up now with your company?'

'No worries. We can send you a brochure and let you decide for yourself.'

'OK.' She draped the towel over her shoulders. 'So what do you need to know?'

'Well, let's start with your name.'

'Vanessa Shaw.'

Jimmy wrote it on his clipboard. 'That's a lovely name, Vanessa. Like Vanessa Redgrave. So, tell me, Vanessa, what would your average monthly electricity bill be?'

'Not that high, actually. I'm only here in the evening so it's only about thirty euros a month.'

'Oh, that's quite low. Do you live alone?'

'Just during the week. My brother comes up at the weekend.'

He smiled again. Mink was right: the young were stupid. Stupid and gullible. 'And what kind of meter do you have?'

'I don't know. Are there different types?'

'Of course.'

'Oh.' She turned her head. 'It's in the hall here. Hold on while I check.'

Jimmy stepped over the threshold, reached out and slipped his arm round her neck. He flexed his biceps under her throat, cutting off her chance to scream. He kicked the door closed behind him and walked her into a sitting room off the hall.

'Now,' he whispered in her ear, 'just relax. Where's Orie?'

He released his arm just enough for her to inhale deeply. He knew she was going to scream so he cut off her air supply again until she almost passed out. When he felt her starting to go limp he eased the pressure. 'Listen to me, girlie. Calm the fuck down, I'm not here to hurt you. OK? I'm not going to hurt you. But this is a choke hold. If I cut off the air to your brain you will die within minutes, do you understand me?'

She nodded.

'Good girl. Now, where's Orie?'

She pointed to the ceiling.

'He asleep?'

She nodded again.

Jimmy flexed his arm again and, true to his word, he didn't hurt her. Within minutes, though, Vanessa Shaw was dead.

35

John and Sarah drove across town in the Manta. The traffic was bumper to bumper and sleet was falling thick and fast, but as cold and as miserable as it was outside the car, it had nothing on the atmosphere inside.

Sarah knew John was angry but she could think of nothing to say that would make it any better. By the time they reached Drumcondra she had a thumping headache.

They climbed the steps and entered the overheated hair salon. It was just as busy as it had been the day before. Sarah unwound her scarf and nodded to the receptionist. 'Hello. I was here yesterday.'

The girl looked up smiling. Her expression changed immediately. 'Oh, it's you.'

'Yep.'

'Hi,' John said. 'I'm John Quigley, nice to meet you.'

John got the smile.

'We were wondering if we could have a few seconds with Vanessa,' Sarah said.

'She's not in today.'

'No?'

'Do you see her?'

Sarah arched an eyebrow at the rude tone. 'What about the girl who does the sweeping?'

'Irina? Why d'you need her?'

'To see if she'd like to join me for a tall glass of none-of-your-business.'

The receptionist got up, stalked across the salon and disappeared into a room off the side.

'Wow, you really made an impression yesterday,' John said.

'I'm just naturally good with people.'

'I can see that.'

'John, I'm really sorry about earlier. I had no right to be so snappy with you.'

'It's OK.'

'No, it's not.'

'Well, it is now. Heads up, here comes your friend.'

The receptionist took her seat and looked pointedly at John. 'Irina will be with you in a second. She's just mixing some colour. You can take a seat there.'

'Thanks.'

They sat down. The chatter never wavered, but although nobody glanced their way, they knew they were being keenly observed.

'I don't know how anybody does this job,' Sarah said. 'It must be exhausting to make small talk all day long.'

'They seem happy enough.'

'I bet it's a front.'

'And secretly they cry themselves to sleep every night?'

'I would.'

'Some people are good with others.'

'Some people are masochists.'

Irina appeared framed in the doorway at the far side of the studio. She was a small, dark-haired woman, unattractive, with a pigeon chest and sloped shoulders. She looked as though she was carrying the weight of the world on those shoulders and had been for quite some time.

'Not a happy camper,' John muttered.

She walked towards them and the look of resigned dread she wore was hard to witness.

'Hello.'

'Irina,' Sarah said softly, 'I was here yesterday, talking with Vanessa. Do you remember me?'

She nodded.

'I think I have something that belongs to you.' Sarah took the passport out of her pocket and handed it to her.

Irina opened it. Her hand shook so badly Sarah was afraid she would faint or burst out crying. And she really didn't want that: the receptionist would probably kick her down the stairs.

'Thank you.'

'Irina, how long have you been in Dublin?'

'Four months.'

'Did a man called Orie get you the job here?'

She nodded, her dark hair hanging over her face like a limp curtain.

'Why did he have your passport?'

Irina shook her head.

John reached out and took her hand. 'Irina, we're not the police. You're not in any trouble. I think Orie was holding your passport until you paid him, am I right?'

She didn't reply, but John knew he had hit the nail on the head. 'Did Orie bring you to Ireland?'

'Yes.'

'Alone?'

'Others, many others.'

She said it so softly that Sarah and John both leaned closer to hear her.

'What happened to them? Were they all women?'

She nodded again, almost imperceptibly. Sarah glanced at John. This was bad.

'Irina, what happened to the other women?'

'I don't know.'

'Well, how did you—'

'I don't know – I don't know!'

'Irina.' John squeezed her hand. 'Talk to us.'

Her face showed anguish. 'Please. I know nothing. I don't want to go back.'

'It's OK, Irina. John, give her our card.'

John took one out of his wallet, but before he gave it to her he turned it over and wrote Kwenzo Howard's name and number on it. 'Irina, this man here,' he tapped the card, 'he can help you and he won't mess with you. He won't try to rip you off and take your money. My number's on there too, so if you need anything give me a shout. I promise, you say the word and I'll help you get that monkey off your back.'

Irina said nothing but she took the card and slipped it into the pocket of her overall.

Sarah smiled. 'Thanks for your time.'

Irina hurried back to the other room, clutching her passport to her chest.

Sarah and John approached the reception desk. 'Do you have an address for Vanessa?' Sarah said.

The receptionist flicked her fringe off her face. 'Here, I can't be giving out the staff's addresses just like that.'

'Is the owner here?'

She sighed. 'No.'

'Get her on the phone.'

'What?'

'Call her.'

'Why?'

'I want to check if Irina's on the books. I want to make sure the salon owner's not abusing her position and paying an immigrant part-time wages in return for full-time work. I want to make sure she knows I'm dead fucking serious when I say one of her stylists is probably in cahoots with a smuggler and, by proxy, therefore she is. I want her to know that the next time I'm talking to my local friendly cop pal I'll be asking him to stick his nose in here to make sure everything's above board. Your boss'll be delighted to hear from me, I'm sure. I'll make sure she understands it was your unhelpfulness that made me cast my eye in her direction, that I wasn't really interested in her or her business, that all I wanted was the address of a girl so that I could talk to her about a missing person, but that now I'm interested in more than just talking to Vanessa Shaw. You following me, sweetie?'

The receptionist glared at Sarah with pure loathing. 'I'll give you her address, but if this lands me in the shit—'

'It won't.'

She opened a small phone book, copied down Vanessa's number and address and handed the piece of paper to Sarah.

'Thanks for your help,' Sarah said.

'You're a real bitch, you know that?'

'I guess it must be true. You aren't the first to call me that.'

They left.

On the way back to the car John gazed at his partner admiringly. 'That was beautifully done.'

'Thanks.'

'You never used to be such a hard arse.'

'I've learned that the only way to get on sometimes is to be as much of a shit-head as everyone else.'

'You never used to be so cynical either.'

Sarah shrugged. 'A cynic or a sap – if those are my choices I know which one I pick.'

36

Jimmy McKellen lowered Vanessa's body to the floor and stood perfectly still, listening for any sign of movement above.

He stepped back into the hall and unsheathed the serrated knife he was carrying in the inside pocket of his jumpsuit. Taking great care not to rest his hands on the banister, he made his way slowly up the stairs.

There were four doors leading off the landing. Two were open, leading to the bathroom and a small boxroom that contained a tanning bed. The remaining two were closed.

Jimmy opened the first door and peered in. It was a small bedroom, and clearly belonged to the absent brother. The décor was mostly blue, and there was a poster of Carmen Electra on the far wall.

He inched along to the last door and used his sleeve to twist the handle and peep in.

The curtains were drawn, casting the room in shadow. But it didn't take Jimmy long to make out the bed and the shape of someone under the pink and white gingham duvet.

He edged into the room, moving softly and quietly, determined to keep the element of surprise.

At the foot of the bed he reached for the duvet and raised the knife. The moment he touched the duvet something moved behind him. He sensed rather than saw it and spun to his left, too late to prevent Orie Kavlar bouncing something off the side of his skull.

Jimmy staggered and dropped to his knees. He tried to get to his feet but Orie was on him in a flash, trying to batter him. Jimmy raised a hand to protect his head and caught Orie's arm as more blows rained down. He was seeing stars from the initial blow and couldn't tell what Orie was hitting him with. He rolled, and as he fell he lashed out with the knife, slicing a long groove across Orie's bare chest.

Orie gasped in pain. He tried to stamp on Jimmy's knife arm and was moderately successful, catching Jimmy on the inside of his elbow hard enough to jar the knife loose. Jimmy dropped it but managed to scramble after it, getting tangled in a fluffy sheepskin rug. Orie dived for the knife too.

They grappled for it, cutting their hands to ribbons in the process. Jimmy got a grip on the shaft and yanked it towards him, cutting Orie's palm almost to the bone. Orie screamed and fell back. Jimmy tried to grasp the knife, but it was slippery with blood and before he could get a decent hold Orie kicked him in the chest, sending him backwards into the wall. Jimmy grunted and went down. He tried to get his feet under him but something hit him square on the bridge of his nose, almost knocking his head off his shoulders.

Jimmy McKellen crashed sideways onto a vanity unit and lay flat on the floor.

Orie bolted. Jimmy tried to get up, but his feet wouldn't support him. He raised his hand to his face and was not surprised to see his fingers come back bloody. What the fuck?

He rolled onto his back and tried again to sit up. Something lay beside him and, as his vision cleared, he saw what had incapacitated him so efficiently. By his hip lay a bloodied pink plastic dumb-bell. He picked it up and squinted at it. One kilo. He had been conked with one kilo of girlie crap.

After a few moments, he lurched unsteadily to his feet and out onto the landing. He went downstairs, grabbing at the walls, leaving smears of blood everywhere, and closed the front door, which Orie had left open. He went back upstairs and straight into the bathroom. He began to wash the blood from his face and hands, which were a mess, and the jumpsuit was covered in his and Orie's blood. He stripped it off and went into the brother's bedroom. He took a pair of jeans and a shirt from the wardrobe and put them on. The jeans were two inches too short, but they would have to do.

He went back to the bathroom and riffled through the cabinet. He found a box of plasters and some painkillers. He taped up his hand and swallowed three Anadin Extra.

He recovered his hat and the dumb-bell, carried his bloodstained clothes downstairs and put the whole lot into a plastic bag he found in a drawer in the kitchen.

He checked the time and considered cleaning the blood off the walls, but what was the point? There was blood everywhere in the bedroom too. The best thing would be to make sure there were no fingerprints and hope he was never called in for a DNA test any time in the future.

He set about removing any fingerprints he might have left. By the time he was finished, it was twenty-five past ten. He put the bloodstained dishcloth into the bag with his jumpsuit, went back downstairs and peered into the sitting room at Vanessa's crumpled body.

Hardly a productive morning.

He picked up the clipboard from where it had fallen in the

hall and his bag, then left, closing the door softly behind him. There was no one on the street and he made his way quickly back to the van.

He called Mink.

'Yes?'

'It's me.'

'Is the problem taken care of?'

Jimmy checked his swollen face in the rear-view mirror. 'I missed him and I had to put the choke on his flame.'

'You . . . What about him?'

'He got the drop on me. I'll get him next time.'

'For fuck's sake, Jimmy! Now he'll surely go to ground.'

'I'll get him through the pregnant girl. He's running out of places to hide.'

'Do it, and don't fuck up again.'

Jimmy hung up and rested his painful hands on the steering wheel. He touched his fingers to his face. If he was lucky only one of his eyes would close. If not, he'd look like a prize fighter for a few days. He hoped no one became too interested in how he'd acquired his injuries.

He started the engine and pulled away from the kerb.

From behind a nearby skip, Orie Kavlar watched him go. He was cut, barefoot and bleeding. When he was sure Jimmy was really gone, he limped back towards the house and let himself in by climbing over the side gate and smashing the patio doors.

He crept into the house and found Vanessa.

He knew she was dead, even before he checked her pulse.

He stepped over her and made his way into the hall. He double-locked the front door in case Jimmy came back and hurried upstairs. He needed to clean up and get the hell out of there.

Lorcan, he thought. His friend would help him.

37

Lorcan was exhausted and the cut over his eyebrow ached. He had slept fitfully, tossing and turning, unable to switch off. When he had finally drifted off to sleep, as dawn was approaching, he had been beset by strange, realistic dreams, in which voices raged and streets melted under his feet.

His old man's words lay heavy on him. The more he thought about them, the more conflicted he felt. He understood his father's anger; he understood Jimmy and Mink; he understood everything. But he was damned if he could bring himself to hand over the only friend he'd ever had. Plus, there was no guarantee that even if he did Mink would let things be. Besides, Orie and him, they were tight, they were like brothers. When he and Orie strolled out and hit the clubs they were players. They had game. People of his father's generation couldn't understand that.

He put an arm behind his head.

His goddamned father: why had Mink gone to him like that? And his father had said he and Orie were 'playing at being gangsters'. Was that what the old man really thought? That this was a game to him?

All his life Lorcan had felt his father disliked him. Nothing he ever did was good enough for the great Darren Wallace. Even the fact that the old man had gone to prison had been a cudgel to beat him with. How many times had he heard the turn-your-life-around speech? That if Darren, with all his disadvantages, could make something of himself then any man or woman could.

It burned him to think of how his father had treated him the night before, how he had spoken to him as if he was no more than a piece of shit. Every time he thought about his father's hateful face, his fists bunched. Coming into Lorcan's home, ambushing him like that. What kind of way was that to treat a man?

Mink and Jimmy McKellen. Orie hated them as much as Lorcan hated his old man. What a two-faced rat Mink was! When Orie had begun going to his casino, Mink had been all over him like a rash. Offering him free hands, drink, drugs, girls, anything he wanted.

But Lorcan hadn't wanted anything from Mink, only to be treated with a little respect. And in the early days Mink had never talked down to him or treated him like a stupid kid. Lorcan had looked up to him, had liked his style and panache. Orie had fallen for his charm, hook, line and sinker. Right up until he started owing money and losing in the casino. He and Orie should never have agreed to work for Mink. They should have formed their own business from the word go. If they had, they wouldn't have been in the mess they were in now.

And he knew what his father was offering. He knew his father was trading Orie. If Lorcan agreed, his debts would be wiped out and Mink would consider him unbonded. All he had to do was turn on the one friend he'd ever had.

But why should he? Why should he bow down to Mink? If

his old man hadn't the balls to stand up to him, why shouldn't Lorcan be the one to do so?

Even leaving aside their friendship, it was short-sighted to lose Orie. Orie had the contacts in London and could make more. He spoke three languages. He knew someone who could forge passports.

Without Mink or Jimmy, their split would be two ways, as they'd always talked about. And none of this dribble-dribble shit either. They could make a good sweep, pack the van up and roll in. Shit, if they divided the money two ways he could pay Slim and play in some of the bigger games where, everyone knew, there was real money to be made.

His future depended on Orie. Without Orie he was tied to his father for the rest of his days. If he let his old man pay off Slim his life was over. Nine to five at the yard, eating sawdust and talking soccer. Day in, day out, him and his old man, stretching on to eternity, just another ordinary Joe.

He lay rigid, transfixed as the horror of his future opened up before him.

His mobile rang.

Lorcan reached for it. He didn't recognise the number. He hesitated – could be anyone: bank, credit-card company, anyone.

He answered after a number of rings.

'Lorcan?'

'Orie! Where the fuck you been, man?'

'I'm in trouble, man, big trouble.'

'Slow down, I can hardly hear you.' Lorcan sat up. 'What's wrong?'

'I knew, I fucking knew. They set me up, Lorcan. They set me up to take fall.'

Lorcan was astounded. Had his old man moved on Orie without his help? 'What happened?'

'McKellen, he kill my friend,' Orie said, with a sob. 'He try to kill me.'

'Shit.' Lorcan couldn't think straight. 'Where are you now?'

'Shankill.'

'Get a taxi and come here.'

'He kill Vanessa.'

'Yeah, man, yeah. That is fucked up.'

Orie began to cry.

'Look, man, just come here. We'll sort something out.'

Orie said something but Lorcan couldn't make out what it was over the crying.

He couldn't think of a single thing to comfort him and in the end he simply hung up.

38

Detective Sergeant Ray Devlin studied the CCTV footage and made another note. God bless modern technology: he had discovered there was not one but two cameras in operation on the road towards Stocks Lane. One camera in particular, a wall-mounted number outside a warehouse, took excellent film and the owner had been happy enough to give him the tape covering the twelve hours before the girl's body had been discovered by the walkers.

Discounting motorbikes, Devlin was still left with a list of thirty-five vehicles that might have been used to transport the girl there. But it was a start and it was a good one. For the first time since he had been given the case, he felt a flicker of adrenaline.

He glanced down the list. He had called seven of the vehicles' owners that morning and confirmed their names. There had been more than one sheepish 'me and the girlfriend' line, which made him wonder just what the hell it was about that particular stretch of road and the surrounding scrubland that inspired thoughts of romance.

So, only twenty-eight more calls to make. Devlin cracked his knuckles and picked up the phone. The next number he dialled was that of Ian Maguire, owner of Maguire Antiques in Rathgar. He was also the registered owner of the Mitsubishi camper van Devlin was now looking at as it was filmed passing the warehouse. The phone rang for a long time, but was finally answered by a shaky male voice. 'Hello?'

'Hello there, my name is Ray Devlin and I'm a sergeant here in Rathfarnham. I was looking to speak with Ian Maguire.'

'Speaking.'

He wrote 'old' on his pad. 'Mr Maguire, are you the registered owner of a 1998 Mitsubishi Camper?' He read out the numberplate.

'Yes, that's mine.' Maguire didn't sound wary. 'A Camper, that's right.'

'Can you tell me what it was doing at twenty past midnight on Friday night?'

'No.'

Devlin sat up. 'You don't remember being on Stocks Lane, Mr Maguire?'

'Stocks Lane? Where's that, now?'

'Sandyford.'

'Well, I don't know what it would be doing there. Mind you, I didn't have the truck this weekend.'

'No?'

'I let one of my employees have a loan of it. He was supposed to be giving his sister a hand moving furniture. Where did you say you saw it?'

'Stocks Lane.'

'In Sandyford?'

'Yes, sir.'

'I see. I can't remember now where Jimmy said his sister lived, but I don't think he mentioned Sandyford. Or maybe he might have. I don't know. My memory's not as hot as it used to be. He might have mentioned Sandyford.'

'Sure I'll ask him myself. Is he there now?'

'No, he's out on a job at the moment.'

'Can you give me his full name and a contact number?'

'His name is Jimmy McKellen – I'll have to get the number for you. Hold on a minute.'

He put the phone down and after what seemed an interminably long time later he returned. 'Now, hold there.'

The sergeant heard pages flicking. He tapped his pen on his leg, hoping the following calls went a bit swifter.

'Ah, here it is, do you have a pen handy?'

'I do.'

Maguire called out the telephone number and he jotted it down.

'Does he have a home number?'

'I don't know – I've never asked him for one.'

'Does Jimmy work for you full-time?'

'Not full-time, no. I don't really need anyone full-time, these days. I hope young Jimmy's not in any trouble now, is he? I'd hate to think he was. He's a good lad, hard-working.'

'It's probably nothing, but we're running a routine check on all vehicles that were on that road over the weekend.'

'I see.'

'Where did you say Jimmy was?'

'He's collecting furniture from an auction in Carlow. He probably won't be back this way now until after two.'

Devlin thought about that. Furniture. There had been furniture oil and wood shavings in the girl's hair. 'Do me a favour, don't mention this call to him.'

'Why? Why would you ask me to do that? You don't think

247

he's involved in a crime, do you? That wouldn't be Jimmy now. He's a good lad.'

'Don't jump the gun, Mr Maguire. The only thing I know right now is that your van was in Stocks Lane on Friday night. I don't know why or who was driving it. Now, could you give me your address, please? I'd like to be there when Mr McKellen returns.'

'Oh, OK. I don't want any trouble. I'm sure, whatever's going on, there's a perfectly good explanation for it.'

'There'll be no trouble. I just want to ask Mr McKellen a few questions, that's all.'

Maguire gave his address and the two men said goodbye.

Devlin sat back in his chair and gazed at the notepad in front of him. McKellen . . . He wondered if he was in the system. He rolled his chair back to his computer and typed in the name.

A few minutes later, the tingle he had felt earlier in the day returned with full force. He took down the information from the screen and checked his watch. He had three hours to kill before he could have a face to face with this McKellen character. Three hours to make more calls and check out some stories. Three hours to go through his list.

Damn.

He picked up the phone again to make another call, and as he did so, his eyes drifted to his notebook once more. He had underlined McKellen's name so firmly that his pen had torn the paper.

Oh, yes. The tingle was very real. He was like a gun dog that had detected a faint scent on the wind. He couldn't explain it, but he recognised it when it happened.

If he nailed this bastard there might be some hope of a transfer back to the city. Stafford would have to take him home. He'd be up for operations again. Devlin listened to the dialling tone and punched in the number of his next car owner, his leg bouncing up and down with barely contained anticipation.

If he nailed this murder, Ravishing Reba might look at him with more than just sympathetic good humour.

Oh, yes.

39

Lorcan paced the floor of the apartment. This was bad: Mink and McKellen were prepared to kill to get to Orie. His old man had been right. This was serious. This was real. What the fuck was he going to do?

He had to make a decision before Orie arrived. Did he turn his friend over to his father? Did he contact McKellen? Mink? Or did he take control of his own life?

All those times he and Orie had joked about going it alone. It didn't seem so brave right now. It was a risk. A big gamble.

He thought of his father, couldn't shake his words out of his head. None of this was really his problem or, rather, none of this need be his problem. But if he handed Orie over, he was effectively kissing his dreams goodbye. His old man would have Lorcan. He'd never be out from under him.

It wasn't fair. All this because some bitch had pitched a fit in the goddamned truck.

'Fuck!'

He flung himself onto his sofa and checked his watch. It was almost half eleven.

The buzzer sounded. He leapt to his feet and snatched up the intercom. 'Is that you?'

'Lorcan?'

'Caoimhe?' Shit. Orie could arrive at any second. 'Caoimhe, now's not a good time.'

'Like, when is? Open the door. It's lashing rain.'

'I'm serious, Caoimhe, I'm busy. I'm on my way out, actually.'

'Oh, sure – are you going to the yard?'

'No, maybe later.'

'Lorcan, stop this. Either buzz me in or I'll let myself in.'

He leaned his head on the wall.

'Lorcan, I mean it. I need to talk to you!'

He pressed the button and listened as she opened the door downstairs. In minutes she was at the apartment door. He let her in.

'What the hell happened to your face?' she said, stepping across the threshold and closing the door behind her. 'Who did that to you? The guy you owe money to?'

Lorcan walked to the kitchen and put the kettle on. 'Dad.'

'What?'

Caoimhe followed him in and watched as he took two cups from the frosted-glass shelves. 'Did you say Dad?'

'Yep.'

'I don't believe you.'

'Figures. It's not like he ever hit us before, right?'

'Why would Dad do that?'

'Why don't you ask him?'

'Because I'm asking you!'

Lorcan spooned instant coffee into the two cups. 'What do you want?'

Caoimhe pushed the damp hair back from her forehead and stared miserably at her younger brother. 'To help you.'

'You can't.'

'I spoke to my bank and they're prepared to give me an overdraft. I can let you have the money and that way Dad won't have to know.'

Lorcan opened the fridge, but it was nearly empty and the milk was more than a week old. He closed it and passed her the cup. 'You'll have to drink it black.'

'Lorcan, did you hear me?'

'I heard you.'

'It's ten thousand, all I could arrange without letting Dad know.'

'He already knows.'

'You told him?'

'Yes.'

Caoimhe sat down on a stool. 'What did he say?'

'He said he'd take care of it.'

'But that's terrific.'

'I'm thinking of turning him down.'

Caoimhe stared at him, stunned. 'Are you for real? Dad's offered to help you out of a hole you've dug for yourself and you're thinking of turning him down? Where's your head? Why on earth would you do that?'

Lorcan shrugged. 'Why does he want to help me?'

'Why the hell do you think? You're his son!'

He looked at her. 'Yeah. I'm his son. His flesh and blood, huh?'

'Why are you acting like this?'

He sat down opposite her. 'Remember that time I got suspended for fighting?'

'Which time? There were loads.'

'In third year, just before the mocks.'

Caoimhe scrunched up her forehead. 'Yeah. You nearly broke some boy's neck, if I remember correctly.'

'Martin Egan.'

'What about it?'

'Dad went mental. He got me home and beat the living crap out of me.'

'I know. I'm not making excuses for him but he was drinking a lot then.'

'He beat me black and blue, and after he was finished, he told me he was sorry I was ever born.' Caoimhe reached out, but he pulled his hand away. 'I never even got to tell my side of the story.'

'What side?'

'That Martin Egan was one year older and twenty pounds heavier than I was. And that the reason I was in a fight with him was because he and his mate jumped me coming out of the basketball courts and started to kick me.'

'They jumped you?'

'Mmm. Someone had told Egan I snitched on him for skipping double maths or some shit. They didn't ask me if I'd done it either.'

'And had you?'

His lip curled slightly. 'Yeah, I snitched on the fat fuck.'

'Dad was sorry, you know he was.' Caoimhe shook her head. 'I'm not excusing him or what he did, I can't, not for that, but I'm not going to keep condemning him for it either. He's tried to make it up to us. You know he wasn't right after Mum died. I mean, ask yourself, did he ever lay a hand on you after that?'

Lorcan pointed to his bruised forehead.

'I mean before all this – whatever the hell is going on.'

'He never got a chance. Up until that arsehole outside the nightclub, I never gave him a reason. I kept away from him, kept my life separate from his. I avoided him like the plague. You ever wonder why I live here and you're still at home?'

'You wanted space of your own.'

'Sure, but Dad was relieved when I said I wanted to move out. He couldn't get this place fast enough for me.'

'So you're angry with Dad for buying you your own apartment, Lorcan? Is that it?'

'No.'

'Then what the hell is it?'

But he had no answer for her – or, at least, not one she would be capable of understanding. Caoimhe had always had a different relationship with their father: she'd never once doubted he loved her, had never seen hatred in his eyes, never had to plead with him to stop hurting her. It was all so simple, really. There was no complication. He hated his father and he'd rather die than be chained to him for the rest of his days.

'I can't go back,' he said.

'Home?'

'Anywhere.'

'I don't understand.'

'I know you don't.'

The buzzer rang. Lorcan stood up and ran his hands down his trouser legs. 'Listen, that'll be Orie, so you'll have to go. Thanks for stopping by.'

'Lorcan, please. Stop being so stupid and listen to me. What about the money? I can—'

'I'll tell you what, sis,' he put his cup down, picked up her bag in one hand, put his other hand on her elbow and guided her to the front door, 'I really appreciate the offer of the money and everything but you hang on to it. Spend it on some paint or plaster or whatever you artists use.'

'What are you going to do?'

He kept her moving. 'You and Dad, I appreciate all your help, I really do, but you know what? It's high time I started doing things for myself, right? Don't you always say shit like that?'

'Yes, but—'

He opened the door and gently pushed her out onto the communal landing. 'I'll talk to you later, OK? I really appreciate you trying.' He handed over her bag. 'See you.'

He closed the door on her bewildered face.

By the time a shivering, faltering Orie arrived upstairs, passing Caoimhe as he did so, Lorcan was calm and collected. He made his friend coffee, cleaned and dressed his chest wound and let him rage and sob. He poured two tall glasses of Jack Daniel's for them and made Orie drink his. Then Lorcan told his friend of his plan.

It was time, he said, to stop being the staff and start calling the shots.

It was time to step up.

Orie, sitting on the couch, chest throbbing, nodded. When you were stuck between with the Devil and the deep blue sea, your options were always minimal.

40

Stacy woke up. She had put her SIM card in an old clunky phone borrowed from her mother, and she immediately checked it to find the stupid thing had turned itself off again. She switched it on and listened to her messages. There were two from the detectives she had hired and one from Melissa, saying she was sorry for upsetting her, but nothing from Orie, not even a missed call.

She lay back and stared at the ceiling. She felt miserable.

She had gone to bed early the day before after cross words with her mother, who kept hassling her and demanding to know what was going on, what she was doing with Nana's money, demanding answers Stacy didn't have. Finally, Stacy had screamed that if she didn't leave her alone, she was going to pack her things and move out. That had shut Pauline up. But the victory had been a hollow one, and afterwards Stacy had cried herself to sleep.

But she had slept badly. The baby was restless, kicking harder than ever. She felt exhausted and wished she could just close her eyes and make everything go away.

She thought of the day she had told Orie she was pregnant. She had been so frightened of his reaction. Would he leave her high and dry? Would he demand she have an abortion? She had almost vomited with nerves, but he had been brilliant. He had taken her in his arms and kissed her, telling her to stop worrying. At that moment, she had fallen utterly and totally in love with him.

But what if she had been wrong? What if it had been a lie, an act? What if he was so used to lying he didn't know what the truth was any more?

She knew Orie liked women and, worse, she knew women liked Orie. When Melissa had told her about Orie and the blonde in Eddie Rocket's she had known it was more than Orie had let on. She had known deep inside that he wasn't true to her. Perhaps her parents had been right all along.

She pulled the duvet up to her chin.

Why hadn't she been more careful? It wasn't like the Pill was hard to take. She should have insisted Orie use condoms – so what if he didn't like them? If she had used even an ounce of common sense she wouldn't be in the mess she was in now.

A tear ran down her cheek onto her pillow.

'Stacy?'

She pushed herself up on her elbows. Pauline was standing in the doorway with a cup in her hands.

'Can I come in?'

Stacy nodded. Pauline came to the side of the bed. She sat down and placed the cup on Stacy's bedside table. 'Would you like a slice of toast with that, love?'

'No, thanks.' Stacy saw that her mother had been crying. 'Mam, listen, I shouldn't have shouted at you last night. I'm sorry.'

'It's all right, love.' Pauline patted her leg through the duvet. 'Sure, we're all up to ninety. I didn't mean to upset you either. I was just worried – you were in such a state.'

'I'm sorry,' Stacy said again.

'It's OK. Are you feeling all right?'

'Didn't sleep very well.' Stacy eased herself into a sitting position. 'I can't seem to get comfortable.'

'When I was pregnant with you I couldn't sleep much in the last month either. You used to kick lumps out of me.'

'Really?'

'All the time. You were only quiet when *Neighbours* came on.'

'*Neighbours*?'

'As soon as the theme music started, there wasn't a squeak out of you. It didn't matter how much kicking you might have been doing beforehand. The same for *Coronation Street*. Your da used to say I had you turned into a soap addict before you were born.'

Stacy smiled. 'There are worse things.'

'That there are, love.'

'I'm scared, Mam.'

'I know.' Pauline took her daughter's hand. 'There's nothing to be scared about. I wasn't much older than yourself when I had you. It'll be all right, everything will.'

'It won't.' Tears filled Stacy's eyes. 'I'm so stupid.'

'Aw, love, what's the matter? Why won't you talk to me? What happened yesterday? You were in an awful state and your da's sure something happened. Was it Orie? Did you and him have a fight or something?'

'It was nothing to do with Orie.'

'Is he being funny about the baby, it that it?'

'No.'

'Look, Stacy, your da told you, and I've told you I don't know how many times. Never mind that fella or what he has to say. He's not good for you. You can't see it, but I can, and your da can. We're knocking round long enough now to know plenty of people like Orie.'

'Stop, Mam, it's not what you think. Orie didn't do nothing!'

'Then what happened yesterday? What happened to your phone? And don't give me any more of that guff about how you dropped it. That phone was smashed in pieces. You didn't—'

'Ah, not this again! I told you last night, I don't want to talk about it. Why can't you just leave me alone?'

'I want to know what happened.'

Stacy shook her head. 'It doesn't matter.'

'Of course it matters!'

'Mam, I'm so tired, I just want to go to sleep.' She slid down under her duvet and rolled onto her side. After a few moments she heard her mother get up and leave the room.

'Oh, Orie,' she whispered, staring at the mobile phone, 'please ring.'

41

John and Sarah were at the office, pondering their next move. Which meant they were at a loss as to what to do next.

Sarah tried Stacy's number again and drew another blank. 'Our client sure doesn't seem too bothered about her missing beau, does she?'

'Still can't get hold of her?'

'Nope.'

'Well, that probably means one thing and one thing only.'

'What, you think Romeo's turned up?'

'No, you idiot. She's probably either gone into labour or is by now the mother of a newborn baby.'

'You'd imagine they'd let us know.'

'Any word on the hairdresser?'

'Her phone's ringing out too.'

'Set adrift on a sea of apathy.' John stretched. 'What do you think about my getting a dog-walker? Sumo's there all day on his own. It might not be a bad idea to have someone call in and take him for a stroll.'

'Why don't you go home and take him out yourself? Or, better yet, get up early in the morning? What happened to the running?'

John patted his stomach. 'Bad weather.'

'Yeah, right.'

'So, what do you think?'

'It's a stupid idea. He's your dog and you ought to look after him better.'

John frowned. 'Not to yank you off your tall pony there, Sarah, but I've been taking care of the business single-handed for a few weeks, I haven't exactly been footloose and fancy free.'

'Don't give me that! You work for yourself. If you organised your hours better you'd be able to fit plenty of stuff into your day.'

'Or if I had a partner who pulled her weight.' As soon as he'd said it he regretted it.

Two bright spots of colour rose in Sarah's face. 'Well, I'm sorry, John, that my mother being ill takes up so much of our precious time together. I'm sorry my injuries caused me to miss some days of work. I'm sorry your dog doesn't get his walk every day. You know what? I'm super, sorry for everything. There! Now you can lay whatever guilt trip you like on me.'

'Sarah, I didn't mean it.'

'Sure you did.' She stood up, grabbed her jacket and bag. 'Now, if you'll excuse me, John, it's lunchtime, and I have to meet my sisters to discuss what home we're putting our mother in.'

'Sarah, wait—'

She ignored him and stormed out of the office, slamming the door so hard the kettle jumped on the shelf by the sink.

Sarah drove across town in a fury. The nerve of him! Pull her weight? Pull her fucking weight? After years of her hounding him to fill in expense forms, of dealing with clients left, right and centre, of answering phones and sitting in the office bored out of her tree while he waffled with Brannigan or Rod downstairs? Pull her weight? The nerve of him. The absolute nerve of him!

She pulled into the gravel drive and parked behind Helen's car. She felt as though her heart was trying to leap free of her chest. And it wasn't just bloody John Quigley, it was her, it was this, it was Vic, it was Rod, it was everything. How much more could she take? 'Arrrrgh!'

She rested her forehead against the steering wheel and forced her breathing to slow down. In and out, in and out. Don't cry, not here, not now. Normal. Just be normal.

She climbed out and closed the Fiesta door softly. It didn't catch so she swung it again, harder this time. A shower of rust filtered down from the frame. It's falling apart, she thought, like everything else in my life.

'There you are. Are you coming in?'

She turned her head. Helen was waiting at the door, her arms crossed over her chest. She was dressed in her version of casual clothing: a pair of D&G jeans and a silk shirt. Flawless Helen, dark bob sharp and glossy, but now there were lines around her eyes and she seemed drawn and older.

Why don't you have any children? Sarah thought. *Why aren't you happy? What's your secret?* 'Hi.' She held up a brown-paper bag. 'I brought French-roast coffee beans from that little place in the George's Street Arcade.'

'Lovely. Come on in. Jackie brought banana bread.'

Sarah walked towards her sister and into the house. She glanced back once at her car, and then the door closed and she was trapped.

'Go on down to the kitchen. Jackie's there.'

'Where's Mum?'

'She and Mrs Higgens went out for a walk a short while ago.'

'Mrs Higgens? Will they be OK?'

'Belinda's gone with them.'

'Oh. Of course.'

'I'll be with you in a moment. I just want to get the brochures.'

Sarah carried on to the kitchen. The house was Victorian, large and generously proportioned. Paul had had it completely remodelled some years back and now Sarah thought it was as soulless as he was, the Great Surgeon, with his thick hair and dry hands.

She stepped into the kitchen. It was a monstrosity of sleek engineering, hidden appliances and modern technology. It had all the atmosphere of a morgue.

She found Jackie sitting at the table, awkwardly pouring a generous helping of red wine into her glass using her left hand. From the colour in her cheeks, Sarah guessed it wasn't her first. Well, why not? She wasn't driving or working now, was she? Sarah's psycho ex-boyfriend had seen to that. A hysterical giggle escaped her.

'Darling!'

'Hello, Jackie.'

'Come in and take your coat off. Doesn't it smell yummy? Helen's made pesto pasta.'

Sarah threw her jacket onto a chair and hugged her. She released her after a moment and took a step back. Despite her scratches and scrapes and the broken arm, Jackie was remarkably fresh-faced and not nearly as worn out as either of her sisters. 'What on earth happened to your cast?'

Jackie grinned. It was covered with drawings and names. 'It's a complete bugger, isn't it? About seven of my Year Five art class arrived at my place bearing flowers, chocolates and felt-tip markers. Who was I to refuse to be a blank canvas?'

'Very creative of them.' Sarah smiled. She was pleased that Jackie's pupils valued her. 'How are you feeling?'

'Well, if I'm honest, pretty good. The arm is a bit of a bother, but Barry's been so wonderful. He even washed and dried my hair for me this morning. Can you imagine?'

She barked a delighted laugh and Sarah couldn't resist joining in. Actually, the thought of Barry playing hairdresser to Jackie didn't surprise her.

'Do you want a glass of wine?'

'Go on, then, maybe a small one.'

Jackie poured her a Jackie version of small, about a third of a litre. Sarah took it and sipped. 'Nice.'

'So, how are you, darling? Still pretty bruised, I see.'

'It's gone down a good bit.'

'Sleeping OK?'

'Better than I was.'

'If you don't mind my saying so, you look a little peaky.'

'Helen told me.'

Jackie inclined her head with a smile. She knew to leave the subject alone.

'So, are you arranging the pictures?'

Sarah gaped at her. 'How did you—'

'Oh, you know Helen, about as subtle as hippo wearing a tutu. Of course I knew. She's been asking me the most ridiculous questions for days now.' Jackie leaned in closer, a twinkle in her dark eyes. 'For God's sake, don't let her frame the landscapes.'

Sarah grinned. 'Don't worry, I promise I won't.'

'Good. I can't let on I know or it will ruin her surprise. So don't tell her anything.'

'Of course not.'

'How's work? Are you busy? How's John doing? He sent me flowers – did I tell you that?'

Sarah was surprised. 'No.'

'Sweet of him. So, how's work going?' Jackie repeated.

'I've got a case.'

'Really?'

'Missing person.'

'Well, be careful.'

Sarah put her glass down. 'Do you think I'm making the right decision here?'

Jackie turned in her chair. 'About Mum?'

'Yes.'

'I think you wouldn't be making it if you hadn't thought it through.'

'It feels wrong.'

'If Mum was going to get better I'd agree but, darling, she isn't going to improve and that's not your fault. You were very brave to take it all on in the first place.'

'I feel I'm letting her down.'

'You have your own life to lead,' Jackie said firmly. 'So do I and so does Helen. It's not as if we're going to hide Mum away and abandon her. From everything I've read on this place she might very well flourish, and we'll still see her, take her out and spend time with her.'

'I know, but—'

'Sarah, you tried your best, but it's taking a toll on you. You can't be expected to tend Mum every moment you're not working. And she's got to the stage now that she just can't be left on her own. That's the bottom line.'

'I guess.'

'Listen to me, you did your best.' Jackie reached out with her left hand and took Sarah's, 'I think it's time you accepted that Mum needs more than you can provide.'

'No, Jackie, I didn't. I've fucked up spectacularly.'

'What do you mean, darling?'

'Nothing.' Sarah withdrew her hand. She took another sip of her wine. 'I'm thinking of heading off for a few months, travel, maybe see a bit of the world. I've dropped the price on my apartment, and once it's gone I might just . . .' She let her sentence tail off.

'But go where, darling? Are you talking about some kind of sabbatical?'

'I just want to travel, to get out of Ireland, see India maybe, or Thailand. Go and find myself.' She smiled acidly. 'Reconnect with my inner wally.'

'What about your business? The agency? You've worked so hard to build it up.'

'I know.'

'And John? Have you told him?'

'No, and I haven't thought it all through yet. The idea occurred to me just recently. The agency will manage fine without me. John does the bulk of the work these days anyway – according to him.'

'I see.'

Sarah took another sip of wine. 'That's why, you know, I'm wondering about my decision. Maybe it suits me to have Mum taken care of so I can go on being a selfish bitch, like I was before.'

'You were never selfish, Sarah.' Jackie patted her hand. 'Highly strung and adventurous maybe, but not selfish.'

'I've made so many mistakes, Jackie.'

'Hah, who among us mortal beings hasn't?'

'Don't mention it to Helen.'

'Oh.'

'I don't want one of her lectures.'

'She doesn't mean to be harsh. She worries about you.'

'She should worry about herself. She's looked so tired lately. It must have been hard for her having Mum here.'

'It's not Mum.' Jackie took a sip of her own wine. 'I don't think she and Paul are getting along.'

'Really?'

'Yes, and you can't tell her I said anything either.'

Sarah lifted her glass in a toast. Jackie smiled and did the same.

'To secrets and lies,' Sarah said.

42

Detective Sergeant Ray Devlin parked his unmarked car outside the antiques shop and put his special badge on the windscreen. He climbed out, stretched and walked to the shop with the enormous gilded mirrors in the front window. An old-fashioned bell jangled as he pushed open the door.

There was barely standing room inside. The air was dead and smelled of dust and age. The shop was stuffed from floor to ceiling with furniture of every shape and make, most of it incredibly ornate and oversized. There were dressers with hand-carved legs and handles that would dwarf his living room, but they were nothing compared to the armoires.

'Hello?'

He heard a muffled shout from the back of the shop and went in that direction.

'Hello there.' A short, grey-haired man wearing bifocals came up a step from a storeroom, wiping his hands on a clean yellow duster.

Devlin showed his ID. 'I'm Detective Sergeant Ray Devlin. I called earlier. I was talking to Mr Maguire?'

'Ah, that'd be me.'

They shook hands.

'Is Mr McKellen in yet?'

'No sign of him now, but he should be here shortly.'

Devlin looked at his watch. 'Is he normally on time.'

'Like clockwork.'

'And you didn't call him and tell him I'd be here.'

Maguire managed to look suitably insulted. 'No, I did not. Look, I've been thinking about this. Jimmy's worked here a while now and he seems a pretty straight sort. Whatever's going on, I'm sure he had good reason to be on the road that night.'

'I'm sure he had too. And that's what I would like to hear.' Devlin looked around him. 'All of this stuff antique?'

'Yes. I restore a lot of it.'

'Tell me this, do you use a lot of chemicals in your work?'

'It depends.'

'What about stripping agents?'

'We hand-strip smaller pieces but we dip doors and shutters. We have a vat out the back for those and anything that might be buried under years of gloss.'

Devlin nodded. 'What about gold leaf?'

'We use that for filigree work. Some of the mirrors are gold leaf and we pick out the filigree with a special paint.'

'Would you mind if I take a sample of it?'

Maguire didn't look too happy about that but he beckoned him into the storeroom. 'Come this way.'

Devlin followed him to a long workbench covered with pieces of wood and tools, some of which he had never clapped eyes on before and couldn't even begin to work out what they were for.

'I use two types. I use a powdered gold leaf, which helps

269

control the pigment content. And then I use a fluid one for wider coverage.'

He took out his notebook and wrote down the names of the products, while Maguire daubed a little of each on some paper for him. Devlin sealed the samples into a clean sheet of paper and folded it.

'I see you've got a lot of brushes here.'

'Of course.'

'What type do you normally use?'

'Well, again, it depends on the job I'm doing.'

'What about for gold-leaf work?'

'Oh.' Maguire looked over his bench. 'I suppose I use the camel-hair brushes for that mostly. They're more stable, you see, less splash-back . . . I don't know what would be keeping Jimmy, it's not like him to be late.'

'Is he a good employee?'

'He is that.'

'Never gives you any trouble?'

'Comes in and does his job.' Maguire sat down on a stool by the bench. 'I know Jimmy's been in trouble in the past. He told me so when I hired him. He was on the level with me.'

'He tell you why?'

'Well, he said him and some fella got into it one night after a night out. He said the fella got hurt but that it was an accident.'

'Did he ever tell you what they were fighting about?'

'No, and I never asked. It was none of my business.'

'They were fighting over stolen goods.'

'Well, it was a long time ago.'

Devlin ran his hand over a copper light fixture, ornate and tulip-shaped, very heavy. 'Yep, Jimmy has quite a track record for being light-fingered.'

'Like I said, I've never had any trouble with him, and before you ask, I've never missed anything from the shop either.'

'What about any of your patrons? Any of them ever miss anything?'

Maguire's eyes were like needles now.

'Because if you thought about it, having a job where you get to go and pick things up from fancy houses must be a godsend for a magpie like Jimmy. Or torture. Which do you think it is?'

Maguire stood up. 'I'll ring Jimmy's mobile, see what's keeping him.'

'You do that,' Devlin said. 'I'll keep an eye out front, see if he shows up.'

43

Jimmy was pulling into the reserved space outside the shop as
Devlin was walking out the door. Devlin recognised the van
from the camera footage. He waited for the driver to alight. A
small man with thick grey hair and a wiry build with roped
muscles came round the side of the vehicle. Despite the cold, he
wore a T-shirt with his cord trousers and workboots, spattered
with many liquids. He also wore leather work gloves. His nose
was freshly broken.

'Jimmy McKellen?'

Jimmy paused at the rear doors of the van. He looked Devlin
up and down. 'Let me guess, you're in the job.'

'Is it that obvious?'

'You might as well be in uniform.'

'You available to answer a few questions for me, Jimmy?'

'Sure, it's not on my dime.'

'What happened to your face?'

'I got mugged.'

'Looks nasty. How does the other fella look?'

'He looked fast. I didn't get a closer look than that. He robbed me and took off.'

'Did you report it?'

'What's the point? Are you going to catch him?'

'Your boss tells me he let you borrow this van to help your sister move over the weekend.'

'Aye – so?'

'Did you manage to get everything moved?'

'What's this about?'

'Does your sister live up near Stocks Lane?'

'Nah, Clonsilla.'

'Stocks Lane's a fair bit away from Clonsilla. Can you give me her phone number?'

'For what?'

'You don't want to give me her number?'

'What do you need to go bothering her for?'

'You haven't asked why I'm talking about Stocks Lane. That's interesting.'

'I thought you'd get round to telling me eventually.'

Devlin tapped the van with his pen. 'What if I told you a security camera picked this baby up on Saturday night, turning right onto Stocks Lane?'

'I'd say what about it?'

Devlin smiled. 'Were you in possession of this vehicle all weekend?'

'Aye.'

'You didn't lend it to anyone?'

'Not that I recall.'

'No one at all?'

'How did you get on the force with that hearing problem?'

'Now, Jimmy, no need to be like that. I'm just curious, that's all, as to why this van entered Stocks Lane just after midnight on Friday night and left not long thereafter.'

'If you wanted to know that why didn't you just ask?'

'I'm asking now.'

Jimmy sighed. He pulled a packet of cigarettes from the sleeve of his T-shirt and stuck one in his mouth. 'Fuck me, you do a turn for someone and this is the thanks you get.'

'A turn?'

'Look, I moved my sister's gear on Saturday afternoon, and the old one, her neighbour Aggie, asked me would I come back when I was done and clear some of the shite out of her garden and take it away for her. She tossed a few quid my way for it. Not much now, but enough to cover the diesel. So I did.'

'You were clearing rubbish.'

'Yeah, so I wasn't going to pay to bring it to a dump, now, was I?'

'No?'

'No. I dumped it up Stocks Lane.'

'You dumped what up Stocks Lane?'

Jimmy looked at him as if he was an idiot. 'Old rubbish, paint pots, wrecked garden furniture, whatever other old shite she had lying around. I think there was an ironing-board too.'

'You were dumping household waste in Stocks Lane on Saturday night? Is that what you're telling me?'

'Look, it's not like she gave me much. I know it's against the law, but everyone dumps shit up there. I didn't think they'd send a bloody plainclothes after me. I thought there'd be a fine or something if I was caught. I don't want to get Aggie in trouble or anything neither. I was only doing her a turn.'

Ray Devlin stared at the irritation on Jimmy McKellen's face. Was this guy on the line? Hard to know, he was so bloody convincing. But what about the gold paint and the camel hair? Maybe Jimmy had contaminated the scene when he had thrown the rubbish out – assuming it was his rubbish. He thought about the pictures. There had been rubbish scattered around. None of it had looked fresh as far as he remembered but, then, he hadn't exactly been paying attention to it. He needed to get a good look at the van, maybe ask Furlong to go over it with a fine-tooth comb. But to do that he needed a warrant and to get that he needed a bit more on Jimmy.

'Would you be able to identify the rubbish? The exact location you dumped it out?'

Jimmy lit his cigarette and glared at him through a stream of smoke. 'Are you kidding me? It was pitch black up there – fuck knows where it is. Why? What's all the big deal over a bit of rubbish anyway?'

'Did you not hear the news?'

'What?'

'There was a girl's body discovered in Stocks Lane on Saturday night.'

'Jesus.' Jimmy took another drag. 'Here, I hope to fuck you don't think that's got anything to do with me. I didn't take no girl up there. I swear on my mother's life.'

'But you admit to being there.'

'Yeah, and I told you why.'

'Yes, you were very cooperative.'

'Look,' Jimmy said, lowering his voice, 'if my boss finds out I was using his van for anything other than helping me sister he'll take a fucking dim view of it, so if I'm straight with you it's only so's you'll fuck off and let me get on with me work.'

'Why were you using his van on the weekend anyway? Do you not have a car of your own?'

'I do, but it's in the shop getting new shocks.'

'So you were stuck.'

'Yeah, you could say that. Me sister would have my guts for garters if I didn't help her out.'

'I'm going to want to talk to your sister to confirm this.'

'Fair enough.'

'Can I have her number now?'

Jimmy gave him his sister's house number.

'What about a mobile?'

'She doesn't have one.'

'Come on out of that, Jimmy. Everyone in the country has one.'

'My sister doesn't. Don't think she can even work one.'

Devlin searched his face, but Jimmy continued to hold his gaze, steady as a rock.

'All right, she's a Luddite, but what about an address? I'm sure she's got one of those.'

'Yeah, 3 Anvil Court, Clonsilla.'

He wrote that down. 'A man of favours, aren't you, Jimmy?'

'I'm a man in need of my lunch, which I haven't had a chance to grab yet. So, if you don't mind, I need to get this shit unloaded.'

'Would you take a run up there with me after work, see if we can track down this rubbish you dumped?'

'Yeah, yeah, whatever.'

'What time do you finish?'

'Six.'

'I'll swing by, if that suits you.'

'Can you drop me over at my gaff after?'

'Sure.'

'All right, then.' Jimmy threw away his cigarette butt, turned back to the van and flung open the doors. Devlin made his way back to the unmarked car and climbed in. He watched Jimmy undo the hoardings in the van and begin to unload it, lugging large pieces of wood and garden ornaments into the shop one by one.

If he was rattled, Devlin thought, he was hiding it well.

44

Sarah was making her way up the stairs to the office when she met John coming down.

She could tell from his face that something was up. 'What is it?'

'I got a call from Orie's neighbour.'

'His neighbour?'

'Little old guy. I left my card with him when I called there.'

'What did he say? Has Orie shown up?'

'No, but he did tell me a pregnant girl got roughed up there yesterday. I tried Stacy again, but no joy, so I called Pauline, her mam.'

'Who was it?'

'I don't know, but Pauline's going spare. She doesn't want to call the guards in case Stacy does her nut.'

Sarah trotted down the steps after him. 'What kind of person roughs up a kid who's about to give birth at any second?'

'The kind who doesn't give a shit about pregnant kids,' John said, pulling open the street door and stepping into the cold air.

By the time John and Sarah got to Cork Street, Tommy was at home and the atmosphere in the small house was turbulent.

Stacy was lying on the sofa, her feet elevated on two pillows. She was swollen and blotchy, her eyes red-rimmed from crying. Pauline was sitting by her hip, her hands resting across her daughter's lower legs.

Stacy looked at John and Sarah reproachfully. 'Thanks a lot.'

'You talk to her,' Tommy said to John, after he had introduced both parents to Sarah. 'See if you can get some sense into that thick head of hers.'

'Stacy, what happened?' John asked.

Stacy opened her mouth to speak but her father cut her off. 'That's what I want to know. I knew there was something wrong yesterday. I knew something had happened.'

'Dad, will you stop?' Stacy said tiredly. 'I told you Orie didn't do anything. He wouldn't.'

'Well, someone did.' He looked at John. 'Who was the old lad that called you? Did he do something?'

'Oh, Jesus,' Stacy said.

'What's going on?' Pauline was clearly bewildered.

'Like I said earlier, I got a call from Orie's neighbour and he said he helped a pregnant girl outside the flat yesterday. He said she'd been attacked, knocked down and—'

'Knocked down?' Pauline gasped.

'Knocked down!' Tommy leaped to his feet. 'I knew it! I knew from the state of you yesterday something had happened! Your poor mother was out of her mind with worry. You come back in pieces, white as a sheet, we can tell you've been crying . . . Who did it? I'll break his fucking neck.'

'Stacy?' John asked.

'Nothing happened. And I don't want you working for me any more. I'll pay you for yesterday.'

'What?' John said, startled. 'Has Orie turned up?'

Stacy turned her head away.

'It probably was him that did it. Her phone was all smashed up,' Tommy said. 'I told you that fella was bad news.'

'Oh, Stacy, love,' Pauline said, 'what have you got yourself involved in?'

Stacy bit her lower lip. Her face was shiny with perspiration, and she refused to make eye contact with anyone.

'Stacy, please,' Pauline said. 'If Orie's threatened you, you've got to tell us.'

'Anything could have happened to her,' Tommy said. 'I'm telling you, we should go to the cops.'

'No, Da!'

'Well, you're hiding something. Maybe it was the old lad. Was it him? Did he do something to you? I'll fucking kill him if it was. All those old flats, you never know what sorts are in them.'

A lone tear escaped Stacy's eye and trickled slowly down her cheek. 'Will you just stop, Da? Will you leave it alone?'

'Excuse me,' Sarah said softly.

Three set of eyes swivelled in her direction.

'Would it be all right if I had a word with Stacy?'

'If you think you can do any better, love, knock yourself out.'

'Alone.'

'Why?' Pauline said. 'Anything Stacy has to say she can say to us.'

'I know that,' Sarah said.

John looked at Tommy, then at Stacy. The girl seemed to have shrunk halfway into the sofa.

'Maybe we could grab a cup of tea,' John said. 'I've been on the go all day and I could murder one.'

Stacy's mother glanced at her daughter again. After a moment, she sighed and hoisted herself up. 'Come on, Tommy, give me a hand getting the cups.'

Tommy followed her out into the hallway without a word of complaint. John went after them and closed the door behind him.

Sarah lowered herself into the chair John had sat in the day before. She undid her jacket and crossed her legs. 'Who roughed you up?'

'I'm not going to tell you anything,' Stacy said, glowering at her. 'As far as I'm concerned, you don't work for me any more, right?'

'What made you change your mind?'

'Nothing. I told you, I'm not talking any more.'

'You don't need to. I can see what's wrong.'

Stacy lowered her eyes.

'You're afraid.'

'I'm not.'

'Sure you are. You got involved with a man you know nothing about, you're carrying his child, he's left you vulnerable and open to attack, and you don't even know why.'

'Orie didn't do this. He didn't do anything to me.'

'Maybe not personally, but whatever Orie has done, you're going to be the one who pays the price. You and your baby girl.'

'Stop it.'

'OK.'

Sarah tilted her head back and gazed at the ceiling.

'Orie loves me,' Stacy whispered.

'Maybe he does. But it doesn't matter. What matters is you, and you're in trouble here because Orie's in trouble. I think you know that, Stacy.'

'I just want Orie to come back. I just want to know he's OK.'

'You have wants and you have needs. You need to stay safe,

you need to protect that little girl you're carrying. Because right now, you're all she has.'

'Why won't he call me?' Stacy began to cry. 'Why would he do this to me?'

'Because he can.'

'But I love him.'

Sarah sighed and sat forwards in her chair. 'Stacy, listen to me, and listen to me well. What I'm about to tell you is something I learned long ago.'

Stacy turned her forlorn face to her.

'Sometimes love is just not enough.'

A few minutes later, Sarah stepped into the kitchen.

Tommy, John and Pauline were seated round a pine table, sipping tea in silence. Tommy spoke first. 'Well?'

'She was slapped around by one of Orie's friends.'

'I knew it. That dirty—'

John frowned. 'Why?'

'He told her to get rid of us, said that if we kept snooping around Orie was going to get hurt.'

'Do you know who it was?'

'I do, and so do you.'

John stood up. 'Come on.'

'You know him?' Tommy asked.

'I've an idea, all right.'

'Give me his name and I'll wring his bloody neck.'

'No, let me find out what the hell is going on first. Then you can wring his neck.'

45

They drove off and quickly became entangled in the late-afternoon gridlock. John inched the Manta along, rolled down the window and lit a cigarette.

'So we're back to the Wallace clan,' Sarah said.

'Don't say it.'

'What?'

'I can hear an I-told-you-so in your voice.'

'I told you to keep an open mind about Caoimhe Wallace. I never said a word about her brother other than that he sounds like a piece of work.'

'He's more than that.'

'Why the hell are monied upstarts rolling with the likes of Orie Kavlar, or whatever his name is? What do you think the deal is with this guy?'

'I don't know, but I'm sure as hell going to enjoy asking Lorcan Wallace when I see him.'

Sarah caught the hitch in his voice. 'You're not going to do something stupid, are you? Let's just talk to him and find out what the hell's going on.'

'What do you mean, stupid? You mean like kick the living shit out of him?'

'Yes.'

'I haven't ruled it out.'

'Don't be ridiculous. This guy obviously knows why Orie's gone off the radar. He probably knows where Orie is too. Look, all we want to do is talk to Orie, get him to call bloody Stacy, and that's it. Job complete.'

'Right.'

'John, listen to me. You've got to calm down.'

'I am calm.'

They inched along in silence until they reached the Quays. John broke a red light and finally they were moving again. The car made it three metres before it ran into the next line of stationary traffic.

'Goddamn it.' John walloped the steering wheel with the heel of his hand. 'Driving in the city would put years on you.'

'I know.'

'So what happened with your mam?'

'I've agreed with Helen and Jackie to let her go to that care facility they tried to show me last year.'

'The place in Santry?'

'Yes. Helen's already spoken to the administrator, and they can take her as early as next week.'

'It's all very sudden, isn't it?' John said. 'Why didn't you tell me you were even thinking of it? When did you decide your sisters were right?'

'Recently.'

'How recently? Last week, yesterday, today?'

Sarah frowned. 'Why does it matter when I decided?'

'I suppose it doesn't. Just you never mentioned it.'

'It's family business.'

'Oh, OK.'

John turned his eyes back to the road. They rolled past Christchurch. 'You're probably doing the right thing. You did your best for her, but it was always a losing battle.'

'Everyone keeps telling me that at the moment. But you know what? You were right when you said I'm not pulling my weight with the agency. I'm not pulling my weight with anyone or anything.'

'Sarah, come on. I didn't mean it. I was being a tool.'

'No, you were right. I'm done with making excuses.' She shrugged. 'I told that poor kid back there that love wasn't enough. And even as I was saying it I knew I was telling the truth. I love my mother, but that's not enough for me to spend my life looking after her. I love my sisters, but it's not enough for me to shape myself into being what they want me to be.'

She turned to look at him directly. 'I love you, but it's not enough to make me trust you again.'

John was astounded. 'Sarah! I know things are a bit weird between us at the moment. I don't know why. But if you give me a chance, I swear to you I'll never let you down again, ever. Everyone deserves a second chance.'

'It's not enough, John.' She turned away and stared out of the window at the traffic. 'It's just not enough.'

John pulled into the gravel forecourt at Fortuna House and switched off the engine. There was no sign of Caoimhe's jeep, but the gates were open and her brother's Honda was parked in front of the house with the boot open.

Lorcan Wallace came out of the front door with a set of golf clubs over his shoulder.

'There's the prick now,' John said, pulling in sharply.

Sarah watched as the hard-faced young man glanced in their direction. 'He doesn't seem too bothered by our company.'

'Wait here.' John climbed out and walked briskly to where Lorcan Wallace was putting the clubs into his boot.

Sarah watched him through the windscreen. She had known he was upset, but now it dawned on her that it was more than that. John grabbed Lorcan by his shirt and head-butted him. 'Oh, shit!' She scrabbled the door open and leaped from the car.

'You like beating up girls, you shite,' John said.

Lorcan reeled backwards towards the front door, his nose gushing blood.

John followed him up the steps. 'You like scaring pregnant teenagers? Huh? Think that makes you a fucking hard man?'

'John, stop!' Sarah galloped after him.

'What the fuck?' Lorcan managed to stay on his feet but he was obviously stunned.

John grabbed him again and hit his head. 'She's about to give birth any second, you dickhead. I don't know what the fuck you thought you were going to get out of her but let me—'

Lorcan swung with a pretty fast uppercut, catching John flush under the jaw. He staggered back, tripped over his own feet and went down. Before he even knew what was going on, Lorcan was strangling him, his blood dripping on John's face. 'I'm going to fucking kill you,' Lorcan snarled, arms rigid, fingers tight around John's throat.

John bucked, trying to bring his knee up between them, but Lorcan was too strong and pushed him back down, locking his arms. John tried to prise his fingers loose but couldn't get purchase. Blood dripped into his mouth and eyes. He turned his head, feeling the pressure build behind his eyes.

Sarah had reached the two men. She lunged for Lorcan and grabbed his hair, trying to wrench him away from John. It might have worked, but Lorcan swung a fist, catching her in the stomach, doubling her over and knocking her back onto the gravel. Without missing a beat, he resumed throttling the life out of John.

It might have ended very badly indeed for John Quigley if Darren Wallace hadn't picked that moment to arrive home. He pulled into his drive and was stunned by the scene before him. His son, bloodied and livid, was intent on suffocating a red-faced man while a dark-haired woman was struggling to get to her feet.

'What the . . .?' Darren jumped out and rushed towards them, grabbed Lorcan and locked his arms behind his son's head. 'Stop, Lorcan! Stop it!' Somehow he managed to drag his son off.

John rolled onto his side and lay there like a landed fish, wheezing and trying to suck oxygen into his starving lungs. He tried to see where Sarah was, but the world still remained black at the edges. He could hear screaming. It was Lorcan – he was yelling at some man, demanding he get off him. Streams of drool hung from his mouth and he looked rabidly crazed.

'John!'

He blinked, shook his head and blinked again. He tried to sit up and now Sarah, ashen and shaken, was kneeling behind his head, holding him steady with her bodyweight.

'John, are you OK?'

He tried to speak but couldn't. He nodded instead.

The screaming had ceased and now Lorcan was lying face down on the concrete, his eyes still wild but no longer rolling. His face was a mass of blood and spittle.

'Who the fuck are you people?' the grey-haired man pinning Lorcan to the ground shouted, slackening his grip a little.

'Detectives.' Sarah tried to get John to his feet, but his legs wouldn't hold him.

'Cops?'

'Private.'

The man glared at them. 'What the fuck's going on here? What did you do to my son?'

'Are you Darren Wallace?'

'Yes – and I asked you a fucking question.'

'Your son attacked our client. We came here to ask him some questions.'

John was finally able to speak. Sarah decided it was a bad idea for him to say anything.

'We came here to question him and he attacked my partner.'

Lorcan started to struggle again. 'That's a fucking lie. I never touched him. He head-butted me in the face. Dad, I swear, he hit me first. I never touched him. I never even saw it coming.'

'That's not what I remember,' Sarah said.

'You lying bitch, I'll kill you.'

'Lorcan, shut the fuck up.'

'Dad, I—'

'Shut up.'

Darren Wallace got to his feet and dragged his son up, making sure he kept himself between Lorcan and Sarah. Sarah kept her eyes on him the whole time.

'If you attacked my son, I'll have you arrested.'

'Your son's a real piece of work. He assaulted a pregnant girl, roughed her up and threatened her, and she's about to give birth any second.'

'I don't believe you.'

'It's true.'

'Even if it is, you two clowns thought what? That you'd come over and rearrange his face? Deliver some street justice?'

'Like I said, we came to talk, then he assaulted my partner. Quite a temper he has.'

'You're lying.' He took a step closer. 'I can tell. Maybe I will call the Gardaí.'

'Go ahead. I don't have a record,' Sarah said, without a moment's hesitation. 'Who do you think they'll believe?'

Darren Wallace's jaw tightened, and for a moment he appeared just as mean as his son. Sarah kept eye contact with him, cool and unblinking.

Darren jerked his head at John. 'Take your shit and get off my property. I don't want to see you here again. You need to talk to my son, you can talk to him through our solicitor.'

Sarah stuck her arm under John and helped him down the steps. She put him in the car's passenger seat and got in on the driver's side. She turned the Manta, squeezed it past Wallace's Mercedes and drove slowly back up the cul-de-sac. A few neighbours were out on their porches, watching.

In the rear-view mirror, she could see both Wallace men watching her go.

'You wouldn't bloody listen, John. I asked you to wait, to cool your jets but, oh no, you had to go in all guns blazing. Didn't you?'

John dropped his head between his knees. He spluttered something.

'What was that?' Sarah said. His neck was mottled red and she could see the imprint of Lorcan's fingers. If his father hadn't come along . . . Her hands tightened on the wheel and she put her foot to the floor.

46

'What the fuck's going on?'

'I told you, I came here to get some things and he attacked me.'

'But who is he?'

'Some private detective.'

'A private detective? Why would a private detective hit you?'

'I don't know.'

'What are you doing here anyway?'

Lorcan was sitting at his father's kitchen table with his head tilted back and kitchen towel wedged up each nostril. 'I came for my stuff that's still here.'

'With all the shit that's going on with Mink, you were thinking of golf?'

Lorcan didn't answer. He had come to steal a cheque and take anything else he could sell. And those detectives had messed it up.

'What pregnant girl were they going on about?'

'How should I know?'

'Don't give me that shit.' Darren got him a glass of water and set it beside him with two painkillers.

'She's Orie's dumb bitch of a girlfriend. She hired them to look for Orie. I told her to get rid of them.'

'So you did rough up a pregnant girl. Are you kidding me? Are you trying to draw more attention to yourself?'

'I was trying to get her to drop them!'

'This gets worse and worse.'

Lorcan squeezed his eyes shut. He had a splitting headache and he was furious. He should have torn the detective's head clean off.

'Do you know where Orie is?'

'No.'

'He hasn't been in contact?' Darren said, in a sceptical tone.

'I saw him earlier, but I don't know where he is now.'

'You saw him? Did you call Mink?'

'No.'

'Why the fuck not?'

Before Lorcan got a chance to answer, they heard the front door open. 'Hello? Dad?'

'We're down here.'

Caoimhe came into the kitchen, in overalls with dust and paint in her hair. She stopped dead in her tracks when she saw her brother. 'Oh, my God! Daddy, no. You didn't.'

'I didn't do that. Some fucking private detective did.'

'John Quigley did this?'

'You know him?'

'I don't know him, but he was here yesterday.'

'Why?'

Caoimhe put her bag down and her hands into her pockets.

'Caoimhe, answer me.'

'He's looking for Orie. His girlfriend reported him missing.'

'You knew about this yesterday?' Darren fixed his gaze on Lorcan. 'Didn't you hear a word I said to you the other night?'

'Daddy, stop. What are you talking about?' Caoimhe said. 'What's happened? What's going on?' She turned to Lorcan. 'Why did John Quigley attack you?'

'Yes, tell her, why don't you?' Darren said, 'Go on. Tell her what you did. Show her what a man you are.'

'I'm out of here.' Lorcan removed the tissue from his nostrils and stood up.

'You're not going anywhere until you tell me what the hell is going on.'

'Doesn't fucking matter what I say or do, does it? It's never good enough for you. It's never enough.'

'Enough? What the fuck do you expect? You've been a screw-up since day one.'

'Dad, stop.' Caoimhe stepped forward and placed her hand on her brother's arm. 'Lorcan, sit down, come on—'

'No.' Lorcan shook her off. 'Fuck him.'

Darren was up so fast his chair tipped backwards onto the floor. 'Fuck me?'

'What?' Lorcan stretched his hands wide. 'Come on, then. Why don't you have another go? Oh, yeah, you won't. 'Cause it's daylight and you haven't had a couple of drinks.'

'You need to watch your mouth.'

'You know what? I'm tired of watching my mouth. I'm tired of being your fucking kicking bag. I'm tired of the dis-respect.'

'Disrespect?' Darren barked out an ugly laugh. 'You want respect? Is that it? Why the fuck would I respect you? You're a disgrace. You're a lazy, worthless article. There are lads down my yard I respect, hard-working young men. But you? Why the fuck would I respect you? You know what? I'm ashamed of you, Lorcan. I'm ashamed to call you my son. I'm ashamed that after everything I've done for you you've turned out like this. Respect? Don't make me laugh.'

Lorcan was staring at his father. All of the colour had drained from his face.

Caoimhe looked stricken. 'He doesn't mean it. Dad, tell him you don't mean it.'

Darren shook his head. 'Respect is earned, Lorcan. You start using your head and I'll start treating you with respect. Start pulling your weight and turning in an honest day's work and I'll treat you with respect. Come down the yard—'

'Fuck you and your yard.'

Lorcan snatched his jacket from the table and left.

'Jesus Christ, Dad.'

'Let the pup go.'

Caoimhe rushed after her brother. She tried to catch him as he unlocked his car. 'Lorcan, wait, he doesn't mean it.'

Lorcan unlocked the door and climbed in. His face was as pale as alabaster. 'Let go of the door, Caoimhe.'

'Lorcan, please, don't do anything—'

'Stupid?' He wrenched the door from her grasp and slammed it shut.

Caoimhe leaped out of the way as he reversed down the drive and pulled a screeching handbrake turn. Seconds later, he spun the wheel and zoomed out of the cul-de-sac.

Caoimhe watched a pale grey cloud of fumes settle in the evening air. Then she made her way slowly back into the house.

47

Ray Devlin knew he was wasting his time the moment Jimmy McKellen's sister opened the door.

'Hello, my name is—'

'I know who you are.'

Devlin smiled at the hard-faced woman. 'Psychic?'

'Huh?'

'How do you know who I am? Jimmy said you didn't have a phone.'

'I didn't have one yesterday. I got one today.'

'Are you all settled in? Must have got everything unpacked quickly.'

She leaned her shoulder on the doorjamb. 'Didn't have much to move.'

'Where were you moving from?'

'Who said I was moving at all?'

Devlin's smile started to slip. 'Jimmy did.'

'Jimmy told you he was giving me a hand moving furniture. Not moving house.'

'So you weren't moving house?'

'I just told you. We were moving furniture.' She tapped the ash off her cigarette. 'Anything else you want to know?'

'Which side does Aggie live on?'

'What d'you need her for?'

'To confirm Jimmy took away rubbish for her.'

'Did he tell you he did?'

'Yes.'

'Then he did.'

'Which side, please?'

She jerked a thumb to her right and closed the door in his face.

Devlin closed his notebook and crossed her scabby lawn to next door's equally scabby lawn. He knocked.

'Who is it?' a frail voice asked.

'Detective Sergeant Devlin. Can I have a moment of your time, please?'

'Who?'

'Gardaí.'

The door opened on the chain and a rheumy pair of eyes peered up at him. She was tiny, birdlike, with long grey hair pinned in an untidy bun on top of her head.

'Hello there.'

'Hello.'

'I was just in next door with your neighbour.'

'Oh, yes.'

'She was telling me her brother gave you a hand over the weekend.'

'Oh, yes.'

'Do you remember him taking away some rubbish for you?'

'Rubbish?'

'Yes, this weekend.'

'Oh, yes.'

They looked at each other for a long time. Devlin decided to try again.

'Did Jimmy help you this weekend?'

'Jimmy?'

'From next door.'

'Next door?'

'Yes, Jimmy. Did he help you with your rubbish?'

'When?'

'This weekend.'

She blinked and looked behind her.

Devlin put his notebook into his jacket pocket. 'Thank you very much. Close that door now and keep the heat in.'

'OK. Thank you, thank you.'

Devlin trudged back across the lawns and knocked on the first door again. Jimmy's sister didn't look any cheerier the second time round.

'Yeah?'

'Does anyone keep an eye on her?'

'I do.'

'So, Jimmy took her rubbish away, eh?'

'If he says so he must have done.'

Devlin looked at her hard. She held his gaze. 'Right. I'll check this out.'

'OK.'

'If I find you've been lying to me you'll be in trouble.'

'Yeah?'

'Yes.'

She closed the door in his face once more.

'Fuck me,' Devlin said, under his breath and headed back towards the car. He sat in behind the steering wheel and rang Maguire's shop.

'Hello?'

'Mr Maguire? It's DS Ray Devlin.'

'Oh, hello there, I was just thinking of shutting up here, Detective.'

'I won't keep you. It's Jimmy I was looking for. Can I have a quick word with him?'

'Jimmy? He knocked off hours ago.'

Devlin's knuckles tightened on the wheel. 'What time?'

'Not long after you left. He unloaded the van and asked me if he could have the rest of the day off, not feeling the best, he said. Probably that injury, awful pale he was.'

'Did he take the van with him?'

'Well, I wasn't going to be needing it and his own is in the shop, so I said he could have it for the day. He's a good man, he'll bring it back.'

'I'm sure he will,' Devlin said. After he's scrubbed every inch of it clean.

48

Mink was not overly impressed by anything he was hearing. 'So, let me get this straight. You killed the girl and you let Orie go free?'

'Let didn't come into it, the wee fuck jumped me.' Jimmy McKellen took a sip of his Gentleman Jack. His left eye had closed, but he had been lucky: his nose wasn't broken and he still had the use of his right eye.

'With a dumb-bell.' Mink shook his head.

'Aye.'

'And now, somehow, you've attracted the attention of a detective – Devlin, you say his name is?'

'Devlin, yeah. He said he's with Rathfarnham. He's just checking out all the cars that were on the road that weekend. Shit, there must have been hundreds.'

'They'll narrow it down.'

'So, he can narrow it all he likes, he won't find nothing.'

'So you say. And yet he came to you.'

'He was doing the rounds, Mink. There's fuck all to link us to that body. But we need to tie her to Orie, and sooner rather than later. You have her passport. We can put it in with his possessions. If they have their killer, they're not going to be looking for another.'

Mink took a seat and leaned back in his chair. 'This is a fucking disaster, Jimmy. I expected you to keep a lid on things, not go making them a hundred times worse.'

'He jumped me. What was I supposed to do?'

'You were supposed to fucking clean the situation. Not add another corpse to the list. Jesus Christ!' Mink slammed his hand on the desk.

Jimmy pressed the glass against his cheek. 'Fucking kid. Slippery as an eel he is.'

'And in the wind.'

'He'll turn up.'

'That's what I'm afraid of,' Mink said, glancing at the monitors on his desk. The evening staff were arriving. 'Any word from Lorcan?'

'No.'

'Little shit, I'm sure he knows something.'

'Orie can't have too many places left and he had fuck all with him when he bolted.'

'You think he'll go back to his digs?'

'On Haverty Road? Yeah, I reckon so.' He took a cube of ice from his drink and pressed it to the bridge of his nose. 'You really think Lorcan would give us a shout if he contacts him? Those two are as thick as thieves.'

'Lorcan's father has dealt with that. The boy is stupid, but he's not a complete fool.'

'Huh, I wouldn't be so sure.'

'Lorcan has too much at stake to make a wrong move like

that. He's lazy. He likes his life, his apartment, the flashy car. He won't risk any of that for Orie.'

'So what do we do? Wait?'

'I suppose so,' Mink said glumly.

Jimmy took another slug of his drink. 'I hate waiting.'

'Maybe you could call out to Orie's landlord, impress upon him how important it is that he contacts you the moment Orie's in touch with him.'

'That's if he goes back there.'

'Well, goddamn it, Jimmy, he has to go somewhere. I want you to sit on his place.'

'Which one? He has two.'

'Well, I don't know, do I?'

Mink's desk phone rang. He picked up the receiver. 'What?' He listened, his face revealing nothing. Then he waved a hand at Jimmy. 'Really? Well, I don't see . . .'

He grabbed a pen and started to write on his notepad. 'Does she live alone? OK, got it. You won't regret this. No, I swear to you, if we put this to bed he's in the clear. You have my word.' He hung up.

Jimmy looked at his employer's face. 'What?'

'That was Darren Wallace.'

'He's got a line?'

'He says Orie was at Lorcan's house earlier today. His daughter saw him there.'

'The little prick! I told you he wouldn't give him up. I'm telling you, Lorcan Wallace is dangerous to us. You can't predict what he's going to do. He needs to be put down.'

'We have a new line.'

'What?'

'You ever hear Orie mention a girlfriend?'

'Which one? He has a few.'

'A pregnant one.'

'Pregnant?'

'That's what I thought.' Mink ripped the sheet off the pad and tossed it across the desk. 'Here.'

Jimmy took it and read the address. 'This his chick?'

'It is indeed.'

'Played that one close to his chest, didn't he?'

'Indeed. I wonder why? You know what this is?'

'Luck?'

'Leverage.'

'We're going to use her?'

'Why not? We make sure Orie knows we have his girl and he'll have to come out of the woodwork.'

'What about Lorcan?'

'What about him?'

'Won't he come out too?'

'Let him,' Mink said, 'If he tries to get in the way, we'll just have to do what we need to.'

'Even if Darren Wallace'll be on our backs?'

'Even if. I'm telling you, Jimmy, if Darren Wallace was half the man I thought he was he'd have made his son hand Orie over.' Mink shrugged. 'It's a sad state of affairs, but going straight softens even the worst sons of bitches.'

Across town two other men were discussing Darren Wallace's supposed toothlessness.

'That's it, Orie, just you and me from now on,' Lorcan said, tossing down half a tumbler of Jack Daniel's. He almost missed his mouth and some of the amber liquid dribbled down his chin. He wiped it off with the back of his hand. 'Fuck them old boys – fuck Mink and fuck my old man. We're gonna do it our way from here on in. We don't need them.'

Orie was drunk and getting drunker. His chest no longer

hurt, his hands no longer hurt. He was filled with the flames of hooch and indignation. 'You and me, brothers.'

'Brothers!' Lorcan poured more alcohol and raised his glass in a toast. 'To brothers.'

'To brothers!'

They drank.

Lorcan slammed his glass down on the coffee table. 'We're gonna make sure they know we mean business.'

'Yes!' Orie tried to focus on Lorcan but couldn't manage it. 'How?'

'Mink's a' – Lorcan hiccuped – 'coward. He gets Jimmy to do his shit.'

'Right,' Orie agreed.

'Without Jimmy, he's just a short-arse with a bad dye job.'

Orie splashed more Jack Daniel's into his glass. He raised his glass. 'Brothers.'

'Brothers!' Lorcan said. He grinned stupidly at Orie. 'You and me, we're gonna be rich. We're gonna be like superstars. Our nightclub is gonna be the best fucking place Dublin has ever seen.'

'The best!' Orie no longer cared that he had reservations about tangling his future with Lorcan's. Lorcan was a jerk, but he was prepared to protect and go out on a limb for him.

'We're gonna take Mink's dog away,' Lorcan said, lurching to his feet. He sat beside Orie and draped an arm over his friend's shoulders. 'We're gonna take his teeth.'

'His teeth?' Orie squinted.

'Yeah, his teeth.' Lorcan raised his glass again. 'Brother!'

'Brother.' Orie gulped the rest of his drink and passed out.

Lorcan grinned. He rested his head on Orie's chest, listening to his breathing, feeling his chest rise and fall under his cheek.

Mink was going to be sorry.

301

49

'What did you mean when you said you don't want to do this any more?' John swallowed a mouthful of Coke and winced. His throat was very sore and bruised. He transferred the phone to his other hand. Sumo lay under his feet, sighing softly.

'Nothing.'

'Then why did you say it?'

'You don't listen to anything I say.' Sarah sounded sleepy, disjointed.

'I do.'

'No, you don't. I'm tired of all the craziness. My back is black and blue from where that jackass knocked me down the steps.'

'I'm sorry about that.'

'I know. Sorry.'

John waited for her to say something else. Sumo sighed again. Time ticked by.

'Sarah?'

'Huh?'

'Did you just fall asleep?'

'No.'

'Are you OK? You don't sound it.'

'I'm tired, John.'

The clock in the kitchen told him it was only half past eight. 'Have you eaten?'

'Yes.'

'What did you have?'

'Pasta.'

He didn't believe her. 'You want to go out? Grab a burger or something?'

'No. I'm going to have a bath and head for bed.'

'You sure?'

'I'm sure.'

'I'll see you tomorrow, though, right?'

'I suppose so.'

'You suppose?'

'Yes, I'll see you tomorrow.'

'Goodnight, Sarah.'

'Night, John.'

He hung up. Sumo lifted his head and gazed at him. 'What? You got something to say too?'

Sumo gave a half-wag.

'You want to go out, is that it?' John groaned and pulled himself to his feet. 'Oh, all right, but no pulling, we clear?'

Sumo got up, his tongue lolling out the side of his mouth, his tail curled high over his back. John ruffled the top of his wiry head. If only everything was as simple to sort out.

They walked through Ranelagh and up into Rathmines, swinging right at the Swan Centre and carrying on towards Portobello. Sumo walked as he always did, out front, nose to the ground. By the time they had reached the canal, John was sweating. He decided to ramble towards Leeson Bridge; that way, he could swing up through Dartmouth and back towards his home.

As he walked, he thought of Sarah. He had never seen her so angry, and maybe she was right to be. He had been out of line with Lorcan Wallace, and he knew it, but damn it, if anyone deserved a slap or two it was that arsewipe.

He wished he knew what the hell was going on with her, or what he had done wrong. What had happened to make her change her mind? "Not enough"? What the hell did that mean? OK, maybe she didn't want to be his girlfriend, but what was the deal about her mother? Why hadn't she spoken to him about it? They used to talk about everything, but now she was shutting him out and he was sick of it.

By the time he had reached Leeson Bridge, John felt aggrieved. Hell, what had he done to deserve the brush-off? Nothing. He worked hard, he had been patient, he had been open, he had backed off, given her time, given her space, given her everything she had asked for, and where had it got him? Nowhere. He was back to being the sidekick, the fool, the work partner.

He jerked Sumo, who had stopped to sniff at a sleeping tramp on a bench. He had nearly quit smoking for Sarah. What more did she want from him?

He was still pondering and feeling sorry for himself when he reached his gate. He didn't see the person sitting in the shadows on his step, but Sumo did, and growled furiously.

'Oh, does he bite?'

'Sumo.' John tightened his grip on the lead. 'Caoimhe? What are you doing here?'

She stood up and brushed off her trousers. 'You attacked my brother. You nearly broke his nose, and I want to know why. What the hell gives you the right to do something like that?'

'Your brother's a jumped-up little bollocks. He deserves a smack or two. I doubt I did any lasting damage one way or another.'

'You can't just do that – you can't.'

She stepped off the step, out of the shadows. John could see she had been crying.

'You don't know him. He's not what you think,' she added.

'I know he roughed up a heavily pregnant girl. I know he would have finished me off if your old man hadn't come along. He's a dangerous man, Caoimhe, and you pretending otherwise won't change that.'

'He has anger issues – he can't control the way he gets.'

'Bollocks. He doesn't want to control the way he gets.'

She looked at him for a long time, her expression one he couldn't read. 'You don't know anything.'

'Look,' John said, 'I don't know what the deal is between your brother and Orie Kavlar, and I don't give a shit, but Stacy Power is a kid and she's pregnant. All she wants is for her boyfriend to come back, kiss her on the nose and tell her everything's going to be OK. If I can make that happen for her, I will.'

'No matter who you hurt in the process?'

'Like who?'

'My family.'

'Your brother has only himself to blame for today. And it strikes me your old lad is well able to take care of himself.'

'Lorcan isn't a bad person.'

'No?'

'No. It's not his fault. He has behavioural problems.'

'So has Sumo here. I keep him on a lead and I don't let him roam the streets.'

'You're an arsehole.' She stepped down the path. John pulled Sumo closer to him to let her pass. 'How did you find out where I live?'

'It wasn't hard. I made a few calls.'

'So why did you come here? To give out to me for lamping your brother?'

'Yes, no.' She raised her hand, then dropped it. 'I don't know.'

John waited for her to go on, but she didn't. 'I won't say I'm sorry for earlier but I'm sorry you're upset.'

'Are you?'

'I don't like to see ladies upset.'

She smiled. 'A gentleman, huh? Defending our honour and fretting over our sensibilities.'

'What's the deal between your brother and Orie? Is he involved in the same shit Orie's involved in?'

'What's that?'

'I believe Orie's a smuggler. I think he smuggles people into the country, then bleeds them dry. Your boy into that, too?'

'Of course not.'

'You sure about that? Why did he threaten Stacy? Why did he want her to drop us?'

'I don't know.'

'I bet I do.'

'You're wrong about my brother! He wouldn't be involved in anything illegal.'

'But he knows why Orie's missing, right? He knows what's going on.'

'No, he doesn't.'

'Did you ask him?'

'Of course not.'

Sumo growled as her voice rose. John leaned back against his gate. 'What are you so afraid of?'

'I'm not afraid. I just don't like to see my family at each other's throats. My father and brother have a very volatile relationship. You coming and accusing Lorcan of all sorts has caused a real rift between them.'

'Is your brother involved in smuggling too? It's all going to come out in the wash if he is.'

She sighed. 'It was obviously a mistake thinking I could talk to you. Would you mind holding your dog tightly, please? I want to leave.'

'Caoimhe, if he's in trouble, I can help.'

'He doesn't need your help.' She walked towards him so fast he barely had time to yank Sumo back towards him. 'Just stay away from my family.'

'If your brother goes near Stacy Power again, I'll make sure he's sorry.'

She didn't answer or look at him as she stepped out onto the street and walked away. The smell of her perfume lingered like smoke on the cold night air.

50

Jimmy sat in the van across the street from Stacy's house and smoked. Just before six, he watched a man he assumed to be the girl's father leave early in the morning, and at twenty past eight he watched a plump woman he took to be Stacy's mother leave for her job.

If the information was good, that left only Stacy in the house.

At nine, he climbed out and crossed the road. His plan was to abduct her and use her as bait, but he wasn't sure how best to go about it. Sometimes it was easiest to play these things by ear.

He rang the doorbell and, after a few minutes, a heavily pregnant girl in a tatty dressing gown opened it. Jimmy smiled at her puffy, sleepy face. She was very young, but kind of plain. He wondered what Orie saw in her. He wouldn't have bothered with her himself.

'Hi, honey, is your name Stacy?'

'Yeah?'

'I'm Jimmy. I'm a friend of Orie. We work together.'

'Orie?' Her face lit up and she looked past him out onto the street. 'Is he with you? Is he OK? Where is he?'

Jimmy couldn't believe his luck. 'He's not with me, but he asked me to come and get you.'

'What's going on? Is he hurt? Is he in trouble?'

'I'm afraid he's been pretty badly beaten up.'

'Oh, my God! What happened?'

'Tell you what, why don't you go and get dressed and I'll take you to him?'

'But where is he? Why can't he come here?'

Jimmy shook his head. 'He's staying at a friend's apartment. He was working with me,' Jimmy pointed to his own damaged face, 'and we were jumped. I'm afraid Orie's in a bad way.'

Stacy bit her bottom lip. 'I knew something had happened to him, I just knew it. Come in. I'll go and get dressed. I won't be two seconds.'

She opened the door and led Jimmy McKellen into her home. He closed the door behind him. The hook was baited.

John got into work just before nine. He dialled Stacy's number but it went to her voicemail. He tried Orie's number without any expectation and was not surprised when he drew a blank there too.

He had just got off the phone with the hair salon when Sarah arrived twenty minutes later. 'Morning.'

'Hi, John.' Sarah slipped off her jacket. She was wearing a dark-red T-shirt and slim-fitting jeans and John saw her as if for the first time. When had she got so thin, so hollow-eyed?

'What's going on?' she asked.

'A big fat nothing. I can't seem to raise anyone this morning. Not Stacy, not Orie, and no squeak from Vanessa either. She was supposed to be in work at nine but she hasn't shown up.'

Sarah glanced at her watch. 'Still early.'

'Yeah, I know. How are you doing? Did you sleep OK?'

She waved her hand in a see-saw motion as she poured coffee into her mug. She didn't comment on what had happened the evening before and John decided not to bring it up.

She made coffee and sat down. John watched her scan her desk as though she was looking for something but didn't know what it might be. 'You OK?' he asked.

'Fine.'

'Guess who came to see me last night.'

'Who?'

'Caoimhe Wallace.'

'What did she want?'

'To tell me to back off her family.'

'Yeah? Is she worried about what we might find?'

'She's worried about something. She says we're causing trouble between Lorcan and his old man.'

Sarah shrugged tiredly. 'Pity about them.'

'Are you sure you're OK?'

'I had to take some of Mum's sleeping tablets – they make me a bit fuzzy-headed.'

'You took sleeping tablets?'

As long as he'd known Sarah, she'd always been against any kind of narcotic, with the exception of the odd painkiller. She barely even drank.

His mobile kicked into life.

It was Pauline Power.

'Pauline, what can I do for you?'

'Have you heard from Stacy this morning?'

'No. I tried her phone earlier and it went straight to voicemail.'

'What about your partner?'

'I don't think so.' John pressed the phone to his chest. 'Sarah, did you hear from Stacy today?'

Sarah shook her head. John lifted the phone back to his ear. 'Is everything all right, Pauline?'

'Well, I don't know. I'm in work and I can't get hold of her. She must have gone out this morning, but it's strange. Her friend Melissa called me – they were supposed to be going into town to buy baby clothes but Melissa says there's no answer at the house or on her mobile. I just thought she might have gone to see you.'

'Well, she hasn't called either of us.'

'Oh.'

'Maybe she's out of range for the mobile or somewhere she can't hear it.'

'She wasn't great last night. She was very pale and the baby was moving something fierce. She shouldn't really be out and about on her own.'

'I'm sure she'll be in touch. I'll try her as well, and if I hear anything I'll give you a shout.'

John hung up and filled Sarah in. As he spoke, Sarah picked up the office phone and dialled Stacy's number. It went straight to voicemail. 'Stacy, Sarah Kenny here, can you give me a call on my mobile whenever you get this? Thanks a lot.'

'Was it ringing?'

'Straight to voicemail.'

'Hmm,' John said.

'Hmm what?'

'Probably nothing.' John picked up the phone again. 'I'm going to see if Vanessa showed up, but if she hasn't I want to take a run out to Shankill.'

'Sure, why not?'

*

Stacy was beginning to think she had made a very big mistake. No sooner had she climbed into the cab of the truck than Jimmy had belted her in and locked the doors. She didn't like the way he kept looking at her, didn't like the questions he was asking or his sneering tone.

'So, are you and Orie a big item?'

'How do you mean?'

He jerked a thumb at her bump. 'Well, you're knocked up, aren't you?'

'Yeah, we're a big item.'

'Funny, I never heard him mention you.'

'Orie doesn't like to talk about his private life. Look, can you just tell me what happened to him? How did he get hurt? How bad is it?'

'Bad enough.'

She looked at his profile. He wasn't nearly as nice now as he had been when he called to the house. She wished she had left a note for her mother. Still, at least she had her phone.

Stacy tried to keep the conversation on track. 'Why didn't Orie call me if he was hurt? Why didn't he go to a hospital?'

'You know Orie, he doesn't like to attract attention. If he'd gone to a hospital they might have called the cops.'

'But why didn't—'

'You ask a lot of questions, don't you?'

Stacy clutched her bag tighter. 'I'm just worried.'

'Yeah, well, don't be. We're here now.'

They pulled into the underground car park of a large apartment complex just behind Smithfield Market. Jimmy drove down the ramp and parked in a secluded section beside the large skips the complex used as bins. 'Come on.'

Stacy unbuckled her seat belt and eased herself out of the truck. Her back was killing her and she had broken into a sweat. The car park was deserted and her anxiety ratcheted up.

Jimmy came to her side of the vehicle, crowding her slightly. 'Come on,' he said again.

'I think I should just give my mam a quick ring to let her know where I am.'

'No reception down here,' Jimmy said, taking her arm just above the elbow. 'You can call her from the flat.'

He led her to the lift and pressed the button. The doors opened and he almost shoved Stacy inside.

Stacy winced. The pain she'd been experiencing during the night had returned with a vengeance. She pressed her hand to the small of her back and tried to stretch.

Jimmy watched her dispassionately. 'What's wrong?'

'I don't know . . . nothing.'

'When you due?'

'Not for another two weeks.' Her bottom lip trembled. 'Did Orie really ask you to come and get me?'

Jimmy smiled. 'Sure he did.'

'I want to call my mam.'

'I told you, you can call her from the flat.'

'I don't want to go to the flat.'

'Don't you want to see your boyfriend?'

'I think I just want to go home. I don't feel well.'

'We're nearly there now.'

'You don't even have to take me. I'll get a taxi.'

'We're nearly there.'

Stacy felt tears building. 'Look, mister—'

'Here we are.'

The doors opened on the top floor. Before Stacy could protest, Jimmy grabbed her by the upper arm and dragged her out of the lift. Stacy tried to free herself. 'Stop pulling me.'

Jimmy glanced to the end of the hall. There were only two apartments on this floor: Mink's whorehouse and the one owned by a German couple who spent half the year out of the country. No one would trouble them up here. 'Come on, he's waiting.'

'No.' Stacy looked fearfully behind her as the lift doors closed. 'I don't want to go with you, I want to go home. Tell Orie I'm sorry, I just had to go and—'

Jimmy socked her one across the jaw. Her legs buckled and she sank to the ground. He grasped her arms and hauled her to the apartment door. Mink had told Poppy to clear it of the working girls. No one would disturb them here.

51

John and Sarah drove to Shankill in near silence. No matter what topic of conversation John introduced, Sarah's mono-syllabic answers starved it into silence.

Finally he could bear it no longer. 'What? What is it?'

'Huh?'

'Are you angry with me about yesterday? Because if you are, you might as well just say what you have to say and get it over with.'

'I'm not angry.'

'You seem angry.'

'All right, I'm angry.'

'Well?'

'Well what?'

'Say what you have to say.'

'I don't have anything to say.'

'You're just going to be angry?'

'Right.'

John was relieved when they reached Dangan Park. He and Sarah climbed out and walked up the path of number 49. John knocked on the door.

There was no answer.

'This is really turning out to be one of those mornings,' he muttered.

Sarah pointed. 'There's a car in the driveway.'

'Might not be hers.'

She stepped over the little chain-link lawn fence and peered through the front window.

'John! Come here.'

He hurried to her side.

'Look.'

He followed her finger and saw a pair of bare feet sticking out from behind the sofa.

He hammered on the window, hard and fast.

'Vanessa? Vanessa!'

Sarah ran back to the door and rang the bell. 'Vanessa!' She pounded on the wood with her fist. 'Vanessa.'

John joined her. 'Stand back out of the way.'

'What are you going to do?'

'Move, Sarah.' He smashed the window with his elbow and unlocked the door. He ran inside, Sarah following.

Vanessa Shaw was slumped on the floor of her living room. John knew even before he checked for a pulse that she was dead. 'She's stone cold.'

'Oh, Jesus.'

John took out his phone and dialled the Gardaí. 'Hello, I'd like to report an accident . . .'

He gave the address and his contact number, then hung up. 'They're on their way.'

Sarah looked at the dead girl. 'Do you think Orie did this?'

'Well, who else?'

'I don't know. We don't even know if Orie's alive.'

'I'm going to try Stacy again.' He dialled her number. When he couldn't get hold of her, he called Pauline. But she hadn't heard from Stacy either and she was starting to sound very frightened. John tried to reassure her, but he wasn't confident that her daughter was fine. If Orie had killed Vanessa, who knew what was going on? 'Call me the moment you hear from her,' he said, as a squad car pulled up outside the window. 'I've got to go. I'll check back in with you later.' He hung up and pocketed his phone.

'What the hell is going on?' Sarah said, wide-eyed.

'I haven't the faintest idea.'

Orie heard the phone first. He sat up and groaned. His head was pounding and his tongue felt as if it was two sizes too big for his mouth. Where was that terrible noise coming from? Lorcan was asleep on the couch beside him, his arm dangling over the side, an empty Jack Daniel's bottle on the floor beside him. He slid off the couch and stumbled into the kitchen. He found the mobile on the worktop and carried it back to his friend.

'Lorcan.'

Lorcan groaned and opened his eyes. 'What?'

'Phone.'

Lorcan took it and pressed it against his ear. 'Yeah?'

'Good morning, Lorcan.'

Lorcan sat up straight. 'Mink.'

'I was wondering if I could have a quick word with Orie.'

'I don't know where he is.'

'I do. He's staying with you. Put him on, please.'

'Fuck you, Mink.'

'Fine, don't put him on. Ask him instead if he likes the idea of fatherhood.'

'What are you talking about?'

'Tell him we have his girlfriend.'

Lorcan looked at Orie. 'What?'

'Tell him unless he meets with us both she and his future child will end up in the Liffey.'

'Yeah, OK, I'll tell him.'

'And say that I expect to hear from him soon.'

Lorcan hung up.

'What is it?' Orie asked.

'Nothing. Mink wants to meet us.'

'Why?'

'To talk. To sort shit out.'

'I don't like.'

'Me neither, but I don't give a shit about Mink anymore.'

'He is angry.'

'Yeah, well fuck him, he's not the only one,' Lorcan said. He managed to get to his feet. 'We need to take care of this problem once and for all.'

Orie nodded. 'What will we do?'

'I don't know. Let's get some food first. Then we can decide.'

When Stacy came round, she was in a small bedroom with only a skylight and a bed. She was on the floor, and when she tried to sit up, the pain was so intense she almost blacked out again.

She lay very still, panting, trying to remain calm. Her jaw was agony, but nothing compared to the pain in her back. She remembered the truck ride, she remembered trying to talk her way out of coming to the flat.

Her phone. She forced herself up and looked around. Her bag was gone.

She scrambled to her feet and tried the door. It was locked. OK.

She sat on the side of the bed and tried to think. Another

wave of pain slammed into her. Her muscles cramped and her back felt as if it was going into a spasm.

'Oh, no.'

Stacy got up and tried to walk it off. This couldn't be it – this couldn't be happening.

She banged on the door. 'Hello? Please. Please . . . somebody—' She doubled over and tried to catch her breath as the pain intensified.

'No no no no no,' she whispered, as she sank to her knees.

A sudden gush of water proved her worst fears.

Stacy Power was in labour.

52

By the time John and Sarah had given their statements and got out of Shankill Garda Station, it was after two. John collected the car from the car park and Sarah called Pauline immediately. 'Did you hear from Stacy?'

'No, and none of her friends have either. I'm going out of my mind.'

'OK, Pauline, here's what you do. Ring the Gardaí and tell them your heavily pregnant daughter hasn't been heard from since this morning. They probably won't do much because she's only been missing for a few hours, but call them anyway. I'll get back to you in a few minutes.'

John pulled up and she climbed in.

'Any word?' he asked.

'No,' Sarah said, 'and she's frantic. I told her to call the Gardaí.'

'They won't do anything, not yet.'

'I know, but still. What do you think? Lorcan Wallace?'

'Maybe.'

'Then we need to find him. Now.'

'Let's go and talk to Caoimhe Wallace.'

'I'll try Stacy again.'

John put his foot down, and as the Manta picked up speed they shared a worried glance.

Half an hour later, John pulled up outside a red-brick building opposite Herbert Park. He rang the bell marked '14', then he and Sarah hurried up to the top floor.

Caoimhe Wallace answered the door and showed them into her studio.

It was a long room, painted brilliant white, with two floor-to-ceiling sash windows and a potter's wheel in the corner. Large chunks of stone lay dotted around and on the workbench a piece of alabaster, on which Caoimhe had been working before they had arrived.

'Look, if you're hear to talk about Lorcan—'

'Caoimhe, listen, I know you're fed up with me, but I want you to hear me out. Your brother, I don't know how he's mixed up with Orie and I don't care, but a girl that Orie was involved with has been murdered, and no one has been able to get in touch with our client today.'

'I don't see what that has to do with me.'

'She's almost nine months pregnant. If you have any idea where Orie Kavlar might be, you've got to tell us.'

Caoimhe sat down at her workbench. 'My brother and Orie are friends, that's all.'

Sarah raised an eyebrow. 'Nobody's saying anything different. Look, we've just come from a garda station, and neither John nor I mentioned anything about your brother, but if you won't help us I'm going to rectify that as soon as I leave here.'

'Caoimhe, please. A woman is dead. I'm not saying your brother is involved but I need to talk to Orie Kavlar.'

She pulled off her goggles and flung them onto the workbench. 'I saw Orie yesterday.'

'Where?'

'At my brother's place. He was arriving as I was leaving.'

'Why didn't you tell me this last night?'

'Because it's none of my business. Or yours.'

'Where does your brother live?'

'In Ringsend – but, look, I don't want anything to happen to him.'

'If he hasn't done anything wrong then what would happen?' Sarah said.

Caoimhe looked away. But, after a moment, she gave them the address. Sarah wrote it down.

'There's something else,' Caoimhe muttered.

'What?'

'Orie looked pretty banged up when I saw him. His hands were destroyed. He was trying to hide them but I could tell he was hurt.' She looked at John. 'Are you happy now?'

Mink was counting the takings when Jimmy called.

'What?'

'Have you heard anything?'

'No, not yet. I told you, Jimmy, I'd call as soon as Orie contacts me.'

'So why hasn't he called yet?'

'Maybe he's weighing up his options.'

'The kid's doing my head in. She's crying and banging on the door like a fucking lunatic.'

'Put some music on.'

'I can still hear her.'

'Then go for a fucking walk or something, or tell her to shut her yap.'

Jimmy hung up.

Mink shook his head. What in the name of Jesus was wrong with people these days?

Lorcan watched Orie stuff the last of his Big Mac into his mouth. He knew he was taking a risk by not telling his friend what Mink had said, but he couldn't be sure Orie wouldn't try something dramatic or foolhardy and attempt to negotiate with Mink for his skank girlfriend's release. At the end of the day, it didn't matter to Lorcan what Mink did with her.

He tried to think about their next step. Last night, he had been so sure, so confident that taking Jimmy out of the equation was the answer. He still thought that, but doing it was a different kettle of fish.

Orie's voice broke into his thoughts. 'We need a truck.'

'Huh?'

'Truck,' Orie repeated, 'or van, to make transport.'

'Right.' Lorcan ran his hands through his hair. 'We're gonna have to hire one, at least for this week.'

'OK, we hire van. I will call contact. He is a shark,' Orie tapped his tattoo, 'like me. He will deal.'

'OK. We get the women in, and then what?'

'Then they pay.'

'It would be easier if we could offload them to someone here, like we do with Mink.'

'Take time to make contact.'

'But I bet we could if we tried. I bet Slim or some of those guys know people who could use girls.'

'You can talk to him?'

'Yeah, why not? We can talk to who the fuck we like now.'

Orie took a slug of his milkshake and grinned. He offered his knuckles, and he and Lorcan tapped.

Stacy was in agony. Sweat was running off her in rivers and her lips were parched. She paced back and forth across the floor of the room, trying to time the minutes between each contraction. There had been fifteen since the last one, and although she was doing everything in her power to keep cool and fight the urge to scream, her terror was growing.

She had to get out of there, but how? The skylight was high above her head. If she could get out she could get help – she could get to a hospital.

She had to do something.

She pulled the bed away from the wall, grunting with the effort, and dragged it to the centre of the room. She climbed on to it but even then she was nowhere near the right height. She needed at least another three feet.

She climbed off the bed and walked in a tight circle. She could feel the ribbon of pain starting in her spine and knew that another contraction was about to start. She checked her watch. How many minutes was that? Was it only ten? Was it—

'Ooh.' The pain almost knocked her sideways. She leaned against the wall and tried to control her breathing. She had been to only two antenatal classes and, for the life of her, she couldn't remember a thing they'd said. Was it shallow breathing that helped or deep?

'Please . . .'

She tried to stand upright but couldn't, so she tried to squat but the pain was too much. She gave in to the fear and the agony and screamed long and hard.

53

John parked the Manta in a space outside the building, then he and Sarah climbed out. They rang Lorcan's buzzer and waited.

Nada.

'He's not there,' Sarah said.

'Or he's not answering.'

'Either way, same result.'

'Fuck.' John put his hands on his hips. 'What are we going to do now?'

'We can wait, see if he turns up.'

'Fuck,' John repeated. 'I've got a bad feeling.'

'I know, but what else can we do?'

'Try Pauline again.'

'I've called her twice now. If she'd heard anything she'd ring.'

'I don't want to wait around. If something's wrong I want to—'

'John, look.'

He turned as Lorcan's hopped-up Honda pulled into the complex. 'Come on.'

He was off before Sarah could warn him not to do something he might later regret.

Lorcan clocked John just as he pulled into the space reserved for him. 'Aw, shit.'

'What is it?' Orie said, glancing behind him.

'Nothing. Stay in the car.' Lorcan got out and walked quickly towards John and Sarah.

'You two again? This is private property so you're going to have to leave.'

'Who's in the car with you?'

'No one.'

Sarah snorted and walked past him. Lorcan tried to grab her arm but John shoved him hard, catching him off-balance and sending him onto the kerb.

She rapped on the passenger window. 'Orie, open up.'

He rolled the window down and smiled at her. 'Hello?'

Sarah gestured to his heavily bandaged hands. 'Must have been painful.'

'Ah, yes, accident in kitchen.'

'Where's Stacy?'

Orie blinked. 'What?'

'Stacy, the mother of your unborn child – do you need a photo?'

'I do not understand.'

'Where is she? What have you done with her?'

'Nothing. She is home.'

'No, she's not, she's missing. We know Vanessa's dead, but I swear to God if Stacy's hurt I'll skin you alive.'

Orie paled visibly. 'I did not hurt Vanessa.'

'Then who did?'

'Not me.'

'But you know about it, right? You know she's dead.'

He swallowed and lowered his eyes.

'Where's Stacy?'

'I do not know.'

'Liar.'

'I do not lie.' He glanced at Lorcan and seemed to be working something out. He turned back to Sarah. 'I tell you, I do not hurt women. I do not hurt Stacy.'

'Yeah, well, I've given your name to the cops over Vanessa so you can tell them that.'

'I will find Stacy.'

'You're a piece of shit, but I'm going to believe that. You'd better work with me on this. If you find Stacy or you know something about where she is, you've got to be straight with me.'

'I do not know where she is.' He looked Sarah straight in the eye. 'But I will find her.'

Sarah pushed off from the window and walked back to John. 'Come on.'

'But what about him?'

'He doesn't know anything. Come on.' She walked back to the Manta and got in.

John joined her. 'What's going on?'

'Drive out of here.'

He started the engine and pulled out of the complex.

'Just go down the street and park again.'

'Why? What's going on?'

'Orie's on the level. He doesn't know where Stacy is, and neither did he know she was missing. But he does know who has her and I'm willing to bet it won't be long before he takes us to whoever that is.'

*

Lorcan was hopping mad. 'But why? Why do you want to talk to Mink?'

Orie held out his hand. 'I want to see something.'

'Mink wants you dead, for Christ's sake!'

'Phone, please.'

'Orie, just calm down and think about it for a minute. Here, let's have a drink.'

'OK, I will go use street phone.'

Lorcan's temper was rising. He flung his mobile at Orie's chest. 'Fine, be a stupid fuck! But don't blame me if he tells you shit you don't want to hear.'

Orie put the phone on the coffee-table. 'So is true. He has Stacy.'

Lorcan's face was sullen. 'Yeah, he has her. He called me earlier to say so.'

'Why he called you?'

'He wants me to run you in. Stacy's his back-up plan in case I don't.'

'You want do business with me?'

'You know I do. We could have a great business together.'

'But you tell me lies.'

'Look, how was I to know for sure that Mink had her? I thought he was just pulling my leg, trying to get me to scare you. Look, they want you, Orie – they want you to take the fall for that other dead girl.'

'But they have Stacy. We must get her free.'

'Orie, listen – listen to me!' Lorcan jumped up. 'Jimmy has her, right? Well, I tell you what, we'll go and get her and we'll do what we said we'd do. I'll call Mink and say OK, you'll meet Jimmy and we can trade for the girl. We'll take Jimmy out. We'll kill two birds with the one stone.'

'We will take Jimmy?'

'Fuck, yeah! Without Jimmy Mink'll back off. You know he

will. Jimmy's hardcore, Mink isn't. Mink's a businessman. He won't want trouble.'

'How we take Jimmy?'

'We'll tase him, then decide. Come on, think about it. He won't be expecting it. He'll think I'm just rolling you to save my own shit.'

'You might do that.'

'Orie, you've got to trust me.'

'We will save Stacy?'

Lorcan furrowed his brow in exasperation. He couldn't understand Orie's affection for that no-hope knacker. 'Yeah, we'll bump her out too.'

'OK. Call to Mink. Say what you need say.'

'I'll tell him my old man's gonna cut me off if I don't hand you over.'

'Is true?'

'He'll believe it.'

Ten minutes later, Sarah and John watched as Lorcan and Orie pulled out onto the street and headed into town.

'Told you,' Sarah said.

54

Detective Sergeant Ray Devlin waited for the lab report with as much patience as he could muster. But Annabel Lynch, the specialist, was not one to be rushed and he was loath to call her back.

He paced the office again. Detective Inspector Derek Hogan, his supervisor, glanced at him over the top of his newspaper. 'You're going to wear a hole in that lino.'

'How can it take so long just to check paint samples?'

'Best to be thorough.'

'I know that.' Devlin took a seat and chewed his lip. He had spent all of the evening before and half of the morning running through the rest of the cars pulled from the CCTV camera outside the warehouse and almost everyone on the list had had a legitimate reason for being on Stocks Lane. He had also gone back to Stocks Lane and had done a complete search of the area where the body had been found. None of the rubbish there was as Jimmy McKellen described, no ironing board or empty paint cans. Jimmy had chanced his arm with that one, Devlin was sure, but he had struck out.

The real clincher was the paint and the camel hair, though. If they could get a match on the paint, they could haul him in for more questioning.

He glared at the phone.

Sarah and John tailed Lorcan down the quays and across into Smithfield. They watched as he pulled up outside a red and brown block of apartments and rang a doorbell.

'Did you see which bell they pressed?' John asked, squinting across the square.

'Nope.'

'Dammit.'

'Let's take a look.'

They got out of the car and walked across to the building. There were twenty different bells.

'Eeny meeny?'

'How about no?' Sarah stepped back to look up.

'We need to get in there.'

'We don't even know what floor they're on.'

'We can split up, try all the doors. You start at the bottom and I'll work down from the top.'

'We have to get in first.'

'That won't be hard,' John said, studying the lock.

Stacy wiped her forehead and tried not to push. She was in so much pain she could barely move. The contractions were less than two minutes apart and were now so powerful she was terrified. The urge to push was stronger with each one.

She had given up calling for help. She knew she was doomed to go it alone. Her baby was coming and there was nothing she could do to prevent it.

*

Orie was nervous as they rode in the lift to the top floor, but not nearly as nervous as Lorcan.

'Now, remember, it's all an act. You're to pretend you think Jimmy's offering a sit-down, a chance to talk, but really he thinks I'm bringing you there because I've decided you're too much hassle. That means at some point he'll make a move on you. The best way to deal with this is zap him before he can do any Jimmy shit.'

'But Stacy – we must be sure she is all right.'

'Yeah, yeah. Well, we'll ask to see her, then zap Jimmy.'

'What we do after we zap?'

'I don't know,' Lorcan said honestly. 'I wish to fuck we had a gun.'

'I have knife.'

'So will Jimmy.'

Orie was pale and sweating. 'Is big step.'

'Come on, man, let's keep our shit together. We'll soon be free.'

'Brothers.'

'Exactly.'

He and Orie banged knuckles. But neither felt confident. Suddenly their situation seemed very perilous and as far from gangster as either had ever hoped to be.

They reached the top floor and stepped out of the lift.

'OK,' Lorcan said, cracking his knuckles and shoving his taser up his sleeve. 'Let's do it.'

They approached the door and knocked.

After a moment, it was opened.

'Hey, Ji—' Lorcan frowned as a huge man opened the door. 'Ga-Ga? What are you doing here?'

'Get in.'

Lorcan and Orie glanced at each other. Something was very wrong.

Ga-Ga took a very businesslike gun out of his pocket and pointed it at them. 'I said in.'

He didn't have to ask a third time.

Stacy took off her tracksuit bottoms and her underwear. She curled on her side and lay gasping for air. The pain was so bad now, but when she put her hand between her legs, she knew that the baby was coming, and there was nothing she could do about it. The veins in her neck stood out like cords as she bore down. Her cries ended in piercing screams as, alone, she began to bring her baby into the world.

Orie and Lorcan walked up the hall ahead of Ga-Ga into the bright sitting room. There were three doors leading off the room, and they could distinctly hear a woman's cries.

'Stacy?' Orie said, but then his attention focused on something else.

The floor was covered with plastic sheeting and on it, in a pool of blood, lay the body of Jimmy McKellen.

'Oh, no,' Lorcan said, raising his hands. 'No, Ga-Ga, listen, please. I told Slim I'd pay him – he said I had weeks. He said we had a deal. Ga-Ga, please, you've got to listen to me. I swear.'

Ga-Ga ignored Lorcan. He pushed Orie onto the plastic and shot him in the back of the head. Orie pitched forward onto his knees and collapsed on Jimmy's body.

Lorcan stared at his friend's twitching corpse. Suddenly, he had no more strength in his own legs. He would have fallen, too, if Ga-Ga hadn't caught him and practically dragged him down the hall and out onto the landing. Together they got into the lift, Ga-Ga propping the trembling Lorcan against the wall.

Ga-Ga pocketed his gun, pressed the button for the ground floor and removed his latex gloves.

'Listen to me.' He slapped Lorcan's face lightly. 'We're gonna take your car and you're gonna drive to your father's house. You can drop me off at Heuston – I'll take a cab into town. You listening?'

'You shot Orie.'

'He's gone, forget him.'

'But why? Why did you shoot him like that?'

Ga-Ga narrowed his eyes. 'He's the mark.'

'You knew I'd bring him?'

'Yeah.'

'But Jimmy?' Lorcan shook his head in confusion.

'Fuck Jimmy.'

They reached the ground floor and walked out without pausing. Ga-Ga used Lorcan's keys to unlock the Honda. 'Let's go.'

Lorcan did as he was told. He was too shocked to do anything else.

55

Sarah was knocking on her third apartment door when John rang her.

'You found them?'

'I don't know. I think I can hear somebody screaming.'

'Where are you?'

'Top floor.'

'I'll be right there.'

Sarah ran up the stairs as fast as she could. By the time she reached the top floor, John was already on his knees trying to pick a lock. 'John! What the hell?'

He held up his hand. 'Listen!'

Sarah stood stock still and pressed her ear to the door. She heard nothing. They waited. And then they heard it, faint but unmistakable: somewhere behind that door a woman was screaming in agony.

'Open it,' said Sarah.

John went to work on the lock, and less than a minute later

he and Sarah were creeping along a narrow hall. The sound was louder now, and there was no doubt that it was a woman. John opened the first door he came to. He and Sarah stared at the scene that confronted them. 'Oh, my God,' Sarah said.

'Jesus.'

They heard another scream, long and guttural.

'Stacy!'

They tried the doors leading off the room they were in. Only one was locked, but the key turned. Sarah threw it open. 'Oh, Jesus Christ! Stacy!'

Stacy's eyes were huge, sweat running down her face. 'Help me!'

'John, phone an ambulance.'

Sarah ran to Stacy and knelt beside her. 'Oh, my God, the baby's coming.'

'I can't, I can't!' Stacy said, tears pouring down her face. 'I'm tearing. She's tearing me open.'

'You've got to relax. Take a deep breath – here, hold my hand.'

Stacy gripped it so tightly that Sarah nearly cried out herself.

'Oh, no,' Stacy moaned, 'here comes another.'

'It's OK, it's OK, we're here now, we're here. Take another deep breath and try to stay calm.' Sarah pushed Stacy's hair back from her face as another contraction racked her. The girl screamed as her baby's head crowned and, in the sitting room, John opened the French windows and stepped out onto the small terrace to plead with the operator for an ambulance immediately.

Ga-Ga caught a taxi outside Heuston station and watched Lorcan drive away. The boy was a gibbering wreck, but that was to be expected. Most mouthpieces were the same when confronted with reality.

He got the taxi driver to drop him off on George's Street and strolled across to Slim's. Slim was playing Man Hunter. 'How did it go?'

'Done.'

'Problems?'

'None.'

'Excellent.'

Slim paused his game and called Darren Wallace. 'Your problems are no more. It's all been taken care of.'

Darren Wallace disconnected and raised his glass. 'Done.'

Mink nodded and took a sip of his own drink. 'I assume there are no hard feelings between us.'

'Business is business.'

'True.'

'To business, then.'

'To business,' Mink said, with a cold smile.

56

John was stripped to his waist and covered with suds. A grouchy Sumo was standing in the bath, grumbling under his breath. It had taken John ten minutes to wrestle him into the tub and another five to keep him there. He himself was now almost as filthy as the dog. 'Shake again, Sumo, and I swear . . . you know those balls you're so attached to? I'm going to have them chopped off, dipped in molten lead and made into ornaments.'

Sumo grumbled and huffed but he didn't shake.

'How many years have we been doing this? You'd think you'd be used to it by now.' John grabbed the shampoo and squeezed a long thin line down the dog's back and ran the shower-head over it. He massaged the shampoo in, working it into a rich foam.

'People pay big money for this but I'm giving you a massage for free and you're objecting.'

John squeezed more shampoo onto his hand and lathered Sumo's undercarriage, then his tail, legs and chest. 'Gotta be done, old fella. Nobody likes a pongy dog.'

He washed Sumo's head last, making sure he gave his ears a good scrub and checked for mites. When he had finished, he ran the warm water over him, taking care not to get any soap in Sumo's eyes. His dog enjoyed the rinsing part.

'Don't move.' John grabbed up the old towels and spread two on the bathroom floor.

'Right, out.'

Sumo jumped out of the tub and managed to get in one good wall-spattering shake before John covered him with a huge bath sheet, from tip to tail.

This was the dog's favourite part of the whole traumatic ordeal. John grinned as he towelled him vigorously.

'See? It wasn't that bad. Why do we have to go through the same battle every time, you big eejit?'

Sumo's head poked out of the towel. He looked like a hairy prize fighter or a particularly startled grinch. He shook off the towel and bounded out of the bathroom. John knew exactly where he was going: to roll up and down the carpet in the hall. He did it after every bath and John's hall smelled of wet dog for two days afterwards.

He had tried to blow-dry him once, with his sister's hairdryer. That had been a disaster. Frankly, the wet dog smell was the lesser of two evils.

He was scrubbing the bath with Cif when the doorbell rang.

Sumo barked, but by the time John had reached the hall, he had stopped and was standing at the front door, tail erect but wagging.

John pushed him out of the way with his knee and opened the door.

'Hey, you.' Sarah stood in the arch.

'Hey.'

Sumo barged out, almost knocking her down.

'Whoa big fella.' She laughed, then bent down and ruffled his head. 'Damp.' She looked up. 'Your dog's damp.'

'I just washed him.' John frowned. 'Have you been drinking?'

'A little. No other way to survive Helen's soirée.'

'Come in – it's freezing out there.'

She squeezed past him, Sumo trotting behind her. 'Why aren't you wearing a shirt?'

'Because I was washing the dog.'

'Oh, yes, so you said.'

'Go on into the sitting room. You want a coffee?'

'Nope. Got any wine?'

'Afraid not.'

'Beer?'

'Beer I can do.'

'All right, then. One of those.'

She went into the sitting room and flung herself onto the couch. John lit two lamps and turned on the fire. 'Are you sure you wouldn't rather have coffee?'

She waved a hand at him and patted Sumo who had plonked himself at her feet and was now content to gaze adoringly at her. Sumo loved the ladies in John's life, Sarah and John's sister Carrie.

John hurried into his bedroom and threw on a white T-shirt. He got two bottles of San Miguel from the fridge and carried them back to the sitting room. Although she had left her coat and scarf on, Sarah had kicked off her shoes and curled her feet under her.

'I like what you've done to the place. You've hung curtains.'

'Actually I didn't, Carrie did that.'

'I always liked her.'

'Was the party that bad?'

'Art people, lot of talking and waffle.'

'How did Jackie's pictures go? She sell many?'

'I don't know exactly, but she seemed pretty happy with the result. But you know Jackie – throw a few glasses of red wine down her and she's pretty easy-going.' Sarah took a sip of her beer. 'I think Helen's going to leave Paul.'

'Really?'

'Yeah. She's miserable.'

'Sorry to hear it.'

'Oh, well. Shit happens, eh?'

'Are you OK?'

'Yeah. I feel bad for poor Stacy.'

'I know, poor kid. It's a pity she had to see Orie's body when they were bringing her and the baby through the sitting room.'

'We should have blocked her view – in all the panic, I wasn't thinking. I went to see her earlier today. She's destroyed, John, and no matter what happens now, she's going to have that memory for ever. What should have been a glorious moment was filled with fear and terror and pain all because people are bastards.'

She stopped talking and gazed into the flames in the fireplace. Then she went on, 'You see how it changed so fast? One minute you're in love, you're happy and making plans for your future. But it's bollocks, isn't it? You can't plan. How can you plan for the future when you can't even leave the past?'

John glanced at her but she was still staring into the flames. 'Orie was a shithead. He was involved with that guy McKellen. So Lorcan Wallace says.'

'I know that, but she loved him.'

'She's better off without him in the long run.'

'Is she?' Sarah chuckled. 'Tell her that.'

'She's still young, like you said.'

'Do you think Lorcan will skate?'

'Probably. After all, we didn't actually see him go into the apartment and there was no trace of gunshot residue on him.

Plus there was that cop Devlin's report. The one that links McKellen with the dead girl they found dumped in Stocks Lane – and they found her passport at his place.'

'Right, passports. Orie's territory.'

'I don't buy Lorcan's innocent play. That boy knows a whole lot more than he's saying.'

'Maybe so, but I don't think he's a killer. He looked pretty shaken when they brought him to the station. I saw him being led in.'

'Course, poor Stacy couldn't tell you who was in the apartment. Imagine what might have happened to her if we hadn't turned up.'

'Might have been a while before she was found.'

'She could have died, her and the baby.'

'She didn't. When it comes to killers, are they born or created?'

John sat back on the sofa and considered. 'Maybe both.'

'I used to think it took a certain type of person to kill. But now I think it's just a certain set of circumstances.'

'Are you thinking of Patrick York?'

She inclined her head.

'You had no choice. If you hadn't killed him, he would have killed me first and you second. You know that. Dammit, he'd already shot you.'

'Choice? I've been thinking a lot about choices lately.'

'You sorry about the ones you've made? Coming home? Working with me?'

'No.' She shook her head slowly. She took another sip of her drink and put it down on the floor. 'I'm sorry I've been so difficult these past few days. That's why I came here tonight, really. To apologise.'

'There's no need—'

She laid a hand on his forearm. 'Stop.' She leaned across and kissed him softly on the mouth. John lifted his hand and cupped the side of her face.

They kissed slowly and tenderly. After a few moments, Sarah pulled back and looked into his eyes. 'It's not your fault, any of it.'

'What do you mean?'

'I said it wasn't enough but that's not true.' Her dark eyes glistened. 'You are enough, John.'

'Sarah—'

She put a finger against his lips. 'I'm going home now, and I want you to remember what I said. You are enough, John.' She stood up, slightly unsteadily, and slipped her feet into her shoes.

John stood too. 'You can stay here.'

'I don't think so.'

He held up his hands. 'No funny stuff. It's late.'

'Goodnight, John.'

She looked at him once more, as though she was drinking in his face. Suddenly John felt anxious. Something was wrong, he could feel it. 'Sarah, please, stay.'

'I can't.'

'Let me call you a taxi.'

'Don't be daft – the rank's just round the corner.'

'Then I'll walk you there.'

She reached the front door and patted Sumo who had followed her. ''Bye, Sumo.'

'Sarah, wait, let me grab a pair of runners.'

She opened the door. 'Brrr, it's cold. I think there might be frost.'

'Sarah.'

She turned once more to him and smiled. 'Go on back inside. I'll talk to you. Thanks for the beer.'

'You're welcome, any time. Are you sure you don't want me to walk you round?'

'I'm sure.'

She went down the path and out of the gate. She waved once and walked away.

John closed the door. What the hell had just happened?

57

John was up early the next morning and discovering just how much of a favour Stevie felt he owed him. He and his friend spent almost six hours clearing out rotting carpets, lino and presses from a run-down old house set on half an acre. Stevie had bought it the month before and wanted to do as much of the work on it as he could. Or, as he put it, he wanted to keep some money in his pocket in case any of his kids needed to eat now and then.

They worked until one, then called it a day. John said he'd be more than happy to give Stevie a hand the following week too. Stevie thanked him and mentioned something about pints. John said he'd definitely hold him to that.

He called Sarah when he got home, but his call went straight to her voicemail. He left a message asking her to call him back. At three, he took Sumo out to get the papers and some milk. He cleared the leaves from the gutters and put on a wash. He got the extension cable out and hoovered his car.

At five, he tried Sarah again, but there was still no answer. He left another message.

At five thirty, Carrie called in on her way home from town. They had two cups of tea and some butterscotch biscuits. She asked him about the case, and shuddered when he told her about Stacy delivering her baby alone. He accepted her offer of dinner later that week. Sumo got his belly rubbed.

At half past six John tried Sarah again.

At seven, he got into his car and drove to Clontarf, telling himself there was nothing strange in Sarah not answering her phone but that it was a nice evening for a drive.

He parked outside her home and climbed out of the car. It was dark and there were no lights on in the house. He rang the doorbell. No one came.

John peered in through the living-room window but nothing seemed out of the ordinary.

So why was his heart beating just a little too fast? Why the gut feeling that something was wrong?

He got out his mobile and phoned Jackie.

'Hello?'

'Jackie, it's John.'

'Well, hello there. How are you? I see you're in the paper again. Terrible story. That poor girl.'

'Yeah, it was pretty bad, all right. Listen, I was just wondering if you'd heard from Sarah today?'

'No, darling, I haven't.'

'OK.'

'Is something wrong?'

'It's just she's not answering her phone.'

'Have you tried the house?'

'Actually, I'm at the house. There's no one here.'

'Well, maybe she's at the cinema or something. Or she's having a quiet day.'

'Probably. If you talk to her, can you ask her to give me a call?'

'Of course.'

'Thanks, Jackie, take care.'

''Bye.'

He hung up and chewed the inside of his cheek. He was being ridiculous – so a grown woman wasn't answering her phone, so what? Big wup. Maybe she was embarrassed about the night before. Maybe she regretted kissing him.

He got back into his car and drove home.

He fed Sumo and hung around the house. He tried to watch television, but couldn't concentrate. He picked up a book, but after he'd read the same sentence five times he gave that up too. He took a delighted Sumo for another walk.

At ten o'clock, he called Sarah. Again, there was no answer. He dithered for a few minutes, then called Jackie again. 'Hey, Jackie, it's me. Have you heard from her?'

'No, and I left a message for her.' Jackie sounded a little more anxious than she had earlier in the day.

'What about Helen?'

'She hasn't heard from her either.'

'Right.'

'John, what's going on? Is there something you're not telling me?'

'It's probably nothing – but it's not like her to be out of contact.'

'Did she say anything to you about going anywhere?'

John thought of the way she'd kissed him, the way her eyes had seemed to roam his face. Why had she been there? 'No.'

'Well, I'll try her again in a while. You know she's been a bit down lately, maybe she just doesn't feel like talking to anyone.'

'Yeah, maybe.'

'If I hear from her I'll call you.'

'Thanks, Jackie.'

The next morning, John got up early. He fed Sumo and had a toasted-cheese sandwich for breakfast. He clock-watched until nine a.m., then called Sarah's house. No one answered.

He tried her mobile.

It went to voicemail.

'Dammit, Sarah!'

At ten o'clock, Jackie called him. 'Hi, John, have you spoken to her?'

'No, have you?'

'No. I'm worried. I'm going out to the house.'

'I'll meet you there.'

'There's no need for that. I'm sure it's nothing. If she's just having some down time I can't imagine she'll be thrilled if we both descend on her.'

'Right.'

'I'll call you as soon as I know anything.'

'Right.' John looked at the kitchen clock again. 'Are you going soon?'

'As soon as I get dressed.'

In the next hour he tidied his bedroom, took a call from his friend Andy, a short one as he didn't want the phone tied up. He cleaned the kitchen counters and was about to make a pot of coffee when Jackie called back.

'Well?'

'She's gone.'

John sat down at the kitchen table. 'What do you mean, she's gone?'

'She left a note here for us. She says she's sorry if she scared us but she was never one for goodbyes.' Jackie's voice shook. 'She says we're not to worry about her and she'll be in touch.'

'That's it?'

'That's it.'

'But . . . gone where exactly?'

'She doesn't say.'

John tried to wrap his mind round what he was hearing. 'I don't understand what you're telling me.'

'The other day, she was talking to me about travelling. I thought she meant in the future.'

'She's just . . . gone?'

'I should have known. It is Sarah, after all.'

'I don't believe it.'

'John, I have to go – I've got to call Helen.'

'Wait, Jackie, please. She has to have said something else.'

'She didn't. I'm very sorry.'

John put his phone down on the table. What the hell? She wouldn't do that – she wouldn't do that to him.

Again, his mind flashed on how her eyes had glistened when she had kissed him.

He jumped up, locked the back door and grabbed his car keys.

He drove straight to the office and took the stairs three at a time. He unlocked the door and hurried inside.

A note was propped against his coffee mug.

Dear John,

I was thinking about what you said the other day, about how everyone deserves a second chance. I think you're probably right, I think you deserve one, but not with me. I've had my second chance and I've made a mess of it.

I seem to do that a lot, make a mess of things. I want you to know I appreciate your friendship, I appreciate your loyalty, I hope you believe me when I say there's nothing in this world I'd rather do than return it. But I can't, John. I can't let you get involved with me any more than I already have. I suppose I thought I could turn back the clock, that I could mend what had been broken.

This all seems melodramatic, but it's the only way I know how to leave things. I don't want to talk about my decision. I don't want to discuss it with you or my sisters.

I hate goodbyes, so don't think of this as one.

You're a good man, John. You're more than enough for anyone.

Love,

Sarah

John put the note down. He settled back into his chair and glanced across the room to her empty desk.

After a while, he lit a cigarette, and as he smoked he listened to the Sunday-morning traffic as it drifted along Wexford Street, three floors below.

ACKNOWLEDGEMENTS

Thanks to my agent Faith O'Grady, my editor Ciara Considine, Hazel the terrific copy-editor and all the staff at Hachette who slog away so hard behind the scenes. The usual shout out must go to my dear friends for being so generous with time and affections. Anna (you looked beautiful and you know it), Antonia (Cocktails!), Bryan and Billy (new neighbours, old chums), Sarah, Tara, Chris and Corinna (ladies who lunch), Con, Fon and Daragh – my running crew (are you sure you don't want to run this year's marathon with me?), Kriss – especially for that joke that made my face ache. A hearty wave for Muriel, your new page looks terrific! Much love to the 'logue homies', Mr M and Mr T. Last, but never least, Andrew and Jordan – reasons why life is so good – all my love, thank you for another wonderful year.